Thorndike Press
32.95
3-10-2005
LBT

QSD 2018

10/0
2/0
6/07

Always

Also by Jude Deveraux
in Large Print:

An Angel for Emily
The Black Lyon
The Conquest
The Duchess
The Enchanted Land
Eternity
Forever . . .
Forever and Always
The Invitation
Remembrance
The Summerhouse
Sweet Liar
Twin of Fire
Twin of Ice
Wild Orchids

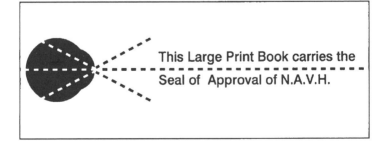

This Large Print Book carries the
Seal of Approval of N.A.V.H.

Jude Deveraux

<+ +>

Always

Thorndike Press • Waterville, Maine

Published in 2005 by arrangement with Pocket Books, a division of Simon & Schuster, Inc.

Thorndike Press® Large Print Core.

The tree indicium is a trademark of Thorndike Press.

The text of this Large Print edition is unabridged. Other aspects of the book may vary from the original edition.

Set in 16 pt. Plantin by Elena Picard.

Printed in the United States on permanent paper.

Library of Congress Cataloging-in-Publication Data

Deveraux, Jude.
  Always / by Jude Deveraux.
    p. cm.
    ISBN 0-7862-6639-2 (lg. print : hc : alk. paper)
    1. Undercover operations — Fiction. 2. Kidnapping victims — Fiction. 3. Missing persons — Fiction. 4. Time travel — Fiction. 5. Psychics — Fiction. 6. Large type books. I. Title.
  PS3554.E9273A79 2005
  813′.54—dc22   2004025307

I dedicate this book to all the readers who were upset because I killed off some of my Montgomerys in a horrible way.

You should have trusted me more.

As the Founder/CEO of NAVH, the only national health agency solely devoted to those who, although not totally blind, have an eye disease which could lead to serious visual impairment, I am pleased to recognize Thorndike Press* as one of the leading publishers in the large print field.

Founded in 1954 in San Francisco to prepare large print textbooks for partially seeing children, NAVH became the pioneer and standard setting agency in the preparation of large type.

Today, those publishers who meet our standards carry the prestigious "Seal of Approval" indicating high quality large print. We are delighted that Thorndike Press is one of the publishers whose titles meet these standards. We are also pleased to recognize the significant contribution Thorndike Press is making in this important and growing field.

Lorraine H. Marchi, L.H.D.
Founder/CEO
NAVH

* Thorndike Press encompasses the following imprints: Thorndike, Wheeler, Walker and Large Print Press.

Part One

2004

Chapter One

Connie and Kayla were almost the same age and about the same size. Even their coloring was nearly the same. But as alike as they were, they couldn't have been more different. Kayla exuded golden blondeness, while Connie was pale and washed-out looking. Kayla's height was statuesque, whereas Connie seemed to tower over people and slumped to keep from doing so. Kayla was a woman no one could overlook, while Connie was easy to miss.

Connie had been working at Wrightsman's jewelry store for six years; Kayla had been there for three weeks. Connie knew everything there was to know about the cut and clarity of jewels. She could tell you the weight and the color number of a diamond at a glance. She knew the provenance of every jewel in the store, knew what was in the safe and who had owned what and why they'd had to sell it.

Kayla asked customers if they liked "the blue ones or the green ones" better.

But in three weeks Kayla had sold more jewelry than Connie had in the last six months. After the first week, Connie had complained to Mr. Wrightsman. "She *models* the jewelry. She wears low-cut dresses, hangs a million-dollar necklace around her throat, then leans over so men can look down her front." Connie had not been pleased by Mr. Wrightsman's answer. He'd told her to "join the real world."

It was late on Friday when the man entered the store. After having worked at Wrightsman's for so long, Connie was used to the rich and powerful stepping into the store. Besides the professionally lit showroom where the customers could show off their wealth by buying something Marie Antoinette had once owned, there was an elegant room in the back where they could sit in private and sell what they could no longer afford.

Connie had met many politicians, movie stars, and jet-setters, but she'd never seen this man before. He was handsome in a masculine way, with heavy black eyebrows, dark eyes, and an aquiline nose set above lips that had a slight, teasing smile, as though he knew something no one else did.

As Connie looked at the man, she felt her knees start to melt. The only other time she'd felt this way was when Sean Connery had walked into the store. This man was wearing a black leather jacket that she was sure had cost thousands; she could almost feel the softness of the leather under her fingertips. His tan trousers had to have been cut to fit him. As he walked toward the door, when she saw that he wore no jewelry, her heart dropped. He was buying for a woman, not himself.

She didn't really think that a man like him would be interested in her, but still, she relished the thought of searching through the vaults for just the right jewel. She prided herself on being a good judge of financial position and this man exuded money. Naked, dripping from a shower, she thought, this man would have an aura of wealth about him.

As he pushed the glass door open, Connie nearly giggled at her thought of this beautiful man being wet and naked. Catching herself, she looked across the cases filled with sparkling jewels on blue satin to Kayla — and was horrified to see Kayla staring at the man with the same expression that Connie was probably wearing.

Connie wanted to scream, "Oh, no you don't. This one is *mine!*" Men like this one, men who possessed old world manners — and old world money — were her reward for putting up with tourists who wanted to see "where Brad Pitt shopped," and with rude rock stars and ego-tripping two-bit actors who wanted the world to know that they bought their jewels at Wrightsman's.

The man entered the store, removed his sunglasses, then stood for a moment as his eyes adjusted. When they did, he looked at Connie and smiled. Yes, she thought. Come to me.

But in the next second he turned his head and saw Kayla — and it was to her he walked.

Connie had to duck behind the counter to hide her anger. Before Mr. Wrightsman had hired Connie, he'd dumped a pile of diamonds on a velvet tray, then sat there in silence and looked at her. He didn't tell her what he wanted her to do with them. Arrange them in order of size? Clarity? Connie had paid her dues at half a dozen retail stores and two wholesale merchants before she'd dared to apply at a prestigious store like Wrightsman's. With no hesitation, she had chosen one diamond out of the pile, one of the smaller ones. She had no loupe so she couldn't judge it for flaws, but for color, the diamond was nearly perfect.

She set the diamond on the side of the tray, then looked at the old man. The tiniest of smiles appeared at a corner of his mouth. "Monday, nine a.m.," he'd said, then looked back at the ledger in front of him, dismissing her.

In the past six years Connie had brought the old, family-owned store into the twenty-first century. She'd put in a computer system, made a website, had arranged for some discreet publicity, and had twice foiled Mr. Wrightsman's youngest son's plans to abscond with the store's profits.

Her life had been nearly perfect until Mr. Wrightsman had, for some unfathomable reason, hired a woman whose only selling advantage was a lot of hair and a lot of bosom.

Now, surreptitiously, Connie watched the man as he bent over the counter in front of Kayla. When she put what Connie called "the tourist tray" before him, she heard the man give a low laugh. His voice was silky-smooth and deep, a voice that made Connie close her eyes for a moment.

And when she did, she dropped the tray

of rings in her hand. Never had she dropped a tray before. Cursing Kayla, cursing Mr. Wrightsman for hiring her, Connie got down on her hands and knees and began to pick up the scattered $20,000 rings. One emerald beauty had bounced under the cabinet so Connie had to bend low to get it — and when she did, she glanced through the glass case just in time to see the man slip a ruby and diamond necklace into his trousers' pocket.

Connie was so taken aback that she sat down on her heels and stared at what she could see of the man through the glass. Surely not, she thought. Slowly, she stood up, then even more slowly, she walked over to where Kayla and the man were standing, keeping her eyes away from him. She mustn't let a pair of sexy eyes distract her.

While Connie had been scurrying to pick up the rings, Kayla had done what she'd been repeatedly told not to do: she'd covered the countertop with merchandise. She'd been told to take one item at a time out so she could keep track of what was where.

It took Connie all of three seconds to see that the case that held the necklace of an empress of Russia was empty, and that the necklace was not in the jumble of jewels lying in a heap. Unaware of what the man had done, Kayla was bent down, pulling three more trays out of the bottom of the case.

Connie raised her eyes to look at the man and when her gaze met his, he smiled in a soft, seductive way that made her want to run to the vault and get out the really good jewels. Maybe he'd like a Fabergé egg or two.

But Connie had morals, and wrong was wrong. The man was beautiful, but he was a thief. With her heart pounding in her throat, she smiled back at him while she reached under the counter, opened the little metal door, and pushed the button of the silent alarm. In six years, she'd only pushed that button one other time.

Kayla saw Connie push the button and looked at her coworker in disbelief. With her head turned away from the man, Connie gave Kayla a look meant to silence her.

After the button was pushed, there was about five seconds of quiet, then all hell broke loose. Sirens sounded outside and heavy iron bars began to drop down across the front of the store.

For a moment Connie's heart seemed to

stop. She locked eyes with the man and she had to fight against screaming at him to run, to try to get away. If he broke a window . . . if he pushed open a door . . . but no, the glass had a high-strength plastic in the middle of it and the doors wouldn't open because of the gates.

But Connie's feelings of compassion, her desire to see the man get away, ended when Kayla stood up. "You mean, spiteful bitch," Kayla said. "You couldn't stand that *I* got him and you didn't."

Flustered, Connie couldn't speak. She hadn't pushed the alarm because she was *jealous*.

"Quiet, little one," the man said to Kayla in his smooth voice, then he picked up her hand and kissed the back of it.

Connie turned away at that and in the next second three policemen were there, and she used her key and a code number to open the gate. "He put a necklace in his pocket," she said, not looking at Kayla.

The police were oddly silent, and when the man held out his hands, they put hand-cuffs on him and told him his rights. It was almost as if they had been told not to ask questions. And throughout it all, as far as Connie could tell, the man had never lost his smile, and she was puzzled by it. Why had he been so stupid? Why wasn't he protesting? After all, until he'd left the store with the necklace in his pocket, he hadn't actually committed a crime. Maybe she'd been hasty in pushing the alarm button.

It was when they reached the front door that Connie heard her own thought. The necklace! Grabbing the empty velvet tray, she held it out to the man. "He still has the necklace," she said.

"You know where it is," the man said, so much sex oozing from his voice that Connie could almost see the two of them sitting on a mile of white beach, margaritas in hand.

She couldn't help herself as she reached forward to slip her hand inside the man's front pocket to retrieve the necklace. And when she did, he bent his head and kissed her. Time seemed to stand still. She could feel his warm thigh under her hand, his chest was touching hers, and his lips were . . . She closed her eyes and she could almost hear steel drums, feel soft tropical breezes on her skin.

"Okay, let's break this up," one of the cops said. "Lady! Get your hands out of his pants and your face off his."

This brought guffaws of laughter from the two other policemen. Connie pulled

17

the necklace from his pocket and, her eyes never leaving his, spread it on the tray.

Standing by the window, the tray in her hand, Connie watched them lead the man to the waiting police car. She could still feel his kiss on her lips.

"Is that the right one?" she heard Kayla ask. Reluctantly, Connie pulled her eyes away from the man and looked at the necklace on the tray. It was not an exquisite ruby and diamond creation but a cheap concoction of glass and gold-toned pot metal.

When Connie glanced up, she saw that the man was about to enter the police car. "He still has the necklace," she shouted, but the thick glass was almost completely soundproof. She banged on the window to get their attention and when the policemen turned to look, the man took that moment to go into action.

His hands were in cuffs, but standing on one leg, he kicked out to send one policeman spinning, then whirled to plant a foot in the chest of the second one. The third cop pulled his gun, but the man knocked it with his cuffed hands, sending the gun flying into the street.

In the next second, the man was sprinting down the street with the speed of an Olympic runner, and Connie saw him disappear into an alley a block away.

"If he gets caught, it will be *your* fault," Kayla said as she flung the door open and went outside.

For a moment Connie stood alone in the shop, then she thought of what Mr. Wrightsman was going to say when he heard that Connie had allowed the thief to take the necklace. She hadn't even looked at it when she'd taken it from his pocket. She'd been so ensorcelled by his kiss that . . . that she was going to lose her job.

Dropping the horrid necklace, she ran out the door, reaching into her pocket to push the electronic door lock as she ran. She *had* to get that necklace back!

By the time she got to the alley, the three policemen had recovered and were searching inside the Dumpster and behind the garbage cans. She stood back, watching them, her heart pounding from her run. If the man had run in here, unless he was Spider-Man, there was no escape. There were twenty-foot-tall brick walls and the few windows were painted over, unused for years. All the fire escapes ended two stories above the ground.

Connie's first impulse was to join in the search, but instead, she stood back and looked. Where could a man hide?

She never would have seen him if he hadn't moved. It was almost as though he wanted to be caught.

There was a tiny ledge on one of the buildings and he was lying flat on it, so still that there were two pigeons on his back. She took a moment to figure out how he'd managed to climb up there. He must have leaped from the Dumpster to catch the bottom of a fire escape, swung upward, crept along the four-inch-wide ledge into the deep shadows where two buildings intersected, then lain flat out, half-hidden under the broken remnants of an old iron and concrete balcony.

Why had he moved? she wondered. Why had he *purposefully* let her see him?

One of the cops saw Connie looking up and drew his gun. But before the policeman could do whatever he was going to do next, two cars screeched to a halt at the end of the alley and six men in suits and dark glasses jumped out. They flashed badges at the cops and one man said, "FBI. We've been looking for this guy for a long time. He's ours."

Two minutes later, the beautiful man, still handcuffed, was standing on the ground, this time surrounded by FBI agents.

Boldly, Connie stepped forward. "He still has the necklace he stole," she said, not looking into the man's eyes. His eyes — and his lips — had the power to make her forget about everything.

"You'll get it back," one of the FBI agents said brusquely as he led the man away.

Standing at the end of the alley, the three policemen behind her, Connie watched them put the man into the car. He winked at her through the window, then they were gone.

Chapter Two

Two FBI agents, one on each arm, shoved the man into Ryerson's office. What a big shot like Ryerson wanted with a lowlife like this guy, they couldn't imagine. They'd run his prints and he had a record longer than the Amazon.

The two agents cuffed the man to a chair that was bolted to the floor, then took their places beside him.

"You may go," Greg Ryerson said.

"He's —" one of the agents began, but Ryerson stopped him with a look.

Silently, the agents left the room, closing the door behind them.

Greg went to the big window and closed the blinds. He wasn't at a high enough level to rate an outside window, but one wall of his office was glass and looked down over the enormous lobby below. He could close the blinds to slits and secretly observe the comings and goings of everyone — something he'd rather do than watch a bunch of birds in a bunch of trees.

Turning back, Greg looked at the man cuffed to the chair. He'd been roughed up. The corner of his mouth was bleeding and the cut over his eye might need a few stitches. Other than that the man looked good. For a second, memories flashed through Greg's mind: a van rolling down a cliff; a man's body flying through the air; a man in a hospital bed, his face covered in bandages.

"So, Jack," Greg said conversationally, "how are you?"

"Bleeding to death. You want to get these things off of me?"

"Think I'll be safe?"

"You won't be if you leave me tied up for another two minutes."

Smiling, Greg opened a box on his marble-topped desk, withdrew a key, and unlocked the handcuffs. As Jack rubbed his wrists, Greg opened a small closet to reveal a sink with glasses above. He took a cloth from a drawer, wet it with hot water, and handed it to Jack. "Want me to get a doctor?"

Jack raised an eyebrow as he held the cloth to his temple. "I'm still recovering from the last time you got me a doctor."

Again, images flashed across Greg's mind: Jack's smashed face, unrecognizable, as he was wheeled into an operating room. "Yeah, I did a good job that time," Greg said, watching Jack relax and smile. The man sitting in front of him bore no resemblance to the boy he'd grown up with. That boy had inherited his father's big, hooked nose and the protruding brow. But that face had been crushed and rebuilt. Out of necessity, Jack had had an "extreme makeover," and he'd come out looking a great deal better than he'd gone in.

"You know, Greg," Jack said slowly, "if you'd wanted to see me, you could have called. Left a message. We could have had lunch. You really didn't need to do all . . . this." He waved his hand to indicate his injured face.

"Where's the fun in that? Besides, all your numbers are tapped."

"By you guys."

"*Us* guys. You're one of us, remember?"

"I try to forget." Jack folded the cloth and wiped the blood from his lip. "So what do you want?"

Greg went to the bar and removed a small glass from behind some junk glasses purchased at the local home store. It was Waterford crystal and only Jack drank from it. Bending, Greg removed a bottle of twenty-year-old port from beneath the sink, then poured the glass three quarters full and handed it to Jack. "I need a progress report. How are you doing? What have you found out? Ready to make any collars?"

Jack didn't answer for a few moments as he sipped his port, seeming to weigh Greg's words. "You never were good at lying," Jack said. "Remember how I always found out the truth when we were kids?" Lifting his head, he looked Greg in the eye. "What's happened and what do you need me for?"

Nervously, Greg moved behind his desk, putting a barrier between him and Jack. "Your father was kidnapped about six weeks ago."

"And here I thought it was something important," Jack said lightly. "By the way, now that you have me in here, how do you plan to get me out? Those boys you sent after me think I have a record going back to when I was nine!"

Greg didn't smile, nor did he answer Jack's question. "I know what your father did to you. I know what he did to my mother after Dad's death. More than anyone else on earth I know what a cold, selfish bastard J. Barrett Hallbrooke is. I lived with it for years, remember?"

Jack sipped his port and studied the glass. "Why do I feel that there's a 'but' in this?"

"There's a big one. But the president wants him. Needs him."

"Needs the Hallbrooke money," Jack said, his jaw rigid. "Good ol' dad can write a check but he can't forgive or —"

"Yeah, yeah, I know all that," Greg said impatiently. "John Barrett Hallbrooke is the coldest bastard on earth. Drop him in a volcano and he'd freeze it. He can't go fishing because he freezes the water for three miles around the boat. The cook stores the frozen food in his bed. I was there, remember? I helped make up the jokes."

"You forgot the one where he kissed my mother and she froze to death. Not the Midas touch, the ice touch."

"Jack," Greg said in a tone of great patience, "I'm not asking you to forgive the man. I just need for you to find him."

"If he's been gone six weeks, he's probably dead." Jack finished his port and set the glass on a table in front of the window, then stood up and looked through the blinds, his back to Greg.

"He's still alive. He's confined, but not being tortured. The people holding him want something other than money."

"Couldn't be any of my relatives then," Jack said, turning back to Greg. "Look, I'd really like to help you on this but I can't. This project I'm on is nearly completed. If you hadn't dragged me out to play jewel thief I would be a lot closer to the end. Did they tell you that I got chased into an alley by some cops? I had to hide facedown on a filthy ledge with a bunch of pigeons on my back. If I hadn't shown them where I was they would have given up. Which reminds me." Jack reached into his pocket, withdrew a ruby and diamond necklace, and put it on Greg's desk. "That girl you planted? Cute but not much upstairs."

Greg glared at Jack. "You're avoiding me."

"Should I take the elevator or the stairs to get out of here?"

"You do know, don't you, that all I have to do is push a button and you'll be locked up? There are only three people in the bureau who know you're working for us, and I'm the only one who knows what you look like now."

Even though Greg had put on his most threatening scowl, Jack just smiled at him. "Pistols at dawn?"

27

Deflated, Greg sat down in his chair, put his face in his hands for a moment, then looked back up at Jack. "This case is driving us crazy! It's top secret and every day it's getting harder to keep it a secret. Your father —"

"Mr. Hallbrooke."

"Yeah, okay. Iceberg Man. Whatever. He was a joke to us as kids, but he's not a joke to a whole lot of people. He practically supports half a dozen charities by himself. And stop looking at me like that! His money helps a lot of people." Greg grabbed a piece of paper off his desk. "This is a letter from the White House. Signed by the president. It's an official command for us to get off our butts and find J. Barrett Hallbrooke the third and get him back at his checkbook."

Grimacing, Jack looked away for a moment, then back at Greg. "Okay, so tell me what you know — not that I'm interested, mind you, but maybe I can tell you which of my relatives has him."

Greg moved to the front of the desk. "We've checked out Gus and Theo and that man she married. Clean, as far as we can tell. We have them bugged and under surveillance. We put a maid in there and they're on camera all day long."

"They're in the house?"

"Sure. They were contacted by us and —"

"Back up. Why you? Who got the ransom note?"

"I have no idea who was told your father was missing and how he or she was told. No one's told me a ransom has been asked for. The only civilians who know about your father's disappearance are his siblings," Greg said.

"And let me guess. The minute you told them they started crying and begged to be allowed to be as near as possible to their beloved brother."

Greg chuckled. "Exactly." Pausing, he shook his head in memory. "Remember what we used to do to them? How we used to lie to them?"

"I remember the time you called Aunt Theo, crying, and said you thought Mr. Hallbrooke had had a heart attack."

"You put me up to it!"

"Yeah, but you *did* it."

Greg laughed. "They got there at, what was it? Three a.m.?"

Jack smiled. "Theo was already crying into her handkerchief, and Uncle Gus had enough luggage to stay forever." He looked at Greg. "What I remember most is how mad your father was."

Greg shifted on his seat. "I still remember that paddling he gave me."

"And wanted to give me." Jack looked at the window blind, then said softly, "You know, I was jealous of you for that paddling. My father . . ." He trailed off.

"Said nothing," Greg said. "He stood at the top of the stairs and told his siblings he was not dying so they could go home. Even though it was the wee hours, he didn't invite them to spend the night."

"And even though he knew I'd done it, he said nothing to me. Not a word. It was the worst punishment I ever had."

Greg gave a melodramatic sigh. "Okay, poor you. Poor little rich boy unloved by his daddy. You got him back, though, didn't you? Drugs, women, a hell-raiser without equal. And now they all think the heir apparent is dead and that the billions are going to go to Gus and Theo and those two criminal-minded kids of hers. No more charities. No more dumping millions into shelters for battered women and abused children. No more paying the salaries of people to find runaway teens. No more —"

"Get off your soap box," Jack snapped. "What's happened since he disappeared?"

"Nothing!" Greg said, throwing up his

hands. His frustration obvious, he went to the bar, filled two glasses with ice, and poured them full of ginger ale. When they were kids they thought ginger ale was alcoholic and that they were pulling a fast one over on Greg's mother — Hallbrooke's cook — when they drank it. They'd spent many afternoons believing they were drunk from consuming great quantities of ginger ale. They stopped on the day they heard Greg's mother and three housemaids howling with laughter over what the boys had thought was a secret. By the time they were exposed, they'd developed a lifelong love of the beverage.

Taking his drink, Jack said, "I'm confused. You say you've heard nothing else but you also said you knew he was still alive. In fact, didn't I hear you say . . . what was it? He is 'confined but not being tortured.' How do you know that if you haven't heard from the kidnappers?"

"Have I ever told you that I've always admired your memory? It's almost photographic, isn't it? Remember how Mom used to ask you to help her remember which cookbook a certain recipe was in?"

Jack didn't reply, just leaned back in his chair, sipped his drink, and looked hard at Greg.

After a moment, red began to creep up the back of Greg's neck. "A psssh . . . ick," he said at last, his mouth on the rim of the glass.

"A what?" Jack asked, then his eyes widened. He set his glass down on the coffee table. "I'm outta here."

Greg put himself between Jack and the door. "You try to leave and —"

"And what?" Jack challenged, his eyes showing anger.

"I'll call my mother and tell her that you faked your death and that you're still alive."

Jack's face drained of color and he sat back down. "No," he whispered. "Your mother . . ."

"She cried hard at your funeral, you know. If I had died she wouldn't have cried harder."

"She'll kill me," Jack whispered.

"Oh yeah," Greg said cheerfully. "And me. She won't be like your dad and be silent. She'll make your life a living hell. You'll go back underground and —"

"Couldn't. Your mom would put my picture on CNN and tell the world what a rotten thing I did."

"True. And all that plastic surgery would be wasted. Everyone would know that John

Barrett Hallbrooke the fourth is alive and well — and rich. You would be the one to have to deal with the charities and your aunt and uncle. And the twins, of course."

"Ah, yes, my young cousins. How are they, by the way?"

"Same as always. Self-centered and bone lazy. The boy, Holcombe, complains if his sheets are wrinkled, and the girl, Chrissy, talks of rebellion and 'the people,' but she makes no effort to get a job."

Jack looked away. When the opportunity had presented itself for him to die, so to speak, he'd eagerly taken it. His face had been reconstructed and a new identity had been given to him by the FBI. He'd never once regretted what he'd done. Greg and his parents, his father's cook and chauffeur, had been his only family.

Taking a deep breath, Jack looked back at Greg. Only his blood relatives had the power to make him feel this bad. "Okay, out with it. What and how?"

Greg leaned back against his chair. "A psychic." He held up his hand to stop Jack's laughter. "You don't have to tell me what you think of psychics. It's what all of America thinks of them. But this one is different. This one is . . ." He looked away.

"Was that a shudder?" Jack laughed,

smirking. "What'd she do? Read your mind? Did she tell you that she knows you've been unfaithful to your wife and now you're scared she's going to tell Sue?"

Greg's voice lowered. "She made me unbutton my shirt and show her where I fell on that iron spike when we were kids. You know that that place has always bothered me. Then she held a little glass ball up to the scar and . . ." He paused a moment. "When she took the ball away, I could move my shoulder more freely than I've been able to since it happened when I was eight. She said the muscle had attached to the bone and she'd freed it."

Jack ran his hand over his eyes. "Lord! A psychic *and* a faith healer."

Greg looked harder at Jack. "You didn't listen to me. I said she *made* me take off my shirt."

"Gunpoint?"

"With her mind."

"Right, Greg," Jack said. "She sent you a thought and you obeyed it."

"Exactly."

"I'm supposed to believe that someone exists on this earth who can do this?"

"Her husband's family has a lot of money so they're able to protect her. At least they're able to keep what she can do out of the press. We know because she helps us on cases."

Jack shook his head. "You've been in here too long. Or maybe you've seen *Men In Black* too often. Gregory, this is the real world, not some teen series on Fox. No Buffy, no kid talking to God. Real. Get it?"

Greg was unperturbed. "She comes in about once a week and goes over pictures and objects. She feels them, and tells us what she sees. She's solved hundreds of cases. Over and over she's proven that she can control things with her mind. Truthfully, people here think she can do a great deal more than she lets us know about. Last year she and Lincoln Aimes —"

"The actor?" Jack asked.

"Yeah, the actor. He was at some resort with her and the place burned down."

"Couldn't she have willed the fire to stop?"

Greg ignored the snide remark. "Nobody died but the guy who started the fire kept yelling that he'd killed Aimes. He said that after Aimes was dead, zombies had carried him away — and brought him back to life."

"He in a psych ward now?"

"Dead. Heart attack soon after his trial. When he was given only four years for arson, he started laughing and saying he got away with murder. He also said he'd 'get the kid' after he got out. Two days later he dropped dead in his cell."

"A crazy man."

"Yeah, but two other women at that spa also said they saw Lincoln Aimes being carried away by 'zombies.' "

"Mass hysteria. Do you have a point to this? Or are you going to tell me that this psychic used her little crystal ball and raised some pretty boy actor from the dead?" When Greg didn't reply, Jack snorted. "I used to think the FBI used science. So where are the rooms full of aliens? How about the people who've been on spaceships?"

"Laugh all you want but I know what she did to my shoulder."

"Okay, I'll bite. Why you? If she can cure people, why isn't she in cancer wards curing little kids?"

"She is. She does. But she has to be discreet or she'll cause riots. The president knows of her, and her powers are being used in ways that are kept from the public."

"Why do I feel as though I'm watching the Sci-Fi channel?"

Greg waited for his friend to stop his sarcasm.

"Okay," Jack said after a while, "let's just pretend this is true. A psychic told you that my father is alive and well somewhere, and the president of the United States wants him found. Why doesn't this psychic just tell you where he is?"

"She doesn't know. She says there's something blocking her from finding him."

"You mean like a truck? Or is it a mountain?"

"Would you cut out the attitude? If your father dies, then all that money goes to your aunt and uncle and her two selfish kids. What do you think they'll do with it? Give it away to help others as your father does?"

"Okay, okay," Jack said. "Point taken. I see why you want to find Iceberg Dad, and I see that you're using any method you can to find him. What I don't see is what *I* have to do with it."

"She, the psychic . . . you see, she really only deals with the top guys in the FBI."

"Not down to your level?"

"No. Not down here. But she asked for me. She said there was someone in the bureau who knew someone who could find your father. I'm sure she knows you're his son and she must know you're deep undercover, but she admitted nothing. She picked me out of a book of photos and I met her alone. She told me to contact the man I know, and that you'd be able to find Hallbrooke."

"I see," Jack said slowly. "And, let me guess, I find myself on the journey."

"You know," Greg said slowly, "I've never wanted to punch you as much as I do right now."

"That left hook of yours could mess up some very expensive plastic surgery."

Greg's eyes glittered. "I can tell that all you're going to do is make jokes, so just go. I'll see that you're escorted out." He began straightening papers on his desk.

"You were always able to get to me, weren't you?" Jack said softly. "As kids you used my who-cares attitude to get me to do whatever you were afraid to do."

"Which is why I'm now safely behind a desk and you're on the streets. We've always made a perfect team."

Jack dabbed at the cut on his eye. "I take it that your psychic is to be here today and that's why I was brought in."

"She —" When the phone on his desk rang, Greg picked it up, listened, then hung up. "She's here now, just arriving."

"Get out the incense and the crystal balls."

Ignoring him, Greg went to the blinds and looked down at the lobby. "There she is."

Jack looked but he saw no one who he thought could be Greg's so-called psychic. There were half a dozen female agents, all of them looking as though they were trying to solve some earth-shattering case — which they probably were — but no one who looked like a clairvoyant.

Greg nodded toward a woman at the counter. When she turned as she pinned her visitor's badge, Jack looked at her. She was small and curvy, with short strawberry-blonde hair. From where he was standing she looked to be a knockout. For a moment he thought that it might be rewarding, so to speak, to work with her.

He watched her walk toward the grand staircase that many agents preferred over the elevator. As she walked, she lifted her hand to tuck a strand of hair behind her ear in a gesture he'd seen before.

"I know her!" Jack said. "Or at least I've seen her before." As he tried to remember, he glanced at Greg and saw that his face was red all the way to his ears, and his mouth was so tightly closed his lips were gone.

Uh-oh, Jack thought as he looked back at

the woman. Was she someone he had had an affair with? There were years of his life that were little more than a blur. After he'd run away from his father he'd spent years in a drug-induced haze. In the four years since he'd been sober he'd met many people he'd once known but now didn't remember.

"It was Houston, wasn't it?" Jack said. "I met her in Houston and we . . ." Trailing off, he kept watching the woman and thinking that that wasn't right. Had he ever been to bed with a psychic? Some woman who said she could read minds? Tell fortunes? Or, as Greg said, make people take off their clothes?

Jack watched the woman reach the head of the stairs and turn toward them. When she did, newspaper headlines flashed across his mind. "The Hillbilly Honey Suspected of Murder," he saw.

Jack dropped the blind. "Is there a back way out of here?"

"I'd like for you to stay and meet her," Greg said firmly.

Jack shot him a look. "You want me to stay and meet the Hillbilly Honey? She killed her husband for his money. And her sister-in-law."

"She didn't. We have proof that she didn't. She was —"

Jack snorted. "She wasn't there? Right, of course she wasn't. Greg, I expected more of you. Just because she wasn't there doesn't mean she didn't kill them. Look at the facts: Poor white trash marries into a rich family and a year later the rich husband dies."

"She's spent years searching for them." Greg took a deep breath. "She's not what the public thinks she is, and she hasn't done what they think she has."

Jack looked at Greg sharply. "You're afraid of her, aren't you?"

"She's done some things," he said quietly. "I've not seen her do anything except, well, heal my shoulder, but I've read the reports. There's a possibility that she can freeze people in place."

"Then she sticks a rock on them and heals them. A great party gag. Look, Greg, I'll help find my father but I'm not working with a so-called psychic. You let her feel all the photos she wants and I'll even listen to what you tell me she's said, but I want nothing to do with the little gold digger."

There was a light knock on the door. "She's here, so sit down and behave yourself or I swear I'll call my mother."

Throwing up his hands in defeat, Jack

took a seat as Greg opened the door. Right away he saw why Greg and this woman's husband, and maybe the entire FBI, were taken in by her. She looked much younger than she probably was, and she had an air about her that made her seem innocent and vulnerable.

Silently, he watched as Greg made chit-chat about the beautiful spring weather. She glanced at Jack and Greg made a cursory introduction. Jack didn't get up, just nodded in acknowledgment, and she looked away.

Jack watched them as Greg poured her a glass of ginger ale. The Hillbilly Honey, Jack thought. There wasn't much in life he hated more than a gold digger. He had sympathy for drug addicts and even some murderers, but for people like his relatives and everyone who'd sucked up to him when they'd learned he was rich, he had no sympathy.

Wonder how she did it, he thought as he watched her and Greg sit down. She was across from the two men, and as Jack looked at her expensive clothes, he wondered what she'd done to get into the exclusive Montgomery family. In his father's wealthy set, the Montgomerys were known to keep to themselves. They were often referred to as "the clan."

But somehow, this woman had used her curvy little bottom to worm her way into the Montgomery clan. Then she'd killed her husband. And her sister-in-law. Had the sister been an accident? Or had the woman been on to her?

Jack looked at the "honey" as she chatted with Greg and smiled. It was a plane wreck, wasn't it? Wonder what she did? Fuel line? A few gauges tampered with? Had she done it herself or paid someone? No, she probably did it herself. Women from her class knew how to use screwdrivers and wrenches.

So what's she done with all the money? he wondered. Men? Or did she like women? She probably had a father who beat her as a kid so she'd probably turned to women.

Sociopath, he thought. Cares about no one or nothing. Her hard-knocks life had made her incapable of love.

"Excuse me," he heard the little honey say.

Still smiling, feeling as though he'd seen through this charlatan, he watched her stand up and take a step toward him. Obviously, she couldn't stand that there was a male in the room who wasn't fawning over her.

When she stood before him, he looked up at her pretty face, then down her body. She had on a conservative dark suit but it only accentuated her curves. She's one hot little number, he thought as he looked back up at her face.

Wham! In the next second she drew back her hand and struck him across the face hard.

For your information I married my husband for love, she shouted at him so loud that his head rang. *And I didn't kill him or his sister.* Putting her hands on the arms of his chair, she leaned into his face. *But I have killed people. I made their heads explode. Would you like for me to do the same to you?*

Try it! Jack shouted back at her. In the next moment he felt a sharp pain in his head, but he looked at her and concentrated on her eyes, and he kept the pain from becoming unbearable.

Seconds later, she stood up straight and looked down at him. *Someone is protecting you,* she said, then she turned on her heel and left the room before Greg could move to stop her.

It took Jack a few moments to recover himself. She'd hit him on his sore mouth and it was bleeding again. "So much for your psychic," he said as he went to the sink to wash his mouth.

In the mirror he caught sight of Greg sitting absolutely still on the sofa. Why wasn't he jumping up and running after the woman? Or at the very least telling Jack what he thought of him?

"Greg?" Jack said, turning to look at his friend. When Greg didn't so much as blink, Jack grabbed his shoulders, then instinctively drew back. Greg's muscles were tightened into rigidity. Jack took his friend's shoulders again and pushed him down onto the couch — where his legs stayed bent into a sitting position.

What could have caused this instant paralysis? he wondered even as he ran to the phone to call for an ambulance. But in the next second Greg's body relaxed and he whispered, "Don't call."

Jack ran to him, but Greg brushed him away, then sat up, rubbing his arms. "What the hell did you do to her?"

At that, Jack went to the bar and poured himself some bourbon. This day had been too much for him. First he'd been told to go to Wrightsman's jewelry store and steal a necklace from an undercover agent and that he'd be brought in. He had not been told of an overzealous clerk who'd looked at him like she wanted him for breakfast, and he hadn't been told he was going to have to fight three policemen while wearing handcuffs. And he had definitely not been told about any pigeons using his body as a platform for a mating dance.

"I didn't say a word to her before she hit me," Jack said after he'd downed a double shot of bourbon.

Greg staggered over to the telephone and pushed a button. "Is she still in the building?"

From the expression on his face, Jack knew the woman had left. "Shouldn't I be the one you feel sorry for?" he asked. "I was just sitting there, minding my own business, and she hit me. Then while I was bleeding, she threatened to *kill* me. She —"

"She didn't say a word to you," Greg said, standing up and flexing his legs.

"Is that how we're going to play it? She didn't say a word to me? Okay, fine by me. It was stupid anyway. She said she'd made people's heads explode."

Greg blinked a couple of times, then sat back down. "I wondered what happened in those tunnels."

"Tunnels?"

"Yeah, she and her husband and her mother and some others cleaned out a

46

bunch of murderers in Connecticut. They called themselves a coven and the ring-leader said she was a witch. Whatever they were, they were a nasty bunch." He ran his hand over his eyes. "They stole kids. Little children. They kidnapped Darci's husband when he was three, but he escaped so the woman — the witch — went after the rest of the family. We believe she killed his father, and after his mother gave birth, she killed the mother and kept that child for her own."

Jack poured himself another bourbon. "But you guys finally got her, right?"

"No!" Greg said sharply. "*They* did. Only we couldn't figure out how the witch and her cohorts had been killed. There wasn't a mark on any of the four people, but the autopsies showed that their brains had been . . . destroyed."

"I see. And you think she — What's her name?"

"Darci Montgomery."

"You think *she* did it? Destroyed their brains?"

Greg was quiet for a moment. "Jack," he said, "Darci didn't say anything to you and you didn't say anything to her. Not out loud anyway."

"You need this more than I do," Jack

said, handing him the drink. "The woman hit me, then shouted at me so loud my ears hurt. I answered her back just as loud, then she said . . ."

"What?"

"She said, 'someone is protecting you.' She couldn't mean my fellow FBI agents because —"

"Jack, I'm telling you that the two of you never exchanged even one word out loud. Whatever was said between you was done in your minds."

"Telepathy," Jack said, smirking. "Thought exchange."

Greg didn't answer, just looked at Jack in speculation. Like the good agent he was, he was thinking how he could use this ability in his cases. Jack could go into situations with no wire and he could relay every word that was being said to Darci. She could tell them what was going on as it was happening. If Jack was in too dangerous a situation he could call for help through Darci.

As for Jack being "protected," that rang true. He and Jack had always had a strong bond between them and several times they'd rescued each other. Well, actually it was Jack who'd been in trouble and Greg who'd come to the rescue. Once when they were in high school together, Greg had "heard" a voice in his head telling him to run to the parking lot. The voice had been so insistent that he'd left class without permission and run as fast as he could. He'd been in time to stop three guys who were in the middle of beating up Jack. Later, the doctor said that a couple more kicks and Jack might have lost a kidney. As it was, it was three months before he recovered.

Greg had always "heard" Jack, but not the other way around. Of course, it was always Jack who'd been in physical danger. Greg had only needed rescuing once and that had been when he'd been accused of cheating on a test. Jack had been the one to figure out who had done it and how. When Greg called him a "genius," Jack said, "No, it was weird, but it was like I could see into your classroom and I could see who had done it. I saw that he'd taped the notes onto your desk, and he read them from the back row with his new glasses." Upon investigation, the glasses turned out to be a form of binoculars the kid had bought at a spy store.

"What's that look for?" Jack asked. When Greg didn't respond, he took a step backward. "I'm not a freak. I'll go undercover in the drug world; I'll go into prison and find out whatever from your worst criminal, but I will *not* work with some voodoo princess. That kind of stuff —"

He broke off because they heard a shout from the lobby below. They went to the window and looked through the blinds. Darci had reentered the building, but since she'd already checked out and wasn't on the appointment book, she'd been asked to leave. When she ignored the request, the agent had put his hand on her arm. He'd yelled when his hand felt as though it had been set on fire. When two other agents tried to grab Darci, they, too, jumped away in pain.

Darci was holding something in her hand and she was looking up at Greg's window. Pulling the cord, he lifted the blind all the way up.

Neither Greg nor Jack said anything as they watched Darci make her way up the stairs toward them. Her focus never left the window, and she didn't seem to be aware of the dozen or so agents who tried to stop her from climbing the stairs.

With their eyes wide in disbelief, Jack and Greg watched as armed men and women fell away from her. Some stopped as they ran, seemingly paralyzed into place. The few who got close enough to touch her grabbed their heads in pain, falling to the floor, unable to get up. She knocked two female agents back against soft chairs, then kept them pinned there as though bound by ropes and gags.

"I think she wants to see us," Greg said with exaggerated calm.

Chapter Three

As Greg walked toward the door, he was unable to believe what he'd just seen. He opened the door to Darci, but couldn't bring himself to speak. What could he say?

Darci held out her hand toward Greg, her fingers closed around something, then she walked past him to Jack. "You," she said to him, extending her hand, meaning for him to take whatever she held.

Greg thought that he'd jump through the plate glass window rather than take anything she offered, but Jack gave the woman a look that said, I'm not afraid of you, then took the object.

It looked to be her car keys.

"What do you feel?" she asked.

"Nothing," Jack answered, looking at the set of keys. "BMW. Your dead husband buy it for you?"

Greg didn't know whether to admire Jack or think he was the biggest fool on earth to not be afraid of this little woman. "Could you . . ." he began, nodding toward the window and the incapacitated people downstairs.

"Oh dear," she said. "Sorry."

Greg watched her relax and in the next second hell broke loose downstairs as people recovered themselves. Within seconds, three agents, firearms drawn, were at his door, and he had to send them away. By the looks on their faces, they would have shot Darci in an instant.

When Greg got the door closed and the blinds drawn, he turned back to look at Darci and Jack. They were still standing, glaring at each other, Jack nearly a foot taller than she. He wondered if they were talking to each other through their minds. He was tempted to go to the bar and grab the whole bottle of bourbon, but he made himself try to deal with what was happening — whatever that was. Darci Montgomery was out of his realm of comprehension.

Mustering his courage, Greg went to the two of them. "You want to fill me in?" he asked.

Jack looked at Greg. "Did you guys rehearse that downstairs?" he asked.

"Rehearse?" It took Greg moments to

realize that Jack was saying that he didn't believe Darci had paralyzed anyone, that it had all been a play put on to . . . to what? To get Jack to believe a lie?

Darci took the keys from Jack's hand and held up one, a small, ordinary-looking key. "Do you recognize this?"

"No," Jack said.

"Do you own something it could open?"

"I make it a point to own nothing," he said, smiling at her in a cocky way.

Greg watched as Darci glared at Jack and he glared back, but nothing happened to Jack. There was no paralysis, no pain in his head, no hands feeling of fire. She can't hurt him, Greg thought.

"Who loves you enough to die for you?" Darci asked.

"Every woman I've ever been to bed with," Jack shot back, then put his hand on his ear. "Ow!"

Instantly, Darci turned to Greg and said, "I didn't do that."

"I would have seen you if you had," Jack said, rubbing his ear.

Greg decided that it was time for him to step in. Jack had agreed to help find his father, but it looked as though this extraordinary young woman was going to have to be involved also. "Jack," Greg said, "why don't you go downstairs and get something to eat?"

"Limp green beans and lumpy mashed potatoes?"

"Exactly," Greg said as he made a call and arranged an escort for a "criminal."

At the door, Jack said, "Get it out of your mind if you're thinking that I'll work with her. I won't."

Greg didn't reply. He just wanted to hear what was going on with Darci and her car keys, but he knew that with Jack's hostility in the room, she'd never tell him anything.

Once Greg was alone with Darci, he didn't know where to begin. On the other hand, she was probably reading his mind. "You didn't do that to Jack's ear?" he said when she was seated.

"No," she answered as she drained her glass of ginger ale.

He saw that she looked tired. Her file said that after what had happened with the witches she'd been hospitalized for exhaustion. After the fire in Alabama and whatever she'd done with Lincoln Aimes, the surveillance crew said she'd not gone outside her house for two weeks.

Pouring her another glass of ginger ale, he handed it to her.

"Would you please tell me what's going on?" she asked.

At that, Greg relaxed and took the seat across from her. Smiling, he said, "That's exactly what I was going to ask you. How can you and Jack talk to each other . . . you know, without words?"

"I don't know," she said softly, looking away. "I thought that I could hear only my husband and even he couldn't hear *my* thoughts."

She looked about twenty years older than when she'd entered his office the first time today. Obviously, holding all those people downstairs had taken their toll on her. In a way he almost felt sorry for her. On the other hand, he was terrified of her. "Maybe you and Jack are soul mates," he said, trying to make a joke.

When she turned blazing eyes on him, the hairs on the back of his neck stood up. What did she do to people who displeased her?

But she just looked away. "No, we're not soul mates. We're — I don't know why he can hear me and me him." She looked back at Greg. "What's he so angry about?"

"His father —"

"No," Darci said, waving her hand. "I can feel his anger at his father — the man who's missing, right?"

Greg nodded.

"That anger is superficial. There's a deeper anger in him, though, and it sets my teeth on edge."

Greg had to take a drink to keep from making a sarcastic remark. What could scare a person who could do what she'd done this morning?

"There's something . . . no, someone from long ago. He is . . . protected."

Greg smiled. "More lives than a cat. He was in a car wreck that should have killed him, but he was miraculously thrown free and survived. His face had been smashed, but when it was fixed he was much better looking than he had been. He was a different person."

"Yes, I'm sure he was. She protected him and changed him."

"She?"

"Yes. I feel that there's a woman around him, surrounding him. She's powerful and she's . . ." Darci looked at Greg, smiling. "She's jealous. She doesn't like me at all."

Greg wanted to light candles and say prayers, but he made himself remain calm. His training hadn't prepared him for discussions about jealous ghosts.

"Has Jack ever had a lasting relation-ship?"

Greg chuckled. "Never longer that a few months, but . . ."

"But what?"

"I think there was a woman a couple of years ago. I'm not sure because Jack was undercover so I didn't see him often. When we did see each other, we talked only of business."

"She died, right?"

"Yeah, in the same car wreck that nearly killed Jack."

Nodding, Darci sipped her drink for a moment. "No, she wouldn't like for Jack to love anyone but her."

"By 'she,' you mean a ghost?"

"In this case, maybe an EF. 'Evil force,' " she added. "She either loves Jack with all her soul, or hates him enough to want re-venge."

"I've known Jack all his life and I'd be willing to bet he's never done anything bad to a woman."

"But who knows what happened a hun-dred or so years ago?"

"Ah. Right. Hundred years ago." Greg swallowed a few times and thought, Why *me*? Why had *he* been chosen by this young woman? But the answer to that question and to a lot of questions in his life was: Jack. Greg cleared his throat. "What was that about your car keys?"

"They were humming," Darci said cheerfully, holding them up. "Here, can you feel them?"

Tentatively, as though he were being asked to hold a hot branding iron, Greg took the keys. He released his breath when he felt nothing. Raising his eyebrows, he looked at Darci in question.

"I found that small key inside a little statue. I've always felt it had some importance to me, to what I'm trying to do."

Greg wanted to ask questions but he restrained himself.

"You see, Mr. Ryerson, I'm trying to find out what happened to my husband. He was kidnapped . . . again."

As Greg watched her struggle to keep the tears back, he was quiet and waited.

"I'm sure you know that my husband was kidnapped when he was a child. The experience so scarred him that when I met him, he was a driven man. I could feel his pain. So much had been taken from him that he was nearly empty inside, but he . . ."

Breaking off, she looked away for a moment, then turned back to Greg. "I'm using what powers God gave me in an attempt to find my husband and his sister, but I've made little progress so far. Last year I met someone —"

"Lincoln Aimes."

"Yes," Darci said, smiling. "A lovely man, inside and out. Through Linc I met someone else, an old blind man who has since told me some things."

Greg waited for her to continue, hoping she'd tell him more, but she seemed to decide against it.

"Let's just say that I know that before I can find my husband and sister-in-law I need to find some other things."

"Things?"

"Objects." She held up the small key on her ring. "I found this key under very odd circumstances and I believe that it opens something that will help me find my husband." She looked at Greg. "Today I knew you wanted me to help you find this Mr. Hallbrooke, and I could feel that this man Jack was related to him. Related by blood, not by caring."

"Yes," Greg said. "There's no love between them."

"She won't allow him to love anyone," Darci said as she looked back at her keys. "I want to help, but I don't like that man

Jack. He sends very ugly thoughts to me. I wanted to hurt him. I'm sorry for that, but as much as I wanted to hurt him, I couldn't do it. I can't reach him. I'm not used to that kind of force around someone."

"Sort of psychic-proof clothing, huh?"

"More or less," she said, smiling a bit. "I wanted nothing to do with him, but when I got outside and took my car keys out, they were humming."

"Humming?"

"Vibrating, and the vibrations became stronger the closer I got to the building. I apologize for what happened down there, but those people weren't going to allow me to follow the key up the stairs."

"I understand completely," Greg said, then smiled for the first time when Darci laughed.

"Wonder what they'll say in their reports?" he asked, laughing with her, glad to see some humor in what he'd seen that morning. "So what happened to the key when you handed it to Jack?"

"It hummed so loudly it was almost operatic."

"But he felt nothing?"

"Nothing at all."

Getting up, Greg paced about the room.

He knew where she was headed. She wanted to use Jack to do some witchcraft-voodoo thing with some key she'd found heaven only knew where.

"I think, no, I *know* that this man Jack, your friend, can somehow lead me to something or someone who can help me find my husband and sister-in-law."

Greg wanted to ask a thousand questions, but the most important one was, Will Jack be safe? Car wrecks and gun battles were one thing, but black magic was another.

Darci stood up. "Why don't I go home and let you think about this? I'll return tomorrow at three. Be sure and put me on your appointment book."

"After today I don't think anyone will try to stop you from entering the building."

"Oh, they won't remember this tomorrow," she said lightly, then swallowed. "I mean, maybe they won't."

Greg was remembering one of the reports he'd read in which an agent said he believed that Darci could do much, much more than any of them knew about. Could she take away people's memories of an event?

"Tomorrow, then," he said as he walked her to the door.

At the door, she put her hand on his arm and looked into his eyes for a moment. It was as though she was trying to say something to him or to read his thoughts, but he heard and felt nothing.

She gave him a little smile, then turned and left.

Chapter Four

"It's the FBI," Darci muttered, "and they couldn't come up with anything more original than for me to be the maid and you to be the chauffeur." The FBI didn't really suspect Jack's relatives of kidnapping, but they thought that if any lead was going to come through, it would be from inside that house, so they wanted an agent there.

Jack gave her a one-sided grin as he looked about the sparse room. "So this is how the servants live."

Darci looked at the two narrow beds in the room and tried to quell her anger at the FBI. Yesterday Greg had told her that she and Jack would be working together in the Hallbrooke mansion. He hadn't said that Jack and Darci were supposed to be a married couple, and that she was supposed to clean the house while Jack lounged around outside, waiting for one of his relatives to want to go somewhere.

But where would they want to go? Until J. Barrett was found, only their living expenses would be paid by the executors of his estate. The bills they ran up outside the house were their own.

Yesterday Darci had spent the day at the FBI building, locked away with Jack and Greg as they experimented with how Jack and Darci could hear each other without using their voices.

Darci tried to tell them that she'd figured out that she wasn't hearing Jack but the voice of an angry, hate-filled woman. It was the voice of a woman who hovered around Jack. She'd tried to explain that, but all she received was Jack's sarcasm.

"Like a rain cloud?" he'd said. "Over me and no one else?"

She narrowed her eyes at him. "Are you using your bad temper to cover what you must have felt all your life? Are you trying to make me believe that there haven't been times when you've *heard* her loud and clear?"

"I'm not working with this nut case," Jack said to Greg, starting to rise from his chair.

Greg turned to Darci. "Yeah, he's heard her, and, yeah, she's protected him." His jaw was clenched tight. This morning the director of the FBI had received another call from the president demanding to know what was being done to find Hallbrooke. Three of the charities supported by Hallbrooke had started to lobby for more government funds. If it leaked to the media that Hallbrooke was missing it wouldn't be healthy for the president's reelection campaign.

It was beginning to look as though Greg's future with the FBI depended on this case, and he didn't want to deal with Jack's hostility toward Darci. Where was the Jack Greg had known all his life? The man who was charming no matter what the circumstances? Years ago, when they'd wheeled Jack into surgery, his face crushed, he'd still been making jokes.

"You two can fight it out *after* you find Hallbrooke," Greg had snapped, then handed each of them a file folder and told them a car was waiting.

Two hours later they'd been hired by Jack's aunt and uncle as maid and chauffeur. Since the FBI had made all the other employees quit, they were to start immediately.

"They don't know where he is," Darci said, dropping her duffel bag onto one of the twin beds. The FBI had packed the bag so she didn't even know what was inside it. She looked at the other bed two feet from hers. If this odious man Jack tried anything, how would she stop him? She seemed to have no power over him.

"Don't flatter yourself," Jack said, sneering, and looking Darci up and down in a contemptuous way.

This morning Greg had pulled Darci aside to talk to her in private. "I want to apologize for the way Jack's been treating you. We've been together since we were toddlers and I've never seen him treat anyone this way."

"It's not him," Darci said. "It's —"

"I know," Greg said, sighing. "It's *her.*"

Hours later she and Jack were inside the Hallbrooke mansion and their jobs were to serve their employers.

Jack knew he had to leave the little bedroom or he'd explode. When he was growing up, Greg's parents had lived in a pretty little cottage at the back of the estate, but the FBI had conveniently burned half of it down last night so Jack and Darci would have to stay inside the main house.

Damn them! Jack thought as he left the house and made his way to the garage. Maybe if he washed and waxed all six of his father's cars he'd release some of his anger.

By the time he reached the garage, he'd settled down somewhat, and as he filled a bucket full of hot water and suds, he began to release more of his rage.

This morning he'd seen his relatives for the first time in years. He knew he looked different now but, somehow, he'd still expected one of them to recognize him. No one did. Aunt Theo had been the one to interview him. She hadn't changed much. She was still scrawny, still haughty. She'd barely glanced at Jack.

Behind her stood her husband Randall, a man with a pedigree back to the *Mayflower*, but with no morals, no ambition, and a truly fabulous ability to spend money.

Half dozing on a couch had been Uncle Gus, someone who believed that luxury was his right.

Theodora and Gus were Jack's father's much-younger siblings. Whereas the eldest son had been raised with an iron fist, these two, the unexpected result of a weekend liaison his widowed grandfather'd had with a much-younger woman, had been indulged and cosseted all their lives. They had grown up believing they were entitled to whatever the world had to offer.

As Jack had stood on the carpet an-
swering perfunctory questions about his
qualifications, he'd easily been able to
imagine what would happen to the
Hallbrooke billions if these leeches got
hold of them. There were some brochures
on top of the piano: cars, yachts, real estate
in Monaco.

When Jack was a child he'd overheard
his father tell his lawyer that he didn't plan
to leave anyone a penny when he died. "I
shall give all of it away before then." It had
taken all Jack's strength to keep from
bursting into the room and shouting that
he didn't want his father's dirty ol' money
anyway.

But as Jack looked at his relatives, he
thought that perhaps when his father had
said he meant to leave behind no money
he'd been doing Jack a favor.

"Of course not," Jack said aloud as he
dipped the sponge into the water and
began soaping the Bentley. His father had
never done a kind thing in his life. He gave
away millions, true, but he refused to meet
with any of the people involved with the
charities. "I pay them to stay away from
me," his father had said when he refused to
accept yet another plaque that honored
and thanked him.

So now Jack was back at his father's house, and he had no idea where to begin trying to find his father. None of his relatives were going to confide in a man they thought was a chauffeur. Jack had seen his twin cousins, seventeen years old and already bored with life. They were both like their mother Theo, snobs to the core, and had barely looked at him.

Jack turned the hose on the car and for a moment he felt rage run through him. There was the girl — that woman — that Darci. Throughout the interview she'd meekly stood behind him, her head down, her hands clasped in front of her. Demure, quiet, insignificant.

Yet throughout the interview she'd been "talking" to him. He'd wanted to shut her out, but he couldn't.

He's not here, she said.

Do you think the house hasn't been searched? he snapped back at her.

He's not here in their minds, she said, then added, *Not that I can read minds.*

Jack could hardly answer the stupid questions his aunt put to him. Did he have a criminal record? Did he obey traffic laws? Had he ever been arrested? Was he an experienced driver?

He'd lied convincingly in spite of the fact

that Darci was playing with his mind. Just before they'd left the FBI building, Greg had asked Jack to "lighten up," but he'd been unable to. His dislike of Darci Montgomery, the Hillbilly Honey, threatened to overwhelm him.

After the interview — Darci had not been asked if she knew how to clean — Theo's son had pointed them toward the kitchen. He'd been too lazy to walk all the way down the corridor to show them their room.

Once they were inside the room, Darci had tried to talk to Jack, but he'd left, unable to bear being near her.

He told himself that he disliked her because she said she was a psychic and he knew that such people didn't exist. Some logic, buried deep inside his mind, knew that he'd seen the way she'd frozen the agents in place, but he still didn't *believe*. It had to have been a trick.

Jack grabbed some clean cloths and began to wipe the water off the car. There was a part of him that knew he was being irrational, but another part just couldn't stop. Never in his life had he disliked a person as much as he despised Darci Montgomery. *Hated* her.

Just thinking about his hatred of her

made him slam paste wax onto the car's surface with renewed energy.

It was late in the day when he went back into the house and what he saw made him blink in disbelief. His aunt Theo was in the kitchen chopping carrots and his uncle Gus was broiling steaks.

Quietly, his mouth open in disbelief, Jack went through the kitchen to the living room. Randall was wearing a ruffled apron and dusting the mantel. He smiled at Jack and kept dusting.

Jack went up the stairs two at a time. In the hallway were dirty plates of food, piles of soiled clothing, and a mound of dirty bed linens. A quick glance showed him that his twin cousins were cleaning out their rooms.

Gritting his teeth, Jack yelled, *Darci!* so loud that it made his body vibrate. When neither of the twins moved, he knew he'd shouted inside his head.

Instantly, a vision of a room came into his head. It was the blue bedroom on the third floor. Again, he took the stairs two at a time, strode down the hall angrily, then flung open the door.

Darci Montgomery was stretched out on the blue damask bedspread, reading a *People* magazine and eating from a ten-pound box of Godiva chocolates.

"You —" he said aloud, jaw clenched and pointing toward the door. "You can't —" He was so angry he couldn't get the words out.

I can't what? she asked and Jack knew she was talking to him without words.

In spite of all the testing Greg had done yesterday, Jack refused to believe that he and Darci could . . . could . . .

She smiled at him. "Someone had to clean and cook and I'm not good at either one. Besides, those two kids had refused to allow anyone to clean their rooms. They even had some rather nasty substances hidden inside books. I can't bear desecration of books, can you?"

"You have no right —" Jack said, then stopped. As he walked to the window, he willed himself to be calm. He needed to get himself under control so they could find his father and get out of here, get away from each other.

"She's afraid you're going to fall in love with me."

Jack's shoulders dropped. "You want to quit that crap? There's no one around me. No one —" He broke off. He'd been through this all day yesterday. Turning, he looked at her, thinking that she looked very good on that bed. The next second, he felt a pain in his head and he rubbed his temple.

Darci held up a piece of candy and studied it. "I think she's afraid that I'll take you away from her. No, send her away from you. She thinks I have the ability to send her away, but your anger keeps me from doing it. Does that make sense?"

Jack didn't answer. "Have you found my father?"

"He's all right. I can feel his spirit in this house. He's a very powerful man. Like you. You two are a lot alike."

"If you're trying to enrage me, it's already been done."

"Yes. Your aura is a deep, dark red. Rather like the eyes of a bull in a cartoon."

Her attitude made Jack so angry that he took a step toward her.

Darci dropped the candy and sat up on the bed, her eyes wide in alarm.

Jack had never hurt a woman, but the fear he saw in this woman's eyes made him feel good. Disgusted with himself, he stepped back. "Look, I think the best thing for us to do is to find my father, then separate."

"Yes," Darci said, moving to sit at the side of the bed and Jack stepped farther away from her. Whatever she was feeling from him had wiped the smile off her face. "Your father left here of his own accord, but I'm not sure he can get away to come home."

"All I need is for you to tell me who and where and I'll do the rest. What do you need? A piece of his hair?"

"I'm not —" Darci began, then when she looked at Jack's eyes, she stopped and took a breath.

Jack could see that she was afraid of him and for a moment he smiled. Obviously she had no power over him. She couldn't hypnotize him into cleaning and cooking — or into doing her bidding.

Darci stood up, straightened her shoulders, and looked hard at Jack, and for a few moments he felt calmer. But in the next second the rage was back.

"You're going to *kill* him!" Darci said aloud, looking at the space above Jack's head. "I don't want him! I'm not your enemy!"

If possible, the anger inside Jack grew. To control himself, he walked to the door and went into the hall. He was calm until Darci stood before him. He could feel his hands shape themselves into circles the exact size of her neck, and he saw her look down at his hands in fear.

Darci took a step backward. "There's a room in this house, a secret room, where some objects are hidden."

"I know of no secret room." Jack stepped toward her. He could almost feel her neck under his hands.

In the next second, Darci was running down the hall. She was small and light and quick. By the time he got down the stairs, he saw just her foot as she disappeared into his father's bedroom. Inside the room, she was running her hands along the bookcase and she glanced fearfully at Jack as she searched for something.

Jack was sure there was nothing there. As a kid he and Greg had explored the big old house endlessly. The bedroom of his often-absent father had been Jack's favorite area as it had been the most forbidden.

When Darci found a button and pushed it — then the bookcase swung back — Jack was stunned. He watched her walk into the dark space behind the bookcase and disappear.

Inside him came a voice that he'd heard before in his life, a woman's voice. He'd never told Greg about the voice he sometimes heard, had never openly admitted it to himself. He'd always thought of it as the "devil's voice." Now that voice was telling him to shut the bookcase and lock it into place. With Darci inside the room.

Using all his willpower, Jack blocked the voice from his mind and walked toward the bookcase.

"You don't have a match, do you?" Darci asked from the darkness. "I think there are some candles here."

"Why don't you use your mind to light the place up?"

"Why don't you ask your girlfriend to show herself? Maybe she could produce an eerie green light."

For an instant, Jack felt like leaping toward Darci's voice, but he controlled the urge. Feeling along the wall, he felt a light switch and flicked it. When the lights came on, he saw Darci staring straight ahead. Jack started to comment on her inability to find a light switch, but then he looked at what she was staring at.

They were in a small room with no windows, the plastered walls painted a dark red. Three walls were blank, but the fourth had a single shelf at waist level with a painting above it. It was a gruesome painting, old and cracked, of a man being tortured, sightless hands placing branding irons on his body. A saint perhaps.

As though she were mesmerized, Darci walked toward the shelf. It was a four-inch-thick piece of wood, pure white and sanded smooth. On the shelf were four objects. There was a little blue glass ball on a marble base, a small ivory statue, what looked to be a precious stone the size and shape of an egg, and a small silver box.

Jack watched in silence as Darci walked toward the box. She didn't touch it, just stared at it, then, slowly, she reached up to her neck and pulled a green cord from inside her shirt. On the end of the cord was the key she'd had on her key ring. She was going to try to unlock the little box.

Jack didn't know what happened next, but one moment he was watching her and the next moment he could feel his hands around her throat. The only thing he wanted in the world was to kill her.

Chapter Five

"Feeling better?" Darci asked as she placed the cool washcloth on Jack's forehead.

Looking up, he saw the coffered ceiling of his father's bedroom, and he realized he was lying on his father's bed. He tried to get up, but dizziness made him lie back down.

"Ssssh," Darci said. "You need to rest. Besides, I've given you a tranquilizer."

"A tranquilizer?" he asked, feeling too befuddled to understand the term. There were bruises on her neck.

"Yes. Your family has an arsenal of drugs so I dissolved three little pink pills in a glass of water and got it down you."

She said all this happily, as though it was an everyday occurrence to give someone pills to knock them out. She removed the cloth from his head, then dipped it into a basin of cold water. When she turned back, she winced from pain in her neck.

"Tell me what happened," he whispered.

"Later. You should sleep now. Those pills —"

He caught her wrist in his hand. "Tell me. I tried to —"

"Kill me," she said. "No, *you* didn't, but *she* did. She seems to know something that I don't, which I think means that she knows I know how to get rid of her. I just wish I did know. I mean, know what I know that I don't know that I know."

"That's clear," Jack said and was pleased when he saw Darci smile.

"When you're in this half-drugged state, she can't make you angry. She needs you alive and awake."

"How . . . ?" Jack asked, reaching up to touch a bruise on Darci's neck.

She looked away, her face turning pink. "You don't want to know."

"Yes, I do." He gave her a crooked grin. "You better tell me now. If I sleep this off I'll wake up hating you, then I won't listen."

Darci smiled. "Too true. Okay, I guess it's that old adage of evil fighting evil. I can't deal with a spirit that has as much hatred as the one around you does, but I know someone who can deal with her." She looked at the far side of the room.

Puzzled, Jack tried to figure out what she was trying to say. "I see. Spirit versus spirit. You called in someone. Who? Jack the Ripper?"

"Worse. Devlin."

"Never heard of him."

"Lucky you. He's a spirit I met . . ."

"At a cocktail party?"

"More or less," Darci said, smiling. "I'm not sure what he is, what he does, or even which side he's on, but I know he hovers around me. When you — she — attacked me, I called on Devlin. I knew he was stronger than she is."

"She," Jack said, closing his eyes for a moment. "It's always her."

"Yes. Devlin pulled her back and that made you quit . . ."

"Trying to choke you to death?"

"It wasn't you. None of this hatred has been from you. It's all her."

"Tell her to go away."

"That's exactly what Devlin said. 'Break the connection and send her away' is what he said I should do. But I said I was afraid that she was powerful enough to take you away with her."

"Did you fight her? Who won? Am I dead now?" For a second, Jack's eyes widened. "Did I kill you?"

Darci put her hand on his chest. "Nope. Two alives and two deads in this room."

"I guess you can see both of them."

"I can see Devlin. You can, too, if you want to. He's —"

"No thank you," Jack said quickly.

Darci sighed. "You're right. Linc hated seeing him."

"Lincoln Aimes? The actor?"

Darci nodded. "My good friend. Anyway, Devlin trapped the woman for a while so I can talk to you. I drugged your body so you'd be calm and not call to her."

" 'Call' to her?"

"Yes, there's a strong pull from you to her — I think. Devlin said we should ask the woman what she wants."

His mind fuzzy, Jack blinked at Darci for a moment. "Not a séance! Please tell me you don't want me to hold hands and hear knocking and —"

"Not at all. Devlin said he could put the woman's spirit into a body and hold it there for about thirty minutes. If we do that, maybe we can get her to talk."

"And tell us why she hates me?"

"To tell us why she wants to kill any woman who gets near you. I think maybe she loved you once and you betrayed her."

Jack blinked at her. "Are you talking

about reincarnation?"

" 'Fraid so."

"Do you have any more of those little pills?"

"Fresh out," Darci said, smiling. "I wish we could call Linc, but he's working on a movie in Turkey. He'd be able to tell you that spirits aren't so bad."

"What's this guy Devlin look like? If he's such a big deal spirit, maybe she'll fall in love with him and leave me alone."

Darci stared at Jack with wide eyes. "That's not a bad idea. Maybe —" She looked up at the headboard. "Devlin says no."

Jack refused to acknowledge the fact that he could feel the bed move with the force of the no's. "Whose body would she be put into?" he asked at last.

"The girl. Your cousin, I believe."

"Chrissy? She's a child. She's just seventeen."

"She has a thirty-five-year-old lover who's ready to kill to get his hands on your father's money. He'll marry Chrissy if we don't find your father, and we can't find him without your help, but you can't help because you have some angry woman hanging over you, telling you to kill any woman you're attracted to. And you're to kill me because maybe I know how to send her back to wherever she came from, except that I don't really know how."

"Couldn't this Devlin send her back?"

"Probably," Darci said, grimacing, "but he won't. He wants me . . . no, he wants the both of us to . . ." She paused. "Truthfully, I think Devlin's up to something very bad, but I have no idea what he's up to this time."

Slowly, Jack sat up in bed. He didn't tell Darci but his body had had a lot of drugs shot into it over the years, so he'd built up a tolerance. What were a few tranquilizers? "So when do we do this spirit transfer?"

"I guess we can do it at any time," Darci said slowly, looking at the bedside table.

Jack followed her eyes and saw the box that had been in the secret room. The bookcase was back in place now. He picked up the box and looked at it, aware that Darci was holding her breath as she watched him.

The box was about six inches long, three inches deep and thick. Not big, but it was heavy, as though it held something substantial. The outside seemed to be of silver, old and tarnished, and hammered into a design of raised curls and waves. He'd never seen a design like it. "Victorian Aztec" came to his mind. "Have you opened it yet?" he asked, turning it around in his hands.

"No," Darci whispered.

He held it out to her and, tentatively, she took it. She held it as though it were rare and precious and fragile.

"Try it," he said. "Try your key."

"No, not yet." Reluctantly, she put the box back on the table, then looked at him. "There's something inside it and I think my key opens the box. It's just that I'm not sure I want to release what's inside."

"Pandora, huh?"

"Exactly. Only no one has warned me not to open it."

"Can you ask this Devlin?"

Darci snorted. "If the box were full of forked-tailed demons, he'd probably encourage me to open it." She looked at Jack hard. "Maybe while you're calm from the pills we should try to transfer her spirit into a body and get her to talk. Once we get her out of the way, maybe we can find your father. I'd really like to know where he got the objects in that room. All of them have power, but the box is . . ."

"The killer?"

"More or less," she said, smiling at Jack. "Greg told me you were actually a nice man, but —"

She halted when the room began to fill with blue smoke. "Uh-oh. Devlin's getting restless. She's getting harder to hold."

Jack was watching the smoke around him, refusing to glance upward to the space where Darci kept looking. If there was a ghost up there, he didn't want to see him — it. "Let's do it," Jack said. "Let's talk to her and see what she wants."

Darci turned toward the bedroom door and stared at it hard.

As Jack watched her, he wondered what the truth was about Darci's husband and sister-in-law. Yesterday, he'd felt as though he knew what the truth was, but now he wondered . . .

He rubbed his hand over his face. It seemed as though he were two people, one who was consumed with hatred, and the other who could think rationally. Part of him was sure there was no such a thing as a psychic, but another part of him had seen some unbelievable things in the last few days.

When the bedroom door opened and in walked his seventeen-year-old cousin, Jack wasn't surprised. Chrissy had dyed her sandy hair black and made it stand up on end. She had a nose ring, an eyebrow ring, and five studs in each ear. Her clothes were all black, with hundreds of steel rivets. Incongruously, she was wearing pink rubber gloves for housecleaning.

"I don't want her hurt," Darci said in a warning voice.

Jack couldn't keep himself from glancing at the bookcase. There, vaguely outlined, was the shape of a man. He seemed to be wearing an Elizabethan ruff and he looked distinctly like Shakespeare.

"You wish you were so talented," Darci snapped at the shape.

Jack watched the shape change, still transparent, but now it turned into . . . a fish?

"He thinks he's funny," Darci said to Jack. "Ignore him." She looked at the shape on the bookcase that was now changing itself into a peacock. "You're not scaring anyone, so stop it. Could you do the transfer, please?"

Chrissy was now sitting on a chair, her eyes glassy and unfocused.

Jack couldn't take his eyes off the shape on the bookcase as he watched it change into a magician. Devlin removed his tall hat, reached into it, and pulled out a rabbit, which he then placed onto Chrissy's lap. Jack drew back when the rabbit seemed to jump straight into Chrissy's stomach.

"You're a real pest," Darci said under her breath, "and I'm going to tell Henry on you."

In the next moment, Chrissy's face changed. "Oh!" she said in a soft voice, then looked down at herself. What she saw didn't seem to please her because the next "Oh!" was of horror. She removed the gloves with distaste.

"What has been done to me?" Chrissy asked as she got up from the chair and went to the mirror over the big mahogany dresser. "How awful," she said, tears in her voice as she looked at her reflection.

Jack moved to sit beside Darci, watching in silence as Chrissy began to remove all the studs from her head. His father's hair-brush was on the dresser and she used that to try and smooth her hair down.

It was as though Chrissy was unaware of anyone else in the room, but after a few minutes she looked at Jack in the mirror and smiled. "You said you'd love me no matter how I looked. I think I'm now testing that love."

When Jack said nothing, Darci nudged him with her elbow. "You do love her, don't you?" she whispered.

"With all my heart," he said out loud.

Turning, Chrissy looked at Jack. Even

though he was sitting next to Darci, Chrissy never looked at her. Her eyes were only on Jack. "My darling," Chrissy said and went to Jack, her arms outstretched.

To Darci's disbelief, Jack held her away. Was he going to ruin their only chance to find out about this woman who haunted him?

"I'm sorry, but I don't know you," Jack said formally. "At least I don't think I do. You see, I have lost my memory."

Darci had to keep from laughing with pleasure at Jack's game. She'd been told that he was excellent as an undercover FBI agent, but she hadn't guessed how good.

"My darling," Chrissy said, stroking Jack's face. "My own true love. You don't recognize me?"

"No, but you're very beautiful."

Chrissy's face turned pink with pleasure. "I am Lavender Shay, and you asked me to marry you six months ago."

"Did you get married?" Darci asked.

Lavender, in Chrissy's body, turned eyes full of hatred onto Darci. "Who is this?" she hissed.

"A relative," Jack said quickly. "My sister. Don't you remember her?"

Lavender stepped back, looked at Darci

for a moment, then glanced about the room. "I do not seem to remember any of this. Where are we? Why did you not return to me?"

"I told you, I lost my memory," Jack said, reaching out his hands to her. "Tell me where we live and when."

"*When* we live?" There was doubt in her voice. "You said you would love me forever but you didn't. You don't even remember me now. You have betrayed me yet again." She was backing away from him, getting closer to the bookcase where Jack could see the outline of that Devlin. He was a mere blob now, as though he were listening so hard that he couldn't be bothered to form himself into a shape.

"I remember my love for you," Jack said quickly.

"The wedding," Darci whispered. "Tell her of the wedding." She'd tried to talk to Jack with her mind, but hadn't been able to. With this spirit in a human body, the mind connection was broken.

"What wedding?" Jack shot back as he said, "Your dress. Lace. I remember a lot of lace."

Lavender smiled at him, her eyes softening. "You must have peeked."

"It's just that I know you so well. You

90

were made to wear lace. Did you decide on the cake?"

"No chocolate, you naughty boy," Lavender said coquettishly, moving toward him again.

"And what about our honeymoon?"

She stopped walking. "You know that will have to wait as Father is so ill."

"Where? When?" Darci whispered.

Lavender turned angry eyes on Darci. "Who are you? Why do you speak?"

"She's to be your bridesmaid, remember?" Jack said, his voice soothing. He extended his hands to take hers, but instead she flung her arms around his neck.

"It's been so long," she said, her lips on his neck. "So very, very long. When you left Camwell I thought I would die."

"Camwell!" Darci said, in spite of her intention to be silent.

"Darling," Jack said, running his hands down the sides of her body, "please set a date for our wedding."

"But it is set," she said suspiciously, pulling back to look at him.

"I'm a man. How can I remember dates?" he said in such a charming way that she smiled at him.

"The twelfth of June, of course. My birthday."

"And which year? This one or next?"

"This one. 1843. You are a silly goose." Pausing, she put her hand to her head. "Something is hurting me. I can't think clearly. It's after the twelfth, but we didn't marry, did we? You weren't there."

She was standing back now, out of reach of Jack. Quickly, she turned to Darci and her face distorted in rage. "You. You stopped him."

Only Jack's quick reflexes kept Chrissy/Lavender from leaping onto Darci. In a re-play of that morning, Darci once again had hands around her throat.

Chapter Six

"Are you all right?" Jack asked.

Slowly, Darci turned her head. In a reversal of roles, she was now lying on J. Barrett Hallbrooke's bed and Jack was holding a cold washcloth to her forehead.

"You and your friends," Darci said through a bruised throat. "Is she gone?"

"Yeah. He . . . it . . . sent her back. I guess. I pulled Chrissy off of you, and she went limp for a while, but then she picked up her gloves and went back to cleaning. All in all, I think I'd rather get shot at than this."

Darci didn't speak for a moment as she closed her eyes and tried to swallow.

"I think we should get you to a doctor."

"No," Darci whispered. "Where is she?"

"He did something with her." Jack didn't turn but he nodded toward the bookcase and Devlin, who had shaped himself into a sleeping baby.

"He's put her asleep," Darci said, moving to sit up in bed. "I think we need to try to find out who she is and why you missed the wedding. I hope you were killed and that you didn't run off with some other woman. Maybe if we show that spirit evidence of your death she'll forgive you."

"Evidence of my death," Jack said. "We'll show a ghost that I'm dead? Tell me, Darci Montgomery, do you live like this all the time?" He held the bedroom door open for her.

"No, only since my husband and sister-in-law disappeared has my life been like this."

He wanted to ask her questions but her manner didn't allow him to. Always, there was a kind of dignity about her that made him keep his distance.

"That's it," Jack said, leaning back in his father's leather office chair. He and Darci had just spent the last several hours on the Internet and on the telephone. It was after midnight now and they were both exhausted — but they'd found out what they wanted to know.

"That poor girl," Darci said, stretched out on the leather couch. On the coffee table were the remnants of the huge meal

Jack's relatives had prepared for them.

It had taken a lot of digging and Darci had had to hex a couple of people into divulging some unlisted phone numbers, but they'd at last found Miss Lavender Shay.

She had grown up in Camwell, Connecticut, in the 1840s, the only child of a rich businessman and his wife.

Lavender had fallen in love with a boy she'd known all her life, a Mr. John Marshall the third, the only child of a rich, widowed landowner. As far as the town was concerned, it was the match of the century, and everyone had been looking forward to the festivities of their wedding.

But on the day of her wedding, Lavender had put on her wedding dress, climbed the stairs to the roof of her house, and jumped off.

The day of joy had turned into a day of mourning.

Darci and Jack had read a single sentence about the suicide in a book about Connecticut ghosts, but could find nothing else anywhere. But after a call to the Camwell library — "You call," Darci had said. "They'll remember *me*" — they'd found out that the house where Lavender had lived and died was still there, as were some of her family's descendants.

Darci watched Jack use a seductive voice — while she used what she'd always called her True Persuasion — to get Lavender's descendants to talk to him. Why? was what they wanted to know. Was Lavender being forced into the marriage? Was the groom a despicable person? Or had he jilted her? Maybe he'd been killed and Lavender couldn't bear to live without him.

"How the hell would I know?" a sleepy man said to Jack. "That old ghost story happened over a hundred and fifty years ago."

"Is there a town historian? Anyone who would know what happened?" Jack had asked the man, a descendant of Lavender's family.

"The only thing this town cares about are witches. Ever since that witch thing a few years back . . . you hear of that?"

"Yeah," Jack said, looking at Darci, who turned away. "I heard about it."

"Nobody here's interested in a girl that threw herself off a roof a hundred years ago. People in this town only care about witches. Tourists come here wanting to see what's left of the tunnels. And downtown now has three so-called witchcraft stores."

Darci was concentrating, trying to send

a message to the man to reveal what he knew.

"Hey! Wait a minute!" the man said. "I just remembered that my wife told me something the other day. Let me ask her."

Jack put his hand over the phone, meaning to talk to Darci while he waited, but her eyes were glazed over with her concentration. Coming from down the hall were muffled sounds of struggle. That . . . "thing," that Devlin, was holding Lavender's spirit prisoner. If she were released, she'd go back to Jack.

And the hatred would return, he thought. But now, for the first time in his life, he didn't feel as though he were full of hate and anger. Now he felt like . . . well, maybe like he might settle down, have some kids. After he buried the hatchet with his old man, that is.

His hand still over the phone, he looked at Darci. She was really quite pretty. Most of the women he knew weren't exactly what you'd want to invite home to dinner, or out to the country club. Maybe if her husband was gone —

"Stop it!" Darci said under her breath.

"Thought you couldn't read minds."

"Any female on earth can read a man's mind."

Chuckling, Jack put the phone back to his ear and listened. The man gave him a phone number of a local high school student who'd been trying to put together a history of Camwell. "With no witches," the man said, laughing. "The kid wants to sell the book to raise money for the school, but who'll buy a book on this town with nothing about witches in it?"

Jack thanked the man, then called the number even though it was after 10:00 p.m. He was rewarded with a young man who was eager to share what he'd found out. Forty minutes later, pages came through the fax machine.

It was from a proposed book about the history of Camwell. The chapter he sent them was entitled "The Lavender Shay Mystery," and Jack read it aloud. Basically, it said that no one had any idea why the young woman committed suicide. When her body was found, her fiancé had been waiting for her at the church.

"Murder," Jack said, putting down the paper. "My guess is that she was murdered."

"That makes sense. She was in love with you — John, that is — but was murdered before the wedding, so now she hangs around you and tries to kill any woman who gets near you."

"More than tries," Jack whispered.

Darci knew what he was thinking. Greg had told her of the young woman killed in the car wreck that had so injured Jack. Since Darci worked every second of her life to stamp down her own pain, she wanted to distract Jack from his. "But if Lavender was murdered, wouldn't she attach herself to the murderer? And it was my impression that the woman we saw tonight wasn't sane, so maybe she did kill herself."

"I'm sure that being a ghost for a hundred and fifty years would make anyone crazy," Jack said.

"Actually, it doesn't. People stay the same." She thought about the chapter the boy had written. He'd spent too much time on the beauty of the young Lavender, but it was clear that he also believed there had been foul play involved in the death. "If a high school kid thinks there was murder involved and we do, why didn't they think of that back then?" Darci asked.

"Because we've been bombarded with blood and gore all our lives. It comes naturally to us."

"Right. And the good ol' days were free of mayhem. Can you think that after reading what happened to John Marshall? To you?"

"He got married, then died when his house burned down."

"Poor man. I wonder if he pined over Lavender all his life. Here, hand me that paper and let me see what I can feel. Maybe —"

"What's that?" Jack asked.

"Oh no!" Darci said, starting toward the door. "It's a vacuum cleaner. I forgot to turn them off."

"Turn them —" Jack began, then grinned. "Mickey Mouse left the broom running."

"More or less," Darci said sheepishly, as she ran from the room. When she returned, she said, "I got them settled and off to bed. I —" She paused to yawn. "I've had about all I can take in one day. You mind if I take that blue room upstairs?"

"It's not my house."

"Legally . . ." She broke off. "Where do you plan to sleep?"

"In my father's bedroom. In the master's bed. King of the palace." He lowered his voice. "You think you could get that . . . that thing to leave the room?"

"Devlin? He has a mind of his own but I'll see what I can do." When she turned to leave, Jack halted her.

"You have something in your hair," he

said. "I'll get it out." He ran his hand over her hair, then tripped over his feet just enough to bump into her. When she seemed to notice nothing, he gave her shoulder a pat and gently shoved her toward the door.

"I don't know when I've been so sleepy," she said, yawning again.

Smiling at her in a fatherly way, Jack closed the door behind her. Alone in the room, he reached into his shirtsleeve and withdrew the green cord. On the end of it was the key that Darci had worn around her neck.

Smiling, he quietly opened the door and looked out into the dimly lit hallway. He'd liberally laced Darci's drink with the same tranquilizers she'd used on him earlier.

All evening he'd been biding his time. He hadn't been the least interested in Darci's boring old ghost story. Who cared if some Victorian chick jumped or was pushed off a roof?

While it was true that he felt as though something dark and ugly had been removed from him, and it was true that some happy, homey little thoughts had been running through his mind, his basic nature hadn't changed. Jack loved adventure, and he couldn't stand an unsolved mystery.

For him, the evening had been a study in self-control. All evening, he'd had to work to control his raging desire to explore that secret room of his father's, to examine the four objects, and to further search for whatever else might be hidden in there. And he wanted to find out what his father was involved in. Did his staid, cold-hearted father have some underworld secrets?

But, first and most, he wanted to open that box Darci had taken to her bedroom. Jack tiptoed upstairs to the blue bedroom. Darci should be sound asleep by now.

Once inside the dark room, Jack stood still until his eyes adjusted. Mainly, he was interested in whether or not that blob that had been swirling about across the bookcase was gone. It seemed to be. Probably followed Darci off to bed, Jack thought.

Now, where was that box? Ah, yes. On her bedside table.

As he reached out to touch the box he could barely see, the light came on.

Darci was on her side on the bed, her head propped on her hand. "Did you think I wouldn't know you'd stolen my key? Now, would you please give it back to me?"

For days, Jack had been sizing Darci up,

and he knew she was a loner, like him. He only told about thirty percent of what he knew and he figured she only told about ten. It was his guess that she'd meant to open the box in private and if she had, he doubted that he'd ever find out what his father had been hiding.

Jack had seen her paralyze people, but he knew she couldn't work her witchcraft on him — when jealous little Lavender was around, that is. But that ghost was stuck in a prison somewhere, so right now maybe Darci *could* control Jack. Maybe she could stop him from opening the box.

Everything happened in a split second. When the bedroom door flew open, and a cold gust of wind filled the room, Darci looked up. Jack grabbed the silver box and jammed the key into the hole as he took a flying leap at Darci. He meant to distract her from casting some spell that would prevent him from opening the box.

But too many things happened at once. Lavender's spirit had escaped just in time to see her beloved jump into bed with an-other woman, and the box opened while Jack, Darci, and Lavender were entangled with one another.

When Darci felt herself falling down, down, down, and felt two other spirits, only one of which was in a human body, falling with her, she cried out, "Jack, what have you done?"

Part Two

1843

Chapter Seven

An acrid smell filled Darci's nose and was beginning to enter her brain. She turned her head away, trying to get away from the smell.

"She's coming around," she heard a man say. "The smelling salts worked. Now, step back. Let her breathe."

Slowly opening her eyes, Darci took a moment to focus. At least six people she'd never seen before were looking down at her, all of them appearing to be anxious and worried. She blinked up at them, not understanding where she was or who they were. She tried to sit up but she couldn't seem to get enough breath to move.

"Out!" a woman said. "All the men must leave so we can loosen her stays."

Seconds later the men were gone and Darci felt hands lift her and begin unbuttoning the back of her dress. When they'd unbuttoned and untied her, she could breathe again.

"Better?" asked a woman and Darci nodded.

As she took several deep, slow breaths, she looked about her. She was in a room with tall ceilings and two tall, narrow windows encased in striped curtains. The wallpaper was blue with big brown pineapples on it. All the furniture was old-fashioned, heavy and dark.

Darci turned to look at the three women hovering over her. Two were middle-aged, with the top of their hair parted in the middle and slicked down, with shiny, tight ringlets over their ears. They didn't have on a speck of makeup and their eyebrows were unplucked.

What made them even more strange-looking to Darci was that they weren't surrounded by the colors of their auras. All her life, she'd seen people bathed in colors that changed with mood and personality. But these women had no colors surrounding them. It was frightening as Darci couldn't read their moods, but it was calming at the same time. Without the ability to see auras, she didn't have to worry who was angry or sad, or who was carrying some dark secret.

Puzzled, she looked at the third woman. She was young — and beautiful. Drop-dead gorgeous beautiful. Supermodel. She had dark hair, full lips — and eyes a lovely purple.

"Lavender," Darci whispered.

"Yes, dear," one of the women said. "Our own dear Lavey."

Darci's eyes widened as she tried to turn around on the couch, but turning was difficult, for she was wearing a long dress with heavy skirts that weighed down on her legs. Lavender took Darci's hand and held it tenderly. "Darci, dearest, you gave us quite a fright. You and Jack —"

"Jack?"

"Yes, Jack," Lavender said, lowering her thick lashes, her cheeks turning a pretty shade of pink.

Darci flopped back against the hard cushion of the hard sofa. "I don't remember what happened." Dramatically, she put her hand to her forehead and peeked out through her fingers. When she touched her head, she found that her own hair was slicked down over her head and she, too, had ringlets over her ears. She could feel a lump of what was surely a lifetime's growth of hair coiled on the back of her head.

Behind Lavender, the two older women were frowning, as though they didn't believe Darci, but Lavender's sweet face was all concern.

"We'd just returned from the rehearsal at the church when Jack told us you'd fainted."

"Church," Darci said slowly. "Rehearsing? For your wedding?"

"Yes, of course, you silly goose, for my wedding tomorrow when I will become Mrs. John Marshall and you and I will become sisters."

"Sisters?" Darci asked, again trying to sit up. "Does that mean that Jack is my brother?"

The two older women exchanged looks, as though to say that Darci had lost her mind.

"You need to rest," Lavender said. "I'm sure that all the work you've done for my wedding has overtaxed you."

"Not to mention this thing that's about to cut me in half," she muttered, pulling at the thick cloth about her waist.

"I agree," Lavender said, smoothing Darci's hair back from her face. "But corsets are a necessary evil. No woman ever looked beautiful without pain."

Darci started to reply that that was absurd, but then she remembered dead lifts and squats. Pain indeed! "Could I possibly see Jack?" she asked.

"Are you well enough?"

"I think so," Darci answered, trying to lift her legs under the heavy skirts so she could sit up. She was still a bit dizzy, completely disoriented, and she needed someone to tell her she'd wandered onto a movie set. The alternate — that she was in a past time — was too ridiculous to consider.

There was a knock at the door and moments later Jack walked into the room. He was dressed in an old-fashioned suit that was nearly as narrow at the waist as Lavender's dress was. There was a moment of rushing about as the two older women pulled Darci upright and tightened the strings on the corset, then buttoned her dress. During this time Jack talked to Lavender. Peering around the women, Darci saw that Jack was practically drooling over the beautiful woman.

Darci tried to send him a mind message. *Where are we? What has happened? How do we get out of here? Do you have the silver box?*

Jack's lack of response made her sure he wasn't hearing her.

When one of the women pulled the corset strings too tight, Darci sent her a mind message to ease off. The woman didn't obey. Curious, Darci turned to the women and concentrated. No response from either of them.

On a table beside the couch was a little beaded bag. All her life, when Darci had touched a personal item belonging to someone, she'd immediately known a great deal about that person. But when she picked up the bag, she felt nothing. She put her hand on the arm of one of the women. Nothing.

"There now," one of the women said, "go to him. Have your last day together."

"Hardly that," Lavender said, smiling. She had perfect teeth. "Are you packed for the honeymoon?"

"I'm getting married, too?" Darci asked, aghast, as she stood up.

Laughing, Lavender kissed Darci's cheek. "No, but you're going on our honeymoon with us. You haven't changed your mind, have you?"

Behind her, Jack was mouthing, *Please don't go,* as he looked Lavender up and down.

Darci moved to clutch Jack's arm firmly. "No, of course I haven't changed my mind, but now I need to talk to my, uh, brother in private."

"Yes, of course," Lavender said. "But remember, tea is at four and dinner is at seven."

"We'll be here," Jack said cheerfully as he escorted Darci out the front door.

"What — ?!" Darci said as soon as they were outside. It was hot and she had on at least thirty pounds of clothes. Before them was a village that looked like a Currier and Ives print. "I need to sit down," she whispered.

"See the white house with the deep porch? That's *our* house, where you and I live with our father — who's rarely at home, by the way."

"Our house?" Darci whispered, feeling faint. To herself, she said, I want to go home. To my daughter and my niece. To my own father.

But the way Jack was acting made her keep quiet. Holding her arm firmly, he led her onto the porch, which was relatively cool. "Watch this," he said, then rang a little bell that was sitting on a wicker table. Within seconds, a pretty red-haired maid appeared and Jack told her he wanted a pitcher of lemonade.

"Yes, sir," the maid said, then disappeared into the house.

Darci did the best she could to breathe, which wasn't easy considering that her rib cage was encased in a tightly laced corset. "You seem to know a great deal more about what's going on than I do," she said, "so tell me everything."

"It seems, my dear sister, that we have done the impossible, which is to travel back in time."

"The box," Darci said. "That's what the box contained." When Jack looked at her in question, she explained. "I was told that there are twelve magic objects and each one has a specific ability. The Touch of God . . ." She glanced at him. "The ball I used on your friend's shoulder can heal. Unfortunately, it can't heal everything. I mean, I can't change a person's destiny to die or not die, but it works on some things, like old wounds. Except sometimes, in certain circumstances, with help, it can do other things," she added, then drew in a breath. "Anyway, it looks like that box your father had hidden away lets people . . ." She trailed off as two women, wearing tight-waisted, full-skirted dresses walked past, bidding them good morning.

She was surprised when Jack addressed the women by name. "Do you know them?"

"My mind seems to be full of two memories. I remember my life in the twenty-first century — except for about four years when I was under the influence of various illegal substances — and I remember this guy's life, this John Marshall's life."

"So why don't I remember being . . . ?"

"Darci, my twin sister?"

"Twin?" She looked back at the street. She was beginning to sweat under her dress and longed for a shower. A shower and a pair of shorts and some sandals. And to be barbecuing shrimp with her husband and daughter, and to be with her father and sister-in-law and their daughter.

"Are you okay?" Jack asked.

"I don't think I have any powers," she said softly. When Jack was silent, she looked at him. He was leaning back in the chair, his long legs stretched out across the porch. She wasn't used to not having the ability to sense what people were feeling. She'd been born with her powers; they were as much a part of her as her skin. "Did you hear me? How do we get back if I have no powers to find out anything?"

The front door to the house opened and the maid came out with a pitcher of lemonade and two glasses. There was a chunk of ice in the lemonade that had what looked to be a couple of sticks frozen inside it. Obviously, the ice had been taken from a pond that winter and stored in an ice house.

Darci decided she had too much to worry about to concern herself with dirty ice. She could be treated for typhoid when she got back home.

Jack said, "Thank you, Millie," and the maid went back into the house. He settled back into his chair as though he . . . as though he were at home.

"You like it here, don't you?" she said.

For a moment he closed his eyes, and when he opened them, he was smiling. "I have no anger inside me, no hatred for a cold father who was displeased by anything I did, no history of drugs and women, and the images of the hideous things I've seen are fading with each passing moment. With every minute here, I feel . . ." He took a drink of his lemonade. "I feel cleaner."

"And then there's Lavender."

Jack's face split into a grin — the first one she'd ever seen on him. Physically, he looked the same as he did when she'd first met him, but here in this foreign place, in this foreign time, there was a big change in him. Here he looked younger . . . and happier.

"Yeah, Lavey," Jack said. "There's not a

movie star prettier than she is, but she's not spoiled, not jaded by modern-day excess. She's —"

"She's going to kill herself tomorrow," Darci said. "Or be murdered."

Jack waved his hand in dismissal. "I'll stay with her and stop that. I'm sure we were sent back here to prevent her death."

"We weren't 'sent' back, as you call it. It was an accident. You stuck your nose into something you don't understand and tried to steal a box —"

"*Steal?!* It was my father's box in his house, so it seems to me that you were the thief."

"That's absurd. I was led to that box by the key I found years ago. I was *meant* to find that box."

"*Steal* the box, you mean. All I did was borrow your key to open a box that legally belongs to my family."

She turned to face him. "Borrow! You cut the cord off my neck! And where is it now?"

"The box or the key?"

She glared at him. "Right now I'd love to give you the worst headache you've ever had in your life!"

"Ah," he said, smiling, "but you can't, can you? You are now just an ordinary person, like the rest of us."

With no way to get us back, she thought, but when she glanced at Jack, she could see that he was happier than she'd ever seen him. He wasn't scowling, wasn't looking at the world as though he wanted to blow it up.

"Casting out demons" is what the Bible called it. The demon spirit that had clung to Jack all his life was now in the curvy body of the beauteous Lavender and Jack was no longer being tortured by her.

As for Lavender, she'd at last got what she wanted: the man she loved.

Darci watched Jack greet two more passersby. She wanted to talk to him, tell him that they had to leave there. They could not possibly stay. She'd never spent much time looking into the past — when she had the power to do such things, that is — but she knew that their presence in a time where they didn't belong could harm things in the future. And, besides, waiting for her in the twenty-first century was her family, the people she loved.

But it seemed that the people Jack loved were in the nineteenth century.

Darci drank more of the lemonade — real lemons, real sugar — and looked out at the street. You're on your own, she told herself. She knew it was up to her alone to figure out why they were there — other than by an accident caused by Jack's thievery, that is — and to figure out how to get them out of there.

Besides her concern for how they'd get out this time, there were some things that puzzled her. The Lavender they'd met in spirit form had been full of anger. She'd turned Chrissy's very ordinary aura into flames of red and orange. Lavender as a beautiful young woman seemed sweet and kind, but Lavender in spirit form was an inferno of anger. The two didn't match.

How Darci wished she could see auras now! Many people who seemed one way showed their true nature by the colors around them. Children bullied into sub-mission often showed their anger in their auras.

Was Lavender that way? One person on the outside and another inside? Or would the events in the next twenty-four hours change her? Was she murdered or did something really horrible lead her to throw herself off a building?

Darci glanced again at Jack and thought that she was going to get no help from him. His plan was simple. He was going to stick by Lavender all day tomorrow so nothing could happen to her, then he was going to marry her and live happily ever after.

A horrible thought came to Darci. What if it was John Marshall who murdered Lavender? What if, on the day of the wedding, he found out something awful about her or she told him something bad, like she didn't want to marry him? What if he hadn't been in church waiting for her but had somehow managed to push her off the roof? That would explain Lavender's anger and why she'd attached herself to him, why she'd made sure his life in the twenty-first century was miserable, and why she'd put him in a car crash that had wrecked his face. It was clear to Darci that Lavender's spirit had stood over the surgeons as they'd rebuilt Jack's face to look just as it had when she knew him in the past.

To cover her thoughts, Darci put the glass of lemonade to her lips. All she knew for sure was that tomorrow something truly horrible was supposed to happen. Whether she or Jack could prevent it was another matter. And *should* they prevent it? If Jack and Lavender married they could possibly produce a child who destroyed the world. Anything was possible.

She put her hand to her forehead.

"Headache?"

"No, I . . ." She couldn't tell him of her thoughts. All she needed to concentrate on was putting the world back the way it was. And the first thing she needed to do was to gather all the information she could.

"What happened before I woke up?" she asked, and when Jack smiled, she leaned back in her chair and listened to his story.

Chapter Eight

After Jack opened the box, he and Darci and the cold, angry spirit of Lavender had fallen through emptiness for several minutes. When Jack awoke, he saw that he and Darci were lying on the ground in a shady woods and they were both dressed in Victorian clothes. Darci seemed to be sleeping, while Jack was groggy. He said he tried to wake her, but couldn't, so he'd walked to the road.

"It was odd," Jack said. "I could remember my modern life clearly, remember my childhood with Greg and his family, and I could remember my father. But what was strange was that the anger I'd always felt toward my father was gone. I'd hated the man all my life. I couldn't forgive him for spending his life locked away with lawyers and always dealing with money. But, suddenly, I saw everything differently. My father's absence had given me the freedom to play with the chauffeur's son and to practically live with his wonderful family. If my father hadn't stayed away from me . . ." Jack grinned. "Let's just say that my dad wasn't a fun person."

He took a breath. "But it was gone. In a flash, all the anger and hatred and the sense of injustice were gone."

He told how he staggered toward a pathway and with every step he took other thoughts that felt as though they were memories came to him. He knew when he came to a fork that one way led to the river where he and his buddies used to go skinny-dipping. The other way led to the main road.

He saw a rock that made him cringe. He knew that when he was nine he'd fallen off his pony and landed on that rock. He'd chipped his left front incisor and cut his face that left a scar over his eyebrow.

Jack had had to stand still for a moment to try to sort out his thoughts. In his "real" life, his twenty-first-century life, he'd fallen on his skateboard when he was eleven and made a scar over his left eyebrow, and his tooth had been broken in the car wreck. The doctors who put him back together years later had repaired both. But when Jack put his hand to his face, he found that the scar was there and the tooth was chipped.

With his head whirling with two sets of memories — two childhoods, two schools, two fathers, two towns, two of everything — he made his way to the road.

An old, toothless man on an old wagon gave him a ride, and when he called Jack Mr. Marshall, the memories of a boy bowling a hoop through the streets began to override the memories of a man who'd been an FBI agent.

Since names were still fuzzy in his mind, Jack told the man to drop him off "you know where." The man had let Jack off in front of Lavender's house.

Here Jack paused for a moment as the memory came back to him. "Lavender was on the porch, laughing with her girlfriends, and she looked at me with complete love. There was nothing guarded in her eyes, no sense of her saying, 'What are you going to do for me?' As I looked at her, I remembered my past life with her. I remembered picnics and going to church together, and stolen kisses behind the barn when we were thirteen. I remembered that I'd been in love with her all my life and I've never stopped."

He looked at Darci. "Did you know that in my twenty-first-century life I've never loved anyone romantically? Not really loved, not the way I love Lavender. Can you imagine that?"

"No," Darci said quietly, "I can't."

"The truth is that I had no idea what it felt like to love, to want what's best for someone else. You'll laugh at me, but I'd . . . I'd jump in front of a moving train if it meant saving her."

"I understand that," Darci said. "I'm just trying to find the train."

Jack smiled. "When I looked at Lavender I knew what had happened to me, to us. I knew that that box had sent us back in time. Maybe I should want to find the way back to the modern world, but it doesn't interest me. All I want to do is be with Lavender for the rest of my life."

He looked at Darci with a one-sided grin. "I knew that you were my sister, but at the same time the modern me knew that I'd never had a sister. Remember that we read that John Marshall was an only child? Like Lavender. When she and I were in the first grade that's what drew us together. Everyone else seemed to have half a dozen siblings, but Lavey and I knew what it was like to spend Saturdays by ourselves."

"I guess history made room for me when I came along with you."

"It looks that way. As far as I can tell,

I'm the only person who remembers that I . . . I mean, John Marshall . . . didn't have a sister yesterday."

"Amazing," Darci said.

For a while they were silent as they stared over the porch rail toward the town. Just down from them was what was probably Main Street, cute and quaint — except for the piles of horse manure in the street. Darci thought that maybe a peek into a hospital might jolt Jack back to reality. Had doctors learned to wash their hands by this time?

"Anyway," Jack said after a while, "Lavender got her father to get the buggy out and we went to where I'd left you sleeping. No one asked what or why so it made me think they were used to . . ."

When he gave Darci a sidelong glance, she wanted to shout, Not fair! "Are you saying that no one said anything because they're used to my doing weird things?"

"I'm not sure, but since you didn't exist before today, you might be able to make up whatever you want to be."

"But no one thought it was strange that your sister was sleeping in the woods and you couldn't wake her up?"

"Apparently not." Jack was smiling. "When we got there, you were just as I'd left you, sound asleep. I picked you up and put you in the backseat of the buggy. You traveled back to the house with your head in Lavey's lap and your feet in mine. And for the whole ride, Lavender and I just looked at each other. We never spoke a word, but it was the most exciting time in my life. Better than any foreplay I've ever had or given." His voice lowered. "She's a virgin and we're waiting for our wedding night. Can you imagine that happening in our time?"

"What then?" Darci asked tightly. She was glad for Jack to experience such happiness, but she kept thinking, He will *never* voluntarily leave here. Could she return to her own time alone? Did she have to return *with* Jack? Did all three of them have to return together? She, Jack, and Lavender's angry spirit? If she had her powers she could have found out this information in an instant. But here she had no powers. Here she had nothing extraordinary or unusual. Annoyed, she said, "What happened then?"

Jack had carried Darci into Lavender's house, put her on the couch in her parents' living room, and her mother's two sisters had all hovered about her, reviving her with smelling salts.

"They smell awful."

Jack grinned. "Young women fainting isn't unusual in this time. It's your under-garments — which I'm not supposed to mention. They're too tight. On you, that is. These clothes feel good to me, but I think the reason everything is strange to you is because you didn't exist here before so you have no memories as I do."

Unnecessarily, Jack said, "I don't want to return to the twenty-first century. I want to stay with Lavender. And I really don't want to talk about returning."

"I'm not sure it'll be our decision whether we leave or not."

"Then whose decision is it?" Jack snapped.

"Whoever made this happen."

"Your Devlin?"

"I don't know that he has enough power to do something like this." But maybe Henry does, Darci thought. Since she'd met Henry in Alabama she'd begun to think that he might have more power than anyone else on earth. Had Henry sent her — and Jack — back to the past for a reason?

"Do you know where the box is?" she asked.

"It's in my room but the key is missing. When I woke up, before new memories came to me, I looked for it on the ground. I looked everywhere but I couldn't find it."

Darci sipped her lemonade and thought back to when she'd first found the key. She'd been walking with her father when they'd passed an antiques shop. She'd felt as though she *had* to go into that shop. Curious, she'd entered and was drawn to a little ceramic man, about four inches high. He was in a bowl full of dirty, broken dishes and glasses. "There's something inside it," she'd told her father. When they got home, her father had used a hammer to try to break it open, but the ceramic didn't even crack. Frustrated, he'd looked at the object under a magnifying glass and thought he saw some markings on it. Since the little man was too dirty to be able to read, her father had taken it to the sink to wash. The second the water touched the little statue, the outer covering dissolved and inside was the key.

Darci wondered what was supposed to have happened as opposed to what did happen. She knew she was supposed to find the box in Jack's father's house but she'd had no intention of opening it while she was in that house. In fact, it had crossed her mind to go to Henry in Alabama and open it in his presence. But

Jack's interference and the spirit that had escaped Devlin had changed all that.

Try as she might, she couldn't believe that it was meant for all three of them to go back in time. Maybe the spirit that had so clung to Jack had known what the box was for and the spirit had meant for her and Jack to return. Did that mean that Darci's return was an accident? That Darci wasn't meant to go back with them?

She glanced quickly at Jack and kept her thoughts to herself. All she knew for sure was that she *must* return to her own time. She had a daughter, and her missing husband and sister-in-law were in the twenty-first century.

As she thought of Jack's story, she wondered if he'd been sent back because he needed to be. Obviously, he had to solve some things in his modern life. If he solved his problems with the angry spirit that had been hanging around him all his life, then what? Would he return to the twenty-first century and take over his father's job of being a philanthropist? The way things were now, if his father died, Jack wouldn't claim his inheritance and his relatives would get everything. What evil would they do with all those billions?

As Darci looked at Jack she decided to

tell him as little as possible about what she was planning to do. She knew what love like his felt like. If someone had told her that something — anything — was going to take her away from her husband, she would have . . .

Unbidden, Darci remembered that horrible night in the tunnels when she'd had to kill four people. She didn't want to remember what she'd had to do to keep Adam from being taken from her.

Yes, if Jack felt the same way about Lavender, then it would be better not to press the issue of his leaving her. He just might save Lavender by pushing Darci off the roof. Ha ha.

When she picked up her lemonade glass, her hand shook a bit. It was scary not knowing whether other people's intentions were good or bad. And it was scary knowing that she couldn't use her mind to control anything.

"Is it all right if I look around?" she asked.

"Sure," Jack said, smiling. "I plan to spend every second with Lavender so you're free."

Standing, Darci smiled back at him and she was glad he couldn't read her thoughts. She was going to do all that she could to find her way back to her own time.

Chapter Nine

After a trip to the outhouse — which made Darci harden her resolve to get out of the nineteenth century — she went through a side door into the house.

It was a nice house, sparse by modern standards, but she liked the furniture. It was newly constructed but it still looked old. She'd never been able to live with antiques before because she'd felt every emotion of the past owners. Every tear anyone had shed near the objects came to her when she touched them.

But not now. Now she ran her hand across the smooth, clean surfaces and felt nothing but the wood. Looking about, she saw that every surface seemed to hold a piece of crochet and she hoped she wasn't the one who was supposed to produce the things.

She walked through the living room — or the parlor, she thought — to the entrance hall and the staircase. Pausing for a moment, she wished she could sense whether anyone was near or not. She didn't like having to rely on her eyes and ears to know whether or not she was being spied on.

She heard no one, saw no one, felt no one, but still . . . still, she felt, well, creepy in the empty house. She knew Jack was on the porch just on the other side of the door, but she didn't want to be so cowardly as to ask him to go upstairs with her.

As she climbed the stairs she thought, So this is how other people feel all the time. Many people had told her she was brave and she'd thought maybe she was. But now she knew she wasn't. All the people who had no powers and went through life not knowing if danger was near were much braver than she was. Right now she was feeling that someone was watching her, and not being able to feel who it was was making the hairs on the back of her neck stand up.

"Devlin!" she hissed under her breath. She'd rather deal with a cantankerous spirit than with whatever was or was not lurking in the shadows.

When Devlin didn't appear, Darci ran up the last three steps.

The first door she opened was her bed-room. She knew it was hers from the lovely four poster with its huge crocheted canopy, and the pretty upholstered chair by the window.

When she realized how well the room suited her, she gave an involuntary shudder. Someone who knew her had planned this.

"Devlin!" she said again. "Henry!" She waited but heard nothing, saw nothing.

Why had this been done to her? A test? But a test of what? Why had she been taken from her daughter, from her niece? From her search for her husband?

Had she been sent? Or was it an accident? If it was an accident, why hadn't someone come to rescue her?

She called for Devlin again, even threatened him, but he didn't appear.

Darci looked through the wardrobe at her clothes. There weren't many dresses and each one contained probably twenty-five yards of fabric. Hot, heavy, and binding, she thought.

At last she turned to look at herself in the mirror. She'd been afraid of what she'd see. In modern times she'd known that Jack's face wasn't his, that it was a beautiful mask, but Lavender seemed to think that's how he'd always looked. It had made Darci wonder what she looked like.

Her first glimpse made her sigh in relief. Her eyebrows were thick and her lashes were so blonde you could hardly see them, but she looked the same as she always had. Her hair was pale blonde, no highlights, and there seemed to be an enormous amount of it. But on the bureau top was a little bun of hair so maybe the lump on the back of her head was artificial. At the sides of her face were long ringlets that to Darci's eye looked ridiculous.

She touched her hair but was careful not to disarrange it. Wonder who twists it into this shape? she thought, and hoped she wasn't responsible for doing it by herself. She could barely manage a blow-dryer, much less ringlets and an artificial bun.

She thought of the pretty red-haired maid and wondered if she doubled as a hairdresser.

Leaving the room, Darci explored the other three bedrooms. The bedroom next to hers was Jack's. "A shrine to Lavender" came to her mind as soon as she opened the door. Nearly everything in the room seemed to be about her. There were four photos of Lavender in silver frames, and there were many knickknacks scattered about, all of them seeming to have some- thing to do with her. There was a pressed flower stuck in the edge of the mirror, a curl of hair inside a tiny wooden frame. A few well-played-with toys were on top of an old cabinet. Toys he'd played with with Lavey?

A tall bookcase contained what looked to be medical texts. Had John Marshall wanted to be a doctor? What had stopped him? He couldn't bear to be away from Lavender long enough to go to medical school?

On top of his bedside table was the silver box — the box that had caused all Darci's current problems. As she slipped it into the pocket of her dress, she thought that she could easily hide a helium balloon inside the voluminous skirt.

The first bedroom across the hall had the blandness of a guest room. She closed the door and went to the fourth bedroom and instantly knew that it was John's fa- ther's room. Since the room had an empty feel to it, she thought she'd ask Jack what he remembered about the man. It didn't seem as though he was planning to attend his son's wedding tomorrow. That no one had mentioned him seemed to mean they didn't expect him to be there.

"There's another woman," Darci said to herself as she left the room, closing the door behind her. "He has a mistress, someone he can't introduce to the family, and he stays with her. Everyone knows it but doesn't mention it."

"Yes, Miss?"

Darci jumped half a foot at the voice. She'd been unaware that anyone had been near her. When she had her power, that never would have happened.

Clearing her throat, she looked at Millie, and thought how with the right hair and makeup the young maid could be beautiful. She wasn't like Lavender, who was gorgeous when she woke up, but —

"You wanted something, Miss?" Millie asked. She had a feather duster in her hand.

"No, I . . . Do you know when my father will be home?"

"Why, Christmas," Millie said, seeming to be surprised that Darci didn't know that.

"Ah, yes, of course. Uh, what do you think of my hair?"

"I can do it for you now if you want."

Relieved, Darci smiled. "No, thanks." Her head came up. "What's that smell?"

"Sorry, Miss, but Cook is making peach

137

jam today. I'll tell her to close the window."

"No!" Darci half shouted as she went to the stairs. "I'll tell her myself." She gave a quick smile to Millie, then hurried down the stairs, following her nose to find the kitchen.

She opened a door to a scene out of a BBC movie. The kitchen was large, with an enormous wood stove against the far wall, and a huge, heavy wooden table in the center of the room. On the floor were many baskets full of peaches that were ripe and fragrant. The tabletop was covered with jars and huge bowls, and two women were slicing and packing the peaches.

Darci hadn't realized she was hungry until she smelled all those heavenly peaches. The aroma made her sway on her feet.

One of the women, the shorter, lighter-weight one, hurried forward and led Darci to a chair at the end of the table.

"No need to faint again today," the older woman said, wiping her hands on her apron. It didn't take any guessing to know that this woman was the cook. "Hurry up, Emmy!" she ordered the younger woman. "You know what Miss Darci's like. She can out-eat any farmhand. Where she puts it all no one knows, but she can certainly tuck it away."

For a moment Darci felt near to tears of gratitude. It wasn't real, but here at last was someone who seemed to actually *know* her.

Within seconds a plate was set before her. It had thick slices of cheese, cold roast beef, three kinds of pickles, slices of tomatoes still warm from the sun, and spiced crab apples.

"Now, go on," Cook said. "Master John's off with his Miss Lavender so no one'll see you in the kitchen with the help. So now, dear, tell us every word of what's going on at the Shay house."

I'm the house gossip! Darci thought, at once horrified and delighted by the news.

"Did you see the wedding dress?" Cook asked.

"No," Darci said, her mouth full. Not one thing on her plate had been pasteurized, homogenized, frozen, packaged, or picked before it was ripe. She thought she might slide under the table from the pleasure of the taste.

"Of course she didn't see it," Emmy said. "That Miss Lavender ain't gonna let nobody see that dress of hers." Her eyes twinkled. "Except our Master John, that is."

Darci started to speak but when she bit into the crab apple, she closed her eyes to the taste.

"He's not seen it," said a voice full of anger. "Oh, pardon, Miss," Millie said, then ran out of the kitchen.

Startled, Darci looked at where Millie had been. "What's her problem?"

Emmy and Cook looked at each other at Darci's odd phrase. Cook recovered first. "She's being left behind. She wanted to go to work for Miss Lavey after the wedding, but Lavender hired some cousin of hers, so Millie has to . . . uh . . ."

"Stay behind with me?" Darci asked.

"It's more excitin' at Miss Lavey's," Emmy said.

"Now that's not so. I'd rather stay here than go there any day," Cook said.

"That's because you'd have to make all them fancy little cakes," Emmy said. "You'd rather cook for Miss Darci than half a dozen of them fancy friends of Miss Lavey's."

"Can I help it if I *like* working for somebody who's not popular?" Cook snapped, then turned red. "Oh! Beg your pardon, Miss Darci."

In the embarrassing silence that followed, they looked in horror at Darci, but she just waved her hand to let them know it was all right. Wonder what makes me weird in *this* century, she thought, sighing.

Still embarrassed, Emmy and Cook began moving quickly about the kitchen while Darci ate. Okay, she thought, trying to push aside her personal feelings and concentrate on the problem. It was early afternoon so she had hours before she was supposed to return to Lavender's for tea. Jack had said Darci was free. But free to do what?

Her first thought was to go to a grave-yard. Maybe if she concentrated she could make contact with a spirit or two and maybe they could get a message to Henry. Or maybe they could call Devlin. But then she knew from experience that ghosts were afraid of Devlin. And, too, ghosts responded best at dawn, not in the middle of a sunny day.

Anyway, maybe with the way I am now I'd be afraid of Devlin, she thought gloomily. Maybe I'd be afraid of all ghosts now that I have no power.

"Well, somebody has it!" Cook said loudly as she put a four-inch-wide piece of warm peach pie in front of Darci.

"Has what?" she asked distractedly.

"My biggest bowl, the one with the

zigzag design on it," Cook said. "Someone has it because it's not here."

Darci paused with a fork full of pie on the way to her mouth, her eyes wide. Yes, she thought, *someone* has it. Maybe she had no power but someone somewhere did. Maybe not power as she had — used to have — but maybe someone could at least conjure a ghost or two. How much power did that take?

Emmy and Cook were over their embarrassment now and were going back to work. They were no longer asking Darci for the latest gossip about Lavender.

Who? Darci thought, and how? How did she find out who had any power? Did these women know?

Darci swallowed her bite of pie. After the time in the tunnels she'd found out that nearly all the people in her hometown of Putnam, Kentucky, had known about her abilities. They hadn't known everything, but they'd known much more than Darci thought they did. It was probably the same in this small town. So how did she ask the question that got them to tell what they knew?

"Is there someone in town who's versed in the occult arts?" Darci asked.

That question stopped the women in

142

place. Cook recovered first. "You don't want to get involved with someone like that. Unless you must," she added as she looked at Darci's midsection.

It took Darci a moment to realize what the cook meant. Unless you're going to have a baby. Obviously, both women thought Darci was asking for an abortionist.

Darci batted her eyes to look as innocent as possible. "Need?" she said, her voice rising. "Yes, I need someone to make him love me as I love him."

The two women blinked at her. This time Emmy understood. "Ah, you want a love potion."

"Yes," Darci said, pretending to hold back tears.

The cook squared her shoulders. "Who is this young man?" she demanded.

Darci put her hands over her face. "You don't know?" she said, sounding hurt. "If *you* don't know, then *he* certainly doesn't know that I've been in love with him since we were in the first grade. If he doesn't love me back I'll just plain *die*."

She peeked through her fingers to see how this was being taken. Cook was obviously eaten up with trying to figure out who Darci was in love with. She patted

Darci's shoulder. "We'll send Tom to Tula's to get what you need."

"I'll have to go with him," Darci said as she grabbed the rest of her pie and ran toward the back door.

"I don't think —" Cook began.

"A lady can't —" Emmy began.

But Darci was out the door before either of them could finish her sentence.

Behind the house was a small stable where a tall, thin, gray-haired man was combing a horse's mane. Darci's impulse was to introduce herself, but she didn't. She tried to think how the daughter of a household in 1843 would treat a stableman. Better to just brazen it out, she thought.

"Could you please take me to see Tula?" she said to the man's back.

He took his time in turning around to look at her. He had piercing eyes that were almost black and they made Darci take a step backward. How she wished she could see his aura! Was this man hiding something? From his look she could believe he was an absolute devil inside.

"You don't wanta see Tula and you don't want no love potion. There ain't no man you're pinin' over."

Darci swallowed. Obviously, he was an

eavesdropper, and he also seemed to be someone who watched what was going on around him. She might be able to get around the household help with an easy lie, but this man was going to take big lies — which happened to be something she was rather good at.

Stepping closer to him, she lowered her voice. "I need someone with second sight, someone who can tell fortunes. For real, not fake." She lowered her voice even more. "Someone sent Lavender a note saying she was going to kill Lavey on her wedding day."

Tom drew in his breath.

"Lavender and my brother laughed the note off but I didn't. The wedding is to-morrow and I need to find out fast who hates Lavey enough to want to kill her. Do you know of anyone who can help me?"

"Simone," Tom whispered. "But girls like you don't go to her."

"This girl does," Darci said and couldn't help the rush of joy that ran through her. Maybe this Simone was why she'd been sent back in time. *If* she'd been sent, that is. If it hadn't been an accident.

"Horseback or the buggy?" Tom asked.

"Buggy," Darci answered quickly, look-ing fearfully at the big horse. It rolled its eyes at her and she gave it a weak smile. "Should I pay her?"

"Not in gold, but she'll take all the food you can carry."

While Tom hitched up the buggy, Darci went into the kitchen and came out bearing a huge basket full of food. Behind her Emmy and Cook carried more baskets. It didn't take a psychic to see that they believed this was "too much."

Once the buggy was loaded, Darci prepared to hop onto the top seat, but Tom gave her a look to remind her of her place. Meekly, she got into the back with the food.

It took nearly an hour to drive to Simone's tiny cottage. They left the prosperous town of Camwell and drove through rural areas with picture-perfect farms with pastures surrounded by fieldstone walls.

Finally, they came to a patch of land that hadn't been cultivated. It grew wild, with giant trees and tangled, thorny blackberry vines.

"Through there," Tom said.

Darci looked at him in disbelief. The place looked like what had surrounded Sleeping Beauty's castle. How could she get through that?

"There's a path and you can find it if you need to," Tom said as he got down.

Darci looked skyward for a moment. May God strike her dead if she ever grew to be so otherworldly that she made people have to search through thorn bushes to find the front door of her house.

She put her hand on a basket, preparing to hand it to Tom.

"Leave it. I know where to leave her food."

If Darci'd had her power she would have known what his cryptic phrase meant. It wouldn't surprise her to find out that Simone and Tom were related.

Tom helped Darci out of the buggy and she took several moments to arrange her huge skirt and her half a dozen slips. "Where's Amelia Bloomer when you need her?" she muttered as she walked toward the blackberry vines and the deep shade. She let out the breath she'd been holding when she realized she'd half expected them to magically part.

The vines didn't part, but on the edge, near a stone wall, she saw an opening and entered. The path had been recently cleared and she wondered who maintained it. Tom?

As Darci walked through the dark forest,

she realized she was nervous. So this is how other people feel when they meet me, she thought. She'd always been on the other end and had always desperately wanted people to see her as normal, as anything but a freak.

But only Adam, her husband, had, she thought. Only Adam had seen the person beneath her ability to see things and change them.

At the end of the path was a cute little stone house that Darci guessed had been there since before George Washington was president. It might have been there in some form when the *Mayflower* landed.

Now what do I do? she wondered. And what was this woman going to see about her? Darci had many secrets and it had never been difficult to keep them to herself, but now . . .

Before Darci could knock, the door opened and she saw a thin little woman with gray, grizzled hair and eyes very much like Tom's. They are related, Darci thought, smiling that she'd guessed that earlier. The woman had a gaudy red shawl around her shoulders and giant gold hoops in her ears. She looked like a caricature of a psychic.

"I see clouds around you," the woman

said in a booming voice that made Darci step back. "Clouds and spirits. The spirits hover over you, watch you, and they take what they need from you. You must be cautious or the spirits will come for you when you least expect it."

"I just wish they'd come when I call them," Darci said under her breath, disappointment in her voice. The woman was a fake, a showman, all psychic mumbo jumbo. Darci well knew that if you mentioned "spirits" people got frightened.

She couldn't repress a yawn as she stepped away from the woman. "Sorry to have bothered you but Tom has some food. He's leaving it . . . Actually, I'm not sure where he's leaving the food, but I assume you'll be able to find it. Thanks." As she said the last she turned and quickly started down the path. Now what was she to do?

"Wait!" the woman called after her, but Darci just waved her hand and kept walking. "You're a ghost," the woman said. "You're not really here." Her voice was normal. No more trying-to-intimidate boom.

Halting, Darci slowly turned to look back at the woman. "What else?"

The woman smiled, showing strong white teeth. "I'm too old to stand out here shouting. Come in and have some tea." All three of you, she said to herself, for, dimly, like pale shadows, the woman saw two spirits just behind young Darci Marshall. Simone didn't know what the spirits meant, but she did know this girl was important. And how odd it was that she couldn't remember ever having seen her before. She remembered that John Marshall had a twin sister, but Simone was sure she'd never seen this girl before.

Inside the house, Simone first turned toward a doorway that was covered by a black curtain embroidered with various astrological signs and a moon and some stars.

She turned away from the curtain. "In here," she said, opening a paneled pine door. Inside was a cozy little room with a cheerful fire in a tiny fireplace. There were fat, upholstered chairs and a tea table laden with many of the things Darci had brought.

Darci looked at the woman in question.

"There's a road around back and a door through there. Tom snitches food from your house and brings it to me." Smiling, Simone removed her shawl and the big earrings. "The customers expect these things," she said, motioning toward the shawl. Once she was in an ordinary skirt and blouse, she looked like a normal little woman. "The tea's hot, so sit and let's eat your food."

Darci took a seat, accepted the cup of tea, and smiled. "My brother can afford it. So tell me what you see."

"You don't want me to tell you that a glorious man is coming into your future?" Her eyes were twinkling.

Darci decided that she didn't have time to be cautious. If this woman had enough ability to know that Darci wasn't really there, then she must have seen and heard a lot in her long life. Darci decided to tell the truth. "The most glorious man has already come into my life, but he's being held prisoner about a hundred and fifty years from now. I think I was making some headway in finding him, but then I got sent back to the past, and now I'm afraid I'm stuck here. Unless I can prevent the death of the future wife of a man who isn't really my brother, that is."

"I see," Simone said as she slowly set down her tea cup. "Are you *sure* you don't want just a palm reading?"

For a second Darci looked at her without comprehension, then she burst out laughing, with Simone joining in. Darci hadn't laughed in a long time.

Finally, Simone said, "Tell me everything."

"What would you say if I told you that I'm from another century and I want to go home?"

When Simone didn't blink an eye, Darci's estimation of her went up. When you dealt with spirits without bodies on a daily basis, it took a lot to shock you.

"I'd say that I've lived a long time and I've seen a lot of things."

Picking up a pecan-filled cookie, Darci looked at it. "So let me guess, Tom listens to everything in town, reports it all to you, and you use it to tell fortunes."

"More or less," Simone said, smiling. "I couldn't very well tell the truth, now could I? I touch a hand and know some young lady will be dead in a year. Or I know that the woman will never have a child. How could I tell them that? I try to fix what I can and leave the rest to God."

"How do you fix things?" Darci held her breath. Perhaps she'd underestimated Simone's abilities.

Simone shrugged. "A girl gets in trouble and goes to my daughter Tula. Sometimes my daughter helps get rid of the child, but sometimes we send the girl away to the country to my relatives. They always tell her the child was stillborn and have a lovely little funeral. It helps the girl. But my cousins bring the child to me and Tom tells the mother who wants a baby so much to come to me. I match them up."

"How nice of you," Darci said in admiration. "What happens if you get caught?"

"I don't want to think about it. Now tell me what I can do for you."

Darci thought for a moment. "If Tom hears everything, has he heard of anyone who wants to kill Lavender Shay?"

Simone leaned back on her chair. "So that's why he brought you to me. I told him over a year ago that I foresaw that girl's death."

"How? Who?" Darci asked eagerly.

"A fall. I saw it in a vision, but I'm afraid my visions are rare and short, and not very clear. As she fell, I saw a figure on the roof behind her, but I couldn't tell if young Lavender had been pushed or someone was trying to keep her from jumping." Simone gave Darci a hard look. "What powers do you have?"

"None, but I did have —" She broke off. "Can you conjure a ghost or two for me?"

Simone seemed to think that was a funny request. "Any particular one? Thomas Jefferson, maybe?"

Darci didn't smile. "If I had a problem with French history he'd be the one I'd call. No, I'm looking for a spirit named Devlin, but he may be difficult to find as I'm not sure he's ever lived on earth as a human."

"Neither have you," Simone said softly. "And, no, I can't call spirits forward. Please don't tell anyone that or I'll never have another customer. Tom and I tried a few séances, but I didn't like such blatant lying, so we quit doing it."

On impulse, Darci held out her left hand. "What do you see?" Part of her didn't want to know. What if she was never to find Adam? "Tell me the truth. Death and all of it."

Simone looked as though she wanted to say no, but she took Darci's hand in her old one and rubbed her palm with her thumbs. "The man you're looking for isn't where you think he is."

"Will I find him?"

"Yes and no. You'll find him but he's not the same man you were looking for."

"Excuse me if I scream," Darci said. "What does that mean?! Do I find him *dead?*"

"I don't know," Simone said. "I'm afraid that most of my ability comes from Tom's snooping."

"I don't think that's true, but who is Tom to you?"

"My son."

"You said I was a ghost, that I didn't belong here."

Simone held Darci's hand tighter and didn't seem to want to say anything.

"Tell me," Darci said softly. "Tell me what you see, even if it's bad."

"I'm not sure, but it may be you who dies tomorrow."

"Dies or just leaves this time and place?"

"Dead. At the bottom of a building. There's a woman in a white dress leaning over you."

"Great," Darci said, leaning back against her chair. "Just great. Nothing like a little pressure on a girl. If I get killed here, does my spirit go back to my own time?"

Simone looked at Darci hard. "You don't know anything about yourself, do you?"

"I'd love to learn."

Simone poured herself another cup of tea and offered some to Darci, but she refused. "We're all put on this earth for a purpose, and as you may know, we keep coming back until we do what we're supposed to."

"Yes, I know that," Darci said impatiently. "I know I was given what power I had for a reason but I've never come close to finding out what it is."

"Have you asked?"

"You mean God?"

"Yes," Simone said softly. "Have you asked God?"

"I've done a lot of praying, but . . ." Darci looked away for a moment. "I'm ashamed to say that most of my prayers — my big wish — has always been to find someone who loved me as I am. You see . . . I used to have rather a lot of ability and it made me, well, different."

At that Simone smiled. "Oh? Is that why there's a golden light around you?"

Darci's face turned pink but she smiled. "If there is, I've never seen it. I know it's selfish of me, but my only interest now is getting my family back."

"If your body dies tomorrow you won't find anyone. I'm not sure about this, but I think God is going to give you only one body."

"No past lives?" Darci asked. "No future lives?"

"I don't think so." Simone smiled. "I wish you could have met my grandmother. She had *real* talent. She would have been able to tell you everything in an instant. She used to go into trances that lasted for days, and she'd come out of them knowing things."

Darci sighed. "That doesn't help me now, does it? Maybe if I found the key . . ."

"What key?"

Darci removed the little silver box from her skirt pocket. "You don't have a key to this, do you? I found the key inside a little ceramic man. We couldn't break him but he dissolved in water."

Simone's eyes widened. "Stay here. Sit right there. Don't move." She quickly left the room.

When Darci was alone, she thought about what Simone had told her, that it could well be her, not Lavender, who died tomorrow. And if Darci died she'd never see her family again. She probably wouldn't be reborn in a twenty-first-century body and get another chance.

Simone returned and in her hand was what looked like an iron egg, but when Darci took it, it was surprisingly light.

"What do you feel?" Simone asked.

"Nothing," Darci answered, frustrated. "I have no power to —"

"Yes, you do. Spirits never change. You have power now but it's . . ." She frowned as though trying to figure out how to explain.

"It's blocked," Darci said. "It's as though someone has wrapped my senses in a thick quilt and I can't find them."

"Think it was this Devlin who you want to contact?"

Darci's eyes narrowed. "I think maybe it was an old blind man who's the sweetest person in the world — and perhaps the most powerful."

"But then isn't the devil exceedingly pleasant?" Simone asked.

"Yes." For a moment Darci put her face in her hands. "I'm out of my element here. Here I can't feel anything, make anything change. It's not *me* here."

"I know you're not where you are supposed to be," Simone said, trying not to show her wonderment. Darci had said she couldn't make anything change. Could someone actually do that? And what mortal had the power to wrap someone else's God-given talent in a quilt?

Simone had to repress the urge to make a cross of her fingers and tell Darci to get out. The truth was, Simone had seen more about Darci than she had ever seen about anyone else. It had been her grandmother who was the real soothsayer, a woman who saw things many years ahead. Simone regretted not having written down what her grandmother said. But all of the family had dismissed the old woman's ranting.

Her gift had been passed to her daughter, Simone's mother, but it was diluted. Simone's mother had hated seeing the future and had stayed at home, refusing to meet strangers or to touch them. Simone had inherited only about a quarter of her grandmother's ability and her daughter Tula, none at all. All Tula had was an old recipe book that Simone's grandmother, who couldn't read or write, had paid a man to write for her. There were about a dozen herbal "spells" in there that Tula used to make her living and support her two children after her husband left them. Simone never doubted for a moment that her grandmother had foreseen Tula's future need and had supplied it.

Now, this young woman had come to Simone and she wished she could tell her more. As always, based on nearly eighty years of experience, Simone didn't tell all she knew. She didn't tell Darci that it wasn't important whether or not she found her lost husband. However, it was very important she leave this place and go back to her own time.

Simone also didn't tell Darci that the beautiful golden light around her was fading fast. In the few minutes since she'd entered Simone's house, the light had dulled.

"You need to find out why you're here, then go back," Simone said. She wasn't sure if Darci was from another time, another planet, or the next town over, but she didn't belong here. Here was killing her rapidly.

Darci held up the egg and looked at it. It was rusty and pitted, but there was no seam along its side from where it had been manufactured. It looked to be one piece of metal. "Have you tried to open it?"

Simone smiled. "When I was a little girl I remember my grandmother cursing quietly as she tried to open that thing. She hit it with hammers, threw it in a fire, then into the snow. She took it to a blacksmith and he couldn't dent it. She boiled it and chanted over it."

Simone looked at Darci. "On her deathbed she told me that I would be the one who would find the person who could open it."

"Ah," Darci said as she put the silver box in one pocket and the egg in the other. "One of the twelve, not that that's any use to me now since I'm stuck here."

"Don't say that!" Simone said. "You

must find your way back. I feel that you *must*."

"But how?" Darci asked. "If I could find the key to the box, maybe I could get back. You don't have a little ceramic man about four inches high, do you? Blue clothes, brown cap, big ears?"

Simone smiled. "No, but my grandmother used to talk to a rock. We children laughed at her, but she said he was a little man, the oldest object on earth and completely amoral. She used to keep him —"

"In a cage made of string," Darci said in a faraway voice, "because nothing else will hold him. And he eats —"

"The salt from Jerusalem," Simone said quietly.

"And one raspberry a year. He likes raspberries."

Simone's face was white. "You know of this creature?"

"Sitting before you is the stupidest person on earth. I had him. When I was a little girl I found him by a stream and I knew everything about him in an instant. I made him a cage and he stayed with me for years. He's very funny. And old. He thinks alligators are newcomers."

"Where is he?" Simone asked.

"Either my mother threw him out or he's in a closet in my hometown. I'll probably never see that place again."

Leaning forward, Simone took Darci's hands. "You must return. If I know nothing else, I know that you must go back to wherever you came from. You can't let your body be destroyed tomorrow."

"How do I go back?" Darci asked. "And does Jack go with me? He wants to stay here with Lavender."

Simone leaned back and thought. "Do you think if you contacted this spirit Devlin or the man Henry you could find out more?"

"I hope so," Darci said eagerly. "I'm ready to do anything, try anything."

"Not far from here is a town called Drayton Falls. About three years ago a young woman there died. I don't think it was her time to go, or maybe the grief of her family has kept her on earth. Whatever the cause, her spirit stays here and she haunts the house she loved. Her spirit is such a strong presence that no one can live in her house. If anyone has the strength to contact another world, she can."

Darci's eyes brightened. "I'll have Tom take me there now."

"No!" Simone said. "If you find the way

back, you must take the two people you came with."

"How did you know that I came here with *two* people?" Darci asked suspiciously.

"Their spirits are with you. Behind you. I see them. Their existence is linked to yours. If your spirit returns, they must go with you."

Darci smiled up. "I think you're more like your grandmother than you know."

"A high tribute, indeed," Simone said.

Darci stood up. "It's nearly time for tea with Jack and Lavender. I'll get them to go to Drayton Falls with me." She turned toward the door, then stopped and looked back at Simone. Pulling the egg from her pocket, she put it on a little table. "I came with the silver box so I think I'll go back with it, but this egg might disappear. I'll look around Camwell and see what I remember, then I'll tell Tom where to hide the egg so I can get it later. All right?"

"Does Camwell survive the coming war?"

"War?" Darci asked, then drew in her breath. The War Between the States. That horrible war where more men died from disease than from weapons. Brother against brother.

Simone watched Darci's face and it told

her more than she wanted to know. "My children are too old for the fight, but my grandchildren aren't."

"Send them west," Darci said softly. "As far west as possible. And, yes, Camwell survives. The buildings last a long time, but its reputation doesn't." She put her hand on the door handle.

Simone started to stand up, but then sat back down. "I think maybe you've aged me today."

"If I can, I'll see you again before I leave."

"No, you go back to where you came from. You're needed there."

"If I return and I get my powers back," Darci said softly, "I'll find you. Wherever you are, whatever body you're in, I'll find you."

"I'd like that," Simone said. "Now go. Go to Drayton Falls with your friends and see what you can find."

Smiling, Darci left the house.

When Simone was alone, she looked at the fire and thought that she should get up and put on a piece of wood, but she couldn't move. The girl said she had no powers, but the energy around her had drained Simone. What had she said? That some old blind man was probably the most powerful person on earth? He'd have to go some to beat that girl, Simone thought, and closed her eyes.

She instinctively knew that she had one more thing to do, which was to bury the egg, then she'd leave the earth. She wasn't sure, but she thought perhaps she'd just done what she was supposed to with her life. Everything else, all the people she'd helped in her long life had been lagniappe, that term from New Orleans that meant "something extra."

Smiling, Simone relaxed in the chair and let herself doze.

On the drive back to Camwell, Darci tried not to allow all that Simone had said to frighten her — but it did. "Must" was a strong word. She must return to her own time, and Lavender and Jack must go with her.

They were nearly back at Camwell when Darci saw a cemetery and called to Tom to stop. As he helped her down, he gave her a sidelong look that told her he knew everything. Obviously, he'd been eavesdropping again.

She had no time to think about what he thought of her; she brushed past him on her way to the cemetery. Some of the headstones were quite old, some new. She wandered about a bit, listening and trying to open her senses to receive any vibrations from any spirits. But all she felt was a soft summer breeze on her stiff hair.

For a moment she thought back to all the times she'd been plagued by spirits swarming around her and how she'd been contemptuous of them. Such a nuisance!

Was that what this was all about? she wondered. To make her appreciate her powers?

Or maybe someone was trying to make her find out about herself. Past lives had never interested her much. As a child she'd been concerned with feeding herself and making sure she had a place to sleep. She'd spent a lot of her life envying other children with mothers who tucked them in at night, and fathers who flew kites with them. No, she'd never developed an appreciation for an ability that set her apart from the rest of the world.

As soon as she graduated from college, she'd gone to New York and met Adam. Since then she'd . . . Lived, she thought. She'd lived as normal a life as she could, with a husband and child, with her father who'd married Adam's sister, and their child. For a very short time, Darci had been the happiest person on earth.

Looking around the graveyard, she thought perhaps she should have done what Simone said and tried to find out why she'd been given such marvelous power. Perhaps she should have looked into her own past — if she had one. Had Simone been right when she said Darci had never lived in another body before? Why didn't Darci know that about herself? Had she been afraid to look?

"I apologize," she said, in prayer, and to the spirits that she knew were around her. "If any of you can hear me, please contact Devlin. Or Henry. Contact —" She broke off as it hit her what Simone had told her. Maybe tomorrow it would be she, Darci, who was thrown off a roof, not Lavender. Maybe Lavender would be wearing her wedding dress as she bent over Darci's broken body.

"It won't be me," she said firmly as she headed back to the buggy. If she had to get Jack to lock her in a closet she'd not leave the ground floor of any building.

On the ride back into the town, she strengthened her resolve to go home to her family. And when she got there, she told herself, she was going to conduct her life differently. She was going to appreciate and learn.

On the edge of town was a church she recognized. She told Tom where to hide Simone's egg, then had him drop her off at Lavender's house.

"Whatever it takes," she told herself. "I'll do whatever it takes."

Chapter Ten

"I'm not going to some haunted house!" Jack said to Darci. "I'm not going to do anything to help you take me away from her. I like it here. I like the people. I like *me* here. You go back if you want to, but I'm staying."

They were in the little garden behind Lavender's house and Jack was shouting as quietly as he could. When he started back into the house, Darci put her body in front of him. "Lavender is going to die and I think maybe you kill her."

"What?!" Jack said, anger making the blood rise in his face. "You're insane."

She put both her hands on his arm, trying to keep him from leaving. "Please calm down and listen to me."

Jack took a couple of deep breaths, but his face was still red. "All right, I'm listening."

"This is the nineteenth century, not the twenty-first, and morals aren't the same.

Here women who get pregnant out of wed-lock have their lives ruined. Things that to us are nothing are horrible to them. I don't have your memories, but is there anything about your past or maybe your father's that someone could tell Lavender that would make her unable to marry you?"

She watched Jack's face go from red to white as the blood drained from his face. Heavily, he sat down on an iron bench. "I've not been a saint in any life," he said softly. "And our father . . ."

"Has a mistress?" she said as she sat down beside him.

"With dyed red hair and a horse laugh and an illegitimate son. She's an embar-rassment to everyone, but he's mad about her. He's not here because we had a fight. He said he either comes with her to my wedding or he doesn't come at all. I told him not to come. Or John did, but I agree with him."

"How much does Lavender's family know of this?"

"Nothing. I've worked hard to keep it from them. I've told so many lies I can't keep them straight."

"I wish I knew what happens tomorrow." Darci smiled. "Somewhere on this earth is a magic mirror that will show the future if you ask it the right questions. If I could get that mirror . . ." She sighed. "Jack, you and I've never been friends so I don't expect you to trust me, but I'm telling you that something is very, very wrong here."

Dully, Jack turned to look at her. What she'd said about some ugly secret being told to Lavender had jolted him. "What could be wrong? It's paradise here. I love everything about this place, the people, the food, even the clothes. I never want to leave here. This place suits me."

Darci stood up, her hands on her hips, and glared at him. "Life in the twenty-first century would suit you, too, if you didn't have some crazy dead woman hanging around you! We're here to keep Lavender from killing herself, then we're to return to our own time." She had to take a few breaths to calm herself. "I'll make you a solemn, sacred vow. I promise you that if we go back to our own time, I'll find where Lavender's spirit is in the twenty-first century and you can go to her."

He looked at her in disgust. "I know where it is. It was hanging around *me*. Remember?"

"Don't you think it's odd that Lavender loves you here in this time but hates you in modern times? What happened to change her so drastically? If she found out something bad about your family and was forbidden to marry you, I could imagine that she'd be so depressed that she'd take her own life. Suicide is a mortal sin, true, but that wouldn't cause the hatred I felt coming from Lavender's spirit. She loves you in this life. What changed her? And, most important, how do we not only prevent her death but also prevent a hatred that lasts for centuries?"

Jack looked at her in silence for a while and she could tell that he was making some decisions. "I guess there are worse things than a night out before the wedding. Does it have to be in a haunted house?"

"Why not? If there's a spirit near here strong enough to manifest herself, I want to talk to her. And you need to keep Lavender away from other people. You have to make sure no one tells her something that might make her so despondent she commits suicide. So why not go together?"

Jack gave a bit of a smile. "So how do we kidnap her? And you don't expect us to spend the night inside the house, do you?"

"I thought you didn't believe in ghosts."

"I didn't until I met you and saw that . . . that thing slime its way across my father's bookcase. Why don't you call *him*?"

172

"You think I haven't tried? You think I've been lounging about in the bathtub all day?"

"From the look of your clothes and hair I'd say you've been mud wrestling. You really should have changed for tea, you know."

"I was too busy trying to save your soul to —"

"My soul! Let me tell you that —"

"I thought I heard loud voices," Lavender said from the doorway. "Why ever are you two arguing now?"

"I need to go to Drayton Falls right now," Darci blurted.

"We couldn't go and get back before dinner," Lavender said.

"She left her best shawl there," Jack said, standing and putting a brotherly arm around Darci. "And she has to take it with her on the wedding trip. I promised her I'd get it for her tonight so I thought we'd all three go."

Lavender looked from one to the other and back again. "When were you in Drayton Falls?" she asked Darci, suspicion in her voice.

Darci's lips tightened. "Lavender, give us a break. The man wants to get you in the back of the buggy and have his way with you."

When Lavender's eyes widened in shock,

Jack gripped Darci's shoulders so hard she nearly cried out.

Lavender said, "I'll be right back," then she turned on her heel and fled into the house.

"She probably went to get her father and his shotgun," Jack said. "You have a vulgar mouth."

"Me! I'll have you know —"

She broke off because Lavender had returned, pulling on gloves, a shawl over her arm, and a bonnet hastily jammed onto her head. "Shall we go? Time's awastin'."

It was difficult even for Jack with his long legs to keep up with Lavender as she hurried through the garden toward the back gate.

"We'll take Father's new buggy, the fast one," Lavender said over her shoulder. "And we don't want a driver so we can . . ." She glanced back at Jack for a moment, her lashes fluttering.

"Looks like people like sex in every century," Darci muttered, envious of Lavender's happiness.

Jack caught Darci's arm. "I can drive a twelve-cylinder Jag, but horses? No way. What about you?"

"Haven't a clue. Can't John Marshall drive a buggy?"

"Probably, but, you know, in the last few hours it seems to be more me than him. It's almost as though I'm taking his memories, adding my own, and creating a new person."

Darci looked at him sharply but said nothing. Was Jack's spirit stronger than John Marshall's? Was Jack's hunger for love and family driving John out?

By the time Jack and Darci got to the stables, Lavender was already there, and the buggy was hitched and ready.

"Aren't we lucky that Father just got home and the buggy is still hitched?" She looked at Jack with such heat that her namesake eyes turned to purple.

"I guess one night before the wedding doesn't matter," Darci said, then caught Jack's arm. "You can't . . . you know . . . with her. What if we do go back? You'll have cheated John out of the wedding night he's waited for for so long."

"Let him suffer," Jack said, hurrying toward Lavender.

When Darci got there both Lavender and Jack were on the driver's seat, with her holding the reins.

As Darci climbed into the back, Lavender said, "Jack is going to allow me to drive. Isn't he the most generous, kind man alive?"

"Oh yeah," Darci said, "the best."

Jack winked at her and the next minute they started off. Lavender sat straight and rigid on the seat and handled the reins competently. Jack — the overactor! — often gave her little admonishments and pointed out potholes to miss, and three times he cautioned her about going too fast. You would have thought he knew all about buggies and horses.

All through their long, slow trek through town, Darci sat in the back and watched the two of them together. They nodded to passersby, calling to them by name, and everyone who saw them smiled back. Everyone in town seemed to find pleasure in the sight of the beautiful young couple.

Darci thought back to Greg Ryerson at the FBI and how she'd felt the deep bond between him and Jack. A deep, die-for-each-other bond. Greg wouldn't recognize Jack now because Jack is no longer an angry young man, she thought.

But Darci knew that something wasn't right. If she had her power, she'd know in an instant what it was, but it was hard to figure out things on a human level. If she had her power, she could just look at people's auras and know what was going on.

She tried to put her mind on Lavender

and Jack but she couldn't. Their giggly happiness made her think of her own husband, of Adam. So far, nothing she'd done seemed to have taken her closer to finding her husband. She'd helped the actor Lincoln Aimes find his son; she'd found Henry, a man with power that she was only gradually finding out about. But still, she hadn't come any closer to finding Adam.

For a moment, she closed her eyes and remembered a happy time when she'd been with her family. Adam had been playing ball with the girls in the back garden. He was laughing and saying it wasn't fair for the girls to throw the ball by using their minds. He'd pretended to read a rule book that clearly stated that "no hands" was illegal. The three of them had ended by tumbling down and rolling on the grass.

But even in her happy memory she saw the shadows that always haunted Adam's eyes. No matter how happy he was, there was always in his aura and in his eyes what had been done to him as a child.

And then there was Boadicea, his sister. She would never be so-called normal. She'd been raised by a truly evil woman, and as a result, she'd never fit into society. Darci's heart would ache when Bo went with them to a mall or to a movie. Bo only felt at home when there were people around her who she knew and loved and trusted.

As they left the town behind them, Darci's thoughts grew more melancholy. Jack had found love, so he wanted to stay with that love. It was easy for Darci to tell him he had to leave, but she wondered what she'd do if the tables were turned. What would she want to do if she found Adam here in this time?

"I'd —" she said aloud, then said no more, because Lavender raised the horse whip, yelled "hee-*yah!*" and the animals took off. Darci was thrown back against the seat and Jack would have fallen onto the road if he hadn't managed to grab the side of the seat.

"Lavender!" Jack shouted but was answered by her laugh.

Darci, trying to stay upright as she bounced along, watched as Jack struggled with himself. The nineteenth-century John Marshall inside of him seemed to want to stop Lavender's wild driving, but the twenty-first-century Jack was loving it.

Jack won. He gave a yell, threw his hat to the ground, pulled off his tight jacket, tossed it back to Darci, then unbuttoned his shirt halfway down his chest.

As Darci banged from one side of the carriage to the other, she knew she'd never seen a more beautiful couple in her life. And she also knew that if she was going to get Jack to leave, she was going to have to use some very powerful magic.

Chapter Eleven

"Yes, I agreed," Lavender said slowly and firmly, "but that was before I knew that you wanted me to go to a haunted house." She was on the driver's seat of the buggy and they were on the outskirts of Drayton Falls, but she was refusing to go any farther.

"You don't have to go in," Darci said patiently. "*I* will go in. You can stay here in the buggy and kiss Jack for an hour or so."

Lavender looked at Darci with narrowed eyes. "You've changed, you know that?"

"Changed from what?" Darci asked, her voice rising. "What was I before today?"

Jack put his hand on Lavender's shoulder and turned her around. "Sweetheart," he said soothingly, "Darci needs to . . ." He gave Darci a look that said he needed help in coming up with a reason why she had to go into a haunted house.

"Tell me about the house," Darci said, trying to get control of her emotions. She needed Lavender so she couldn't afford to anger her. Lavender knew where the house was and could save them a lot of time by just taking them there. Ever since her first encounter with Connecticut, Darci didn't trust the place, so she didn't want to have to go knocking on doors and asking directions. "I want to know what happened to make the house haunted."

Lavender seemed to relax as Jack held her hand and caressed it. "A man and his wife and their two young children lived there. It's an old, old house, one of the first to be built in the state. I think it had something to do with the Revolutionary War, but I'm not sure what. It's been in the Drayton family for a long time. They came from England and somehow kept the land no matter what happened."

She glanced at Jack. "All right, I'm hurrying. Old Mr. Drayton died when I was a girl and that left young Mr. Drayton as the heir to it all. When he didn't get married right away, my mother used to say she hoped he'd wait for me. But he didn't."

When Lavender looked at Jack, he lifted her hand, kissed it, and she said, "I'm glad he didn't wait."

"But he did marry?" Darci asked.

"Yes. He went away for a few years and

returned with a wife from somewhere else. They moved into the old house and right away had two children. I didn't know them as they're quite rich. Not our set."

"What happened to her?" Darci asked.

"It was all anyone could talk about for months. It seems that she just dropped dead one day. I heard that she was in her garden and just fell down. She was dead instantly. Her husband shut himself in his room for weeks and left the care of his children to the nanny. When he finally left his room, he moved to the other side of the town and locked his old house up."

"So he didn't move because of a ghost?" Darci asked.

"Oh no. In fact, my mother told me that Mr. Drayton refused to believe that there was a ghost. I heard that he yells at anyone who says there is a ghost. But everyone within a hundred miles has heard the stories of the poor woman. She's been seen in windows and in the garden and walking in front of the house. It isn't just one person who's seen her but dozens. I heard a story that a bunch of boys tried to break into the house one night and they ran out so terrified that one of them never recovered his mind."

"Lavender, please take me to this

house," Darci said softly, her voice pleading. "If you don't I'll go into the nearest liquor establishment and ask the men in there."

"You wouldn't," Lavender said, aghast.

"She would," Jack said, "so I really think you should take us there. We'll leave Darci there, then you and I will —"

"You would leave your own sister in a haunted house?" Lavender sounded out-raged. "You'd leave her to the mercy of the spirits? What kind of man are you?"

"I wouldn't marry a coward like him," Darci said. "I'd call the wedding off right now."

Jack gave Darci a look to tell her that he was going to happily wring her neck the moment they were alone. "All right, I'm outnumbered," Jack said. "Take us to the house and I'll . . . guard the entrance, I guess." He shot a lascivious look at Lavender. "If I get scared, will you hold my hand?"

"You are incorrigible," Lavender said, but she was smiling as she picked up the reins. "What I want to know is why Darci wants to go to a haunted house."

Darci decided to take a chance. "Because Simone said I had to."

Lavender hesitated a moment, then

flicked the reins of the horses. "You should have told me that earlier."

"Did I miss something?" Jack asked. "Who's Simone?"

"She's not for any man to know about," Lavender said tightly, then glanced back at Darci. "Be careful what you say around Tom. He snoops and he tells."

"I've already learned that," Darci answered.

Minutes later, Lavender turned the horses down a narrow dirt road. Weeds ran down the middle of the road and trees hung over them; Jack was constantly brushing branches away so they wouldn't hit him or Lavender. As they neared the house the atmosphere seemed to grow darker and quieter. From behind, Darci could see Lavender and Jack begin to stiffen their backs, and Lavender slackened the reins so the horses were walking slowly.

But with every step closer to the house, Darci began to smile more broadly. Yes, she thought, this was the place. She couldn't feel it as she did when she had power, but merely as a sensitive human she could still tell that the very air was different. The horses began to twitch their ears and snort. When the horses stopped, Lavender flicked the whip above their heads, but they refused to move.

"I think this is as close as they'll go," Lavender said, trying to be brave. "We'll have to walk the rest of the way."

Jack got off the seat, then helped Lavender down, but neither of them moved toward the house that Darci was sure was just out of sight behind the trees. When she was on the ground, she turned to them. Both their faces were white, their eyes wide.

"Please let me go alone," she said. She could see that both of them wanted to protest, but at the same time they were dying to get away from what they feared. "Food!" Darci said. "We're going to miss dinner and I'm starving. I don't want to faint again, so maybe you two could go get us some food. Is there a McDonald's around here?"

"Do you mean the MacTavish Tavern?" Lavender asked, puzzled.

Jack took Lavender's elbow firmly in his hand. "She'll be all right," he said. "Trust me on this, but she's had experience and she knows what she's doing. Let's go get something to eat and bring it back here in, say, about an hour?" He looked at Darci in question.

"Make it an hour and a half," she said,

glad to get rid of them.

Within seconds, Lavender and Jack were in the buggy and were maneuvering it back out of the narrow lane. When they were gone and Darci was alone, she breathed a sigh of relief.

She didn't know for sure, but she doubted if the spirit occupying the house was dangerous. To Darci, the woman sounded as though she was very lonely and missed her family very much. Like me, Darci whispered into the still evening. The late afternoon was waning, but it was summer so it would be hours before it was completely dark.

She walked down the road and soon came to a turn. When she pushed aside some overhanging willow branches, she saw the house and instantly knew that Lavender had been right: the house was very old. The upper story was wider than the lower, a holdover from medieval times when the houses were built over narrow streets. They couldn't widen the ground floor so they widened the upper floors to make as much room as possible. What had once been a necessity had become a design concept. This house, with its dark wood and small windows, was obviously from the earliest period of building in the

United States, and done by people who were used to seeing medieval buildings in Europe.

Weeds had grown around the place and it had that forlorn air that was so common to abandoned houses. She saw that some of the roof shingles were loose and if they weren't replaced soon water would get into the house. Once water entered, a house didn't have long to live.

She stared at the house until her eyes hurt, hoping to see the movement that the locals claimed to see, but there was nothing. The wind was soft and sweet on her face, and in the distance the birds sang. It was a nice place for a house and she could see why the original builders had chosen the site.

As quietly as she could, she went up the overgrown drive to the house, her heart pounding loudly. Perhaps inside this house was the answer to going back home. Perhaps she could meet the spirit of this woman who'd loved her husband and children so much that she couldn't leave them, and maybe Darci could appeal to her. If the woman hadn't been a ghost for so long that she'd become hardened with anger and frustration, maybe Darci could get her to empathize with her plight. Maybe the woman would go to Devlin or Henry, or maybe . . .

Darci didn't want to think too much, to get her hopes up too much so that they'd be shattered. But she couldn't stop thinking. Maybe she'd been sent back in time to find that iron egg that Simone had given her. If that was true, then she could now return to her own time. Maybe the ghost would know about the box that had caused them to go back in time in the first place. Darci patted the box in her pocket and vowed to ask the spirit where the key was.

By the time Darci got to the door, her heart was racing, and when she put her hand on the knob, she was shaking. Maybe what was inside this house would lead her home.

The door was locked. And so were all the windows she could reach. At the back of the house she sat down on the broken bricks of what had been an old well casing. "Is anyone home?" she called out. Lavender had said the ghost had been seen in the garden so maybe she'd come outside to meet Darci.

But no such luck. Darci hesitated only seconds, then picked up a brick, hefted it for a moment, then threw it through a pane of glass. That it was probably seventeenth-century glass and irreplaceable wasn't lost on her. Minutes later, she'd used the bricks to form a little staircase so she could climb up to the window. Getting through wouldn't have been a tight squeeze if Darci'd had on a pair of jeans and a T-shirt, but with the heavy skirt and petticoats she was barely going to fit. She thought about removing some of her garments, but with only an hour and a half before Jack and Lavender returned, she didn't have the time. Besides, if she were caught in her underwear, Lavender would probably be so shamed that she'd have to call off the wedding. "And then everything bad would be my fault," she whispered.

When Darci landed on the floor amid the broken glass, she was smiling. It was good to think of something lighthearted in all this.

"I'm here," she whispered to the empty house. There was no furniture so even her whisper echoed off the walls. "Please come and talk to me," she said, a bit louder this time. "I've lost my husband, too. Please help me find him."

She waited but heard nothing. When she thought she heard something from upstairs, she ran through three rooms before she found the narrow, steep stairs. She ran up them, thinking that she wished she'd asked Lavender what the woman's name was.

"Mrs. Drayton," Darci called. "Please help me. Please help me find my husband."

Nothing. No sound.

Darci wandered through the upstairs rooms. They were made in the old-fashioned way of one room leading into another. No hallways, so people had to walk through other bedrooms to get out.

"If I had my power," Darci whispered, "I'd know which room had been hers." She tried to imagine which room she'd want for the master bedroom if she lived in the house, but she couldn't seem to make up her mind. This one and this view, she said at last, looking out a front window at the road leading to the house. She could see a church steeple in the distance. Had the Draytons gone to church there?

"Please help me," Darci whispered as she leaned her forehead against the cold window glass. "My husband left and I never saw him again. He got on an airplane one day — do you know what an airplane is? — and he never came back. I've tried to find him."

She drew in her breath. "You see, when I was in my own time period, not now, but a long time in the future, I had some abilities." Turning, she looked at the room. "If I were myself right now you wouldn't be able to hide from me. If you're in here I'd know it. But right now I'm just a normal woman, like you were, and like you, I've lost my family. Please," she said, "please help me. I've come such a very long way."

There were tears rolling down her cheeks, and her throat was clogged with more tears. Putting her hands over her face, she sank down to the floor. "Maybe I'm never going to find him," she said. "Maybe I wasn't supposed to go back in time. Maybe it was an accident and now I'm stuck here. Jack doesn't want to go back, and Simone said that I couldn't go back without Jack. No, I can't go back without Jack *and* Lavender. But they don't want to go and it doesn't matter anyway because I don't know how to get out of here."

"You could use the front door," said a cold voice — a voice she never thought to hear again.

Darci lifted her face to see a man standing in the doorway. The sun was setting behind him so all she saw was a silhouette — but it was the silhouette of Adam, her husband. It was a body she knew every inch of.

Weakly, she began to pull herself up by holding onto the windowsill. Slowly, never taking her eyes off the dark shape of the man, she tried to stand. "Adam?" she whispered.

"Yes, I'm Adam," he said, his voice still cold.

It was Adam's voice, Adam's body. The tears started rolling down her cheeks again. She was determined to stand so she used both hands on the windowsill. "Adam," she said, this time a statement, not a question.

The man stepped forward into the light and she saw his face. Darci looked into the frowning, angry face of her husband, Adam Montgomery, for only a second before everything started going 'round and 'round and she fainted.

Chapter Twelve

Darci slowly opened her eyes, and for a moment she couldn't focus. She lay still, blinking in the pale light of what looked to be a golden candelabra.

"Feeling better?"

Turning her head, she looked into the beautiful face of her husband, Adam Montgomery. For a moment she just gazed at him, drinking in what, to her, was the most beautiful face ever created. His hair was as black as she remembered, and there were the wings of gray just above his small, flat ears. Her stare moved from his deep-set blue eyes down to his soft lips, to his cleft chin. She glanced down at his strong body, the body that had given her so much pleasure for the few years they'd had together.

She looked back up to his eyes. They were Adam's eyes, still seeming to carry the weight of the world in them — but yet, there was a light inside them now, something new that she'd never seen before.

When she lifted her hand and put it to his cheek, he turned and kissed her palm. For a moment she closed her eyes, then held out her arms to him. "Come to me," she whispered. "Come to me."

Adam looked as though he meant to envelop her in his strong arms, but the next moment the door opened and Jack stood there. Adam moved away.

"How are you?" Jack asked, genuine caring in his voice. He took Adam's seat beside the chaise where Darci lay.

Puzzled by everything, Darci looked past Jack to Adam and he put his finger to his lips for her to be quiet. She tried to get the frown off her face and look at Jack, but all she wanted to do was put her arms around her husband.

"What happened?" Darci asked.

"You passed out on us again," Jack said, smiling. "Lavey and I came back with half a boar's head and Mr. Drayton was carrying you out the front door. We put you in the buggy, let Lavey drive, and you were here faster than an ambulance could have done it. I think she ran over four chickens, a cat, and two pedestrians."

Darci managed a smile at his joke. "Where is here?"

"At my house," Adam said. He was wringing out a white cloth in a basin of water. "I should introduce myself. I'm Adam Drayton and I found you in my old house."

"He's been great," Jack said. "He caught you trespassing and when you fainted he still helped you." His eyes were warning her not to say too much and screw things up.

"I think she should rest now," Adam said. "Perhaps you and Miss Shay would care to dine with me."

Jack's back was to Adam, and he winked at Darci. "Please get well, dear sister," Jack said, then leaned forward as though to kiss her cheek. "He likes you, he's rich, and he's a widower. Maybe we'll stay here after all."

Jack stood up and looked at Adam with a little smile. "We'll have dinner, then we'll all go back to Camwell."

"It's much too late to be on the roads," Adam said. "You must be my guests for the night. I'll send my driver to tell your families where you are."

"How kind of you," Jack said facetiously, still making faces at Darci. "Well, I guess I'll just mosey on downstairs and see what Lavey's up to. You two behave now. Just like we're going to."

Both Darci and Adam watched the door close behind Jack, then Adam said, "You can't choose your relatives."

Darci laughed — and cried at the same time. It was so wonderful to again hear Adam's sarcastic humor. She opened her arms to him. "Come to me."

Adam sat down on the chair beside her, but he didn't take her in his arms. "We must talk. You were in your faint for nearly an hour so I had time to think. I don't know what cruel trick fate has played on us, but we must lift ourselves above it."

When Darci tried to sit up, Adam put a pillow behind her head. As he leaned near her, she could smell the fragrance of his skin. She inhaled it, closing her eyes for a moment.

Adam moved away from her, and stood behind the chair. "I am not who you think I am, and you are not my Diana."

"Diana?" Darci asked, still trying to understand what was going on. It had been easier to adjust to having awakened in a different time in history than it was to understand what Adam was saying. "You are my husband," she said.

"No, I'm not." He walked to the far side of the room.

Darci lay back against the pillow, watching him, and trying to understand. She tried to look at the room they were in. It was a pretty sitting room, much like the ones in the other houses she'd seen since she'd traveled back in time. But there was a subtle difference here. The carvings on the furniture were finer, the porcelains over the fireplace had the look of art rather than what could be bought at the local flea market. Here and there was the sparkle of silver. The paintings on the walls looked to be one of a kind. Lavender had said the Draytons were wealthy and this room showed it.

Just like at home, she thought. If her Adam had lived in the 1840s, he would have lived in a house like this one.

She watched Adam go to a cabinet on the wall, open it, and reach inside. "I brought you up here to this room to show you something," he said as he withdrew a beautiful silk case from inside the cabinet. Slowly, he began unbuckling the straps from around it.

"As I said, I've had more time to adjust to this than you have. When I first saw you in that room I thought you were another intruder, one of the sick people in this town who can't allow a man to have any peace. But

197

then you looked up at me and I saw . . ."

Turning, he smiled at her. "I saw what I think you see in me." From the package he withdrew what looked to be a framed picture, but she could only see the back of it. "You say that I look like your husband. This is my wife," he said, and handed the picture to her.

It was a portrait of Darci. It was her as she looked in modern times, with strawberry-blonde hair and dark lashes and eyebrows. She doubted if the woman in the portrait was wearing makeup, but she looked like Darci did after about an hour's worth of work.

"Your wife?" Darci managed to ask. If she had her powers now maybe she'd be able to see that this Adam was not *her* Adam. Their auras were probably so different that anyone with any psychic ability would never confuse them. Looks are superficial, she told herself.

As Darci looked at the portrait of a woman who was as much like her as this man was like her husband, she knew that being sent back had been no accident. It looked as though Jack and Lavender's problems might be secondary, or maybe they were the catalyst to get Darci back to this time.

"Is she the woman who haunts the old house?"

"She haunts nothing!" Adam said fiercely. "Don't you think that if there was a chance she was there that I'd never have moved from that house? If I could see her for another moment . . . if I could touch her . . ." For a long moment he looked at Darci with such longing, with such lust, that her heart seemed to leap into her throat.

Adam looked away. "Is this God's sense of humor to play such a trick on me? To give me a woman to love then take her from me, then to give me a replica?"

Darci put the portrait on the table by the chaise and lay back. She felt defeated. Was this why she'd been sent here? To find a man who looked like her husband? Or was she to make a choice? Adam was in one century, but her daughter was in another century.

"My husband disappeared," she said slowly. "He and his sister left one day and never came back. I've been searching for them for years, but I can't find them."

Adam was frowning at her as he took the portrait and carefully put it back in its silk sheath. "But I thought you lived in Camwell. Your brother —"

"Jack isn't my brother. He's —" How could she explain something that she didn't understand? "Will you call the local witches' council if I tell you that I'm from another time period?" she asked, trying to sound lighthearted.

Adam sat back down on the chair near her and crossed his legs in a way that was so familiar to Darci that she wished she could faint again. How many times had she sat down on her husband's lap and wiggled until he . . . ?

"Time travel? It's been debated, of course, but it's not possible."

"I wish it weren't," she said, trying not to look at him.

"All right," he said, leaning back and smiling, "tell it to me as a story. I rather like stories."

She smiled back at him. Where should she begin? "I am born" as Charles Dickens did in *David Copperfield*? No, that would take a lifetime, and she didn't have . . . It was difficult to think of time when she was in this man's presence. It was difficult to think of trying to find a man when he seemed to be sitting in front of her.

"Jack and I were working together and —"

"As his secretary, perhaps?"

"Not quite. I was the boss."

Adam looked at her in astonishment. "I see. And what year do you come from?"

"Two thousand and four," she said, then watched the blood drain from his face. In the next second he got up and poured himself a drink.

"I want to say here and now that I know this could not possibly be true, but there is something odd in all this. I look like your husband and you look like my dear wife. I think there's more to this than mere coincidence. Please go on."

She didn't comment on the fact that he didn't offer her a drink. "Jack and I were searching for his father, who has disappeared, and by accident we found a room that contained four objects, one of which I could feel had magic powers."

"Feel?" Adam asked. "How did you *feel* this?"

"I had certain abilities that . . ." She trailed off. How could she explain all this? "Why do you think this has happened to us?" she asked. "Whether I'm from this time or not, why do you think this has happened? Or do you believe it's just coincidence?"

He set down his drink and looked at her. "I don't believe in chance or coincidence.

Everything is for a purpose, but I don't think either you or I know what that purpose is. I think you and I have been put together for a reason."

"All I know for absolutely sure is that I want to find my husband and sister-in-law."

"Are you sure they aren't dead?"

"Yes, I could tell that much."

"You could tell this through these — what did you call them? — abilities you have."

"Had."

"Ah, yes. Had."

She didn't like his tone. She didn't put up with it from Adam Montgomery and she wasn't going to put up with it from this man. "I could do wonderful things," she said. "I could paralyze people, make them do what I wanted them to, see things that other people couldn't." His expression was mocking. He was laughing at her, and not believing one word she said — which made her say too much. "I killed people and I raised a man from the dead. I went into the light, grabbed his hand, and pulled him back to earth."

"I see," Adam said.

"Stop that! I told you that you sound like Abraham Lincoln when you say that."

"And who is he?"

"The man who will be president during the Civil War."

"Civil War? And when is that?"

"Soon. But maybe not so soon to you. Twenty years," Darci said, her anger subsiding. This was the North and they wouldn't be affected much by what was coming, but she hated to think about what was going to happen in the South.

"Slavery," he said.

"Yes," she whispered. "And economics."

Adam began to pace the room in a way that she'd seen her husband do a thousand times. She thought he was thinking about the coming war and wondered if he'd want her to tell him of the future, but he asked nothing. He kept pacing and she knew to leave him alone and let him think. At least that's what *her* Adam needed.

Why? she wanted to scream. Why had this been done to her? Why dangle this man in front of her? He was food to a starving woman, but she couldn't have him.

At last he turned to her. "What you said just now, it couldn't be true."

"About the war?"

"No, I know that's coming. I can't believe that it'll hold off for a whole twenty years. The institution of slavery must stop, but the Southerners —"

"It's you Yankees —"

He looked at her in surprise, then waved his hand. "No, not about that. I mean about the other. You say that you raised a person from the dead. Can you do that?"

"I did it, but I had help. A *lot* of help. Two of the people who helped didn't have bodies."

"No bodies. Ah, I . . . I mean, I understand." He gave her a small smile. "Is this Jacob Lincoln so bad?"

"Abraham Lincoln. Great man, but you wouldn't want to look like him, and you wouldn't want his wife. Spends much too much money. The man I raised from the dead had been dead only minutes, not . . ." She stopped, unable to say what was in her mind: I couldn't raise your long-dead wife from the grave even if I had my full powers.

"I understand. You need a healthy body." For a moment he looked at her in speculation.

"No, you can't put your wife's spirit into me," she said calmly. "I have my own spirit and I plan to keep it in this body."

He grinned at that, then sat back down in front of her. "Can you do things such as you said? Really?"

"I did," she said cautiously. When he was so close to her, all she could think of was touching him.

He got up again. "Tonight has made me remember how much I missed my wife. She was a funny little person, always happy. Sometimes I think she knew she wouldn't be on this earth long. Shall I tell you how I met her?"

Darci nodded.

"A cousin of mine was interviewing for the job of governess. She wanted a young woman from a good background and well educated, and in came Diana. She was so small and delicate-looking that I didn't think she could handle those horrible children of my cousins, but she did. What's wrong?"

"Nothing," Darci said. "It's just that your meeting is much the same as my husband's and mine. He hired me to work for him."

"As what?"

"A sort of secretary," she said, then smiled when Adam nodded, as though things were once again in their proper order. She couldn't help but think how much fun it would be to teach this man that women could and did do things besides cook and clean.

What if I stayed here? she thought. What could I do for the future, knowing what I do? She had no power in this century, but she had a good knowledge of history. Could she prevent some of the more awful things from happening?

For that matter, *did* she remain in the nineteenth century? Did she remain and maybe help Abraham Lincoln? Or did she work with suffragettes? Did she help in hospitals with her fundamental knowledge of medicine?

Stay with this man? Here in this time? Her woman's instinct told her that it wouldn't take much to put herself in the place of his late wife.

While she was thinking, the door burst open and two little girls wearing beautiful white cotton nightgowns came into the room. Darci collapsed back against the chaise because the girls were the exact replicas of her daughter and niece. She watched Adam swoop both of them up in his arms and twirl them about. She heard the girls' squeals of delight, could see their adoration of their father.

Gradually, the girls became aware of Darci. Standing in the doorway was a stout woman with a disapproving look on her face, obviously the nanny, and obviously she didn't think the master should be alone in a room with a woman. Or maybe she disapproved of Adam's horseplay.

One of the girls, the one who looked like Darci's daughter, Hallie, stopped laughing and stared at Darci, then the other girl also became still. Adam set the girls on the floor, took a hand of each, and walked toward Darci.

"May I introduce my daughters, Miss Marshall? This is Henrietta, who we call Hitty, and this is Isadora."

"But I'm not Izzy!" the girl said.

"Certainly not," Adam said formally.

Darci felt weak from all the emotion going through her, but she managed to sit up and held out her hand to shake. "How do you do? I have a daughter very like you, Hitty, and I have a niece who is like you, Isadora."

"What are their names?" Hitty asked.

"The name for you is Hallie, and your name is Isabella."

The girls smiled at that and looked at their father. "They're very like our names."

Adam's eyes locked with Darci's and he seemed to say, There is a reason for this.

"I think the girls should be in bed now," the nanny said from the doorway, and hurried forward to take the girls.

"May I put them to bed?" Darci asked, her eyes on Adam's and pleading. "I haven't seen my own children in a while and . . ."

"Yes, of course," Adam said. He gave the nanny a dismissive look and she left the room.

Darci had to hide her smile. It had always been that way with her Adam. He could make an employee obey him with a mere glance. For Darci, the only way she could get the cleaning lady to get off her cell phone and actually clean was to use her True Persuasion.

"Thank you," Darci said as she took a hand of each girl and led them out of the room. "Show me where your bedroom is." She knew without asking that the girls shared a room. Her own Hallie and Isabella wouldn't be separated. The girls pulled her down the hall to a beautiful room with a big four-poster bed. On one wall was painted a woodland scene, with little bunnies peeking out of the trees and deer in the distance.

"Are you going to be our mother?" Isadora asked as she climbed into the bed beneath the hand-embroidered coverlet.

"Why would you ask that?"

"Because our father never talks to ladies.

They want him to but he won't. He's rich, you know."

"Yes, I know, but rich doesn't make a person good or bad."

"I know, but the ladies don't know that. Papa says that all they want is what he has in the bank."

Chuckling, Darci tucked the coverlet about both of them. "What makes you think I'm any different from them? Maybe all I want is his money, too."

"No, you look at him differently and he looks at you differently. We know about these things."

At that, Darci's eyes widened. *Know?* What did they mean by that? "Do you two ever play games that are unusual, not like the other children play? Like making your dolls dance about?"

When the girls gave Darci a blank look, she let out her pent-up breath. Her daughter and niece had abilities that Darci thought might outstrip hers. They could work together to make objects move, and Darci thought perhaps they could read minds. She could block them from reading her mind, but too often the girls knew things that only mind reading could have told them.

"Will you tell us a story?"

"Do you have a favorite?"

"Tell us a story that no one has ever heard before."

"How about if I tell you about two little girls who look just like you and are magic? One is named Hallie and the other is named Isabella."

"Is it a true story?"

"Yes, but it hasn't happened yet, not for a hundred and sixty-one years."

"Do they live on the moon?"

"No, but men have been to the moon, and people drive automobiles everywhere."

Smiling, Darci began to answer questions about what the world would be like in a hundred and sixty-one years, and this took so long that she never got around to telling about Hallie and Isabella. When the girls were yawning, she kissed their foreheads, tucked them in, and said good night. At the door, a sleepy Hitty said, "I wish you'd stay. We don't like Miss Colby, but you're nice. I'm going to pray that you stay here and be our mother. Papa says that God answers prayers."

Darci could think of nothing to reply to that so she left the room, closing the door behind her. In the hallway, she leaned against the door. Should she stay or leave?

It was the thought of her daughter and

niece that pulled her away from the door. If she stayed these little girls would get a mother and a father, and Darci was sure that, even without any powers, she could help the Victorian world.

But what about her own daughter and her niece? Neither Hallie nor Isabella would have a mother. Hallie would have no parents at all, and Isabella would have only her father, Darci's father. And what good would he be? Darci thought. The man would be so miserable that he'd neglect both girls.

"Are you all right?" Adam asked, smiling down at her.

When she looked up at him she wanted to slide her arms about his waist, as she'd done to her husband a thousand times. And from the look in his eyes, he'd welcome her touch.

But as he stepped toward her, she said, "I'm starving."

Adam laughed, a laugh that came from inside him. "Don't tell me that you're like Diana and can eat more than the gardener."

She wanted to laugh with him and tease him back, but she didn't. "I'm not Diana," she said softly. "And you're not my husband. This is not my house and your children aren't mine."

"No, of course not," Adam said, and stepped back from her, the veil coming down over his eyes again. "Perhaps we should join the others for dinner," he said. "I have a good cook and she has roasted a joint of meat that could feed half the armed forces."

"We'll see if it's enough," Darci said and swished her skirt as she walked ahead of him. I cannot stay, she said to herself. I cannot stay. I cannot stay.

Chapter Thirteen

Downstairs, Darci and Adam surprised Jack and Lavender entangled in each other on the parlor sofa. From the look of the empty glasses on the table and Lavey's glazed expression, Jack had been plying her with drink. Darci was embarrassed by the sight of them, but not so Adam.

"Good, you haven't eaten yet," Adam said, ignoring their disarranged clothes and Lavender's hair, which was cascading messily down about her shoulders. Darci wouldn't have thought it was possible, but Lavender looked even more beautiful than usual. "Shall we go into the dining room?" Adam asked.

As Jack helped Lavender to stand, Darci got behind him. "You are truly despicable," she hissed in his ear. "How could you do that to her?"

He tossed a roguish smile over his shoulder. "In college I majored in drinking and fornicating."

"You can*not* do this to her. She's to marry someone else tomorrow."

"Nope. I've decided for sure that I'm going to stay here."

She wanted to say more to him, but he clasped Lavender's arm close to his body and walked with her toward the dining room. He didn't seem to be the least bit affected by the alcohol he'd consumed, but Lavender was obviously quite happily drunk.

Behind them, Adam took Darci's arm and led her into the dining room. The room was as quietly and as lavishly rich as the rest of the house. The tablecloth was pristine white linen, and on it were porcelain dishes that Darci'd seen only in museums. There was a huge silver platter with a haunch of roast beef the size of a car engine. Half a dozen bowls were brimming with steaming vegetables, relishes, sauces, and breads. A sideboard held two cakes, three pies, a tart, and a big pudding with a white sauce dripping down the top of it.

"And you want to leave this," Jack said under his breath to Darci.

"They don't all eat this way," she answered back.

Adam held out a chair for Darci, and

Jack seated Lavender, but she slipped to one side and he had to push her upright.

"Should we tie her to the chair?" Darci said under her breath to Jack, but he just grinned.

Adam sat at the head of the table, Darci on his left, Lavender on his right, and Jack beside the woman he loved.

"I thought we'd serve ourselves tonight," Adam said, "so I've dismissed all the staff except the nanny, and she's upstairs. Please pardon the lack of courses and formal service." He seemed oblivious to the undertones of what was going on around him, but Darci was sure he was aware of everything.

Jack was looking at Lavender, not interested in Adam Drayton, but Darci was watching him intently. Her Adam was good at disguising what was really on his mind. Due to his good acting, the only way Darci knew when her husband was planning to do something dangerous was when his aura changed colors. Which took her back to the day he disappeared. Why hadn't his aura changed that day?

"And what do you have on your mind, old man?" Jack asked, finally seeming to be aware that Adam had something to say.

"Miss Marshall was telling me some rather interesting things tonight, and I also overheard her telling my daughters about the future."

"Did she now?" Jack asked, raising his wineglass to Darci as though to say that she had a big mouth.

"I'm interested in what caused you two to come back — if you did, that is."

Jack looked at Lavender to see if she was listening, but she was smiling at nothing and seeming to hear little. "We did, but I'm not sure how we did. The why is easy. We came back to save my dearest Lavender. She's to —" He lowered his voice. "There would have been an accident tomorrow, but we're going to prevent that."

"Can you do that?" Adam asked.

"Yes, we can," Jack said with conviction.

"But mightn't that change things?"

"Change history?" Darci said before Jack could speak. "That's been my worry. If we change anything at all, it could affect everything in the future."

"Why does everyone assume that to change the future means only bad?" Jack asked. "Every movie has it that if you change history one tiny bit, then the future world will explode. What if to change history were to make it better? What would happen to the world if someone assassinated Hitler?"

"Hitler?" Adam asked.

"Mass murderer on an unimaginable scale," Jack said, his eyes on Darci. "How do we know that if we save Lavender we don't change the world for the better? Did you know that she wanted to be a doctor? She couldn't because —"

"Because she's a woman," Darci said, thinking about his words. "What you're really saying is that if you stay here with her you might be able to change the world for the better."

Jack leaned back in his chair, his wineglass in his hand, and looked at her. "You could, too. If both of us stayed, with our combined knowledge, and what I know how to do, we could eliminate a lot of the true evil in the world."

"And what do you know how to do?" Adam asked as he put thick slices of roast beef onto the four plates.

"Jack's a spy," Darci said quickly. "More or less, anyway. He pretends to be friends with people, finds out what illegal things they're doing, then turns them over to the law."

Adam looked at Jack for verification.

"True," Jack said, "but not how I'd state it. My problem has been . . ." He trailed off.

"Her," Darci said, looking at Lavender, who was beginning to look like she wanted to go to sleep.

"Yeah, me," Lavender said, her eyelids drooping. "Did you know that Jack's different than he used to be? He won't even let me call him John anymore. I had decided not to marry him. He was so very boring. I only agreed to marry him because my father was threatening me. I wanted to go to college and become a doctor, but Father said I had to get married. He's broke, you see. Nobody knows it but he is. So Father made a deal with Jack's father to marry me off to him. That's why nobody in town says anything about Jack's father's lady love. You see, my father has no money but he has influence in Camwell."

Jack and Darci looked at each other in astonishment. Had Lavender's drunken revelation just told them why she'd killed herself? Maybe she'd told John Marshall she didn't want to marry him, and her father told her he was going to do something awful to her. Lock her up? Send her away? Men in the 1840s had absolute power over the women in their lives.

"But I like this Jack," Lavender said, smiling. "He's a different man in the same body. I'm the only one who knows he's different. The other one, the one I was supposed to have loved all my life, he wasn't very nice."

Darci leaned back in her chair and smiled at Jack. "There's our answer."

"And if I leave the day after tomorrow, she'll find herself married to a man who 'isn't very nice.' Is that what you want for her?"

"That's not our business," Darci said. "We must go back."

"And *how* do you go back?" Adam interrupted.

Smiling happily, Jack said, "We have no idea."

"How did you get here?"

Darci gave Jack a look of disgust. "He opened a box that he shouldn't have opened and suddenly we were here. But when we got here, we had the box but no key." At that, she pulled the little silver box from her pocket and put it on the table.

Putting down his fork, Adam picked up the box and looked at it. "You've tried other keys?"

"Not here, but we did when we were —"

"In your own time," he finished for her.

"Yes," Darci said. "When we were in our own time." She looked at Jack. "When we were in the time we belonged in."

"Where did the key come from?" Adam asked as he set the box back on the table.

"I found it years before I found the box," she said. "It was hidden, and I happened to find it. Actually, I'm sure I was directed to find it, and I had it a long time before I could use it. When I found the box —"

"In my father's secret room," Jack said.

"Yes, his father had the box and I had the key, so which denotes ownership?"

"The one who knows how to use what's inside the box," Adam said quickly. "So you put the key in the box and you ended up here?"

"You sound as though you believe this impossible story," Jack said.

"I really don't care whether it's true or not. Tell me, Mr. Marshall, have you ever loved anyone?"

"If you'd asked me that last week I would have said yes, but I would have been lying. Not knowingly lying, but I was. Years ago I thought I was in love with a young woman who was killed in a car wreck, but then I met Lavender. I haven't even known her twenty-four hours but I know that I love her. I know that I'd die for her. I'd risk anything for her."

"Yes, that's the kind of love I mean," Adam said, then looked at Darci in question.

"Yes," she whispered. "I know that kind of love. A love forever."

"Forever," Adam said. "That's the very word I want. That's the way I loved my wife. Like you, Jack, I knew within minutes of meeting her that she was the only woman I'd ever love like that. But she was taken from me. She was young, healthy, happy, but she died. I don't know why. One minute she was alive and the next she was dead. What does your modern medicine say to that?"

"It happens in our time, too," Darci said, "but in our time many things can be detected before they happen. She could have had a blocked artery, which is easily found and easily fixed."

Adam was looking down at his food. "In the three years since she died, I've done everything I know to bring her back in any form possible. I've paid every charlatan within five hundred miles of here to conduct séances and raise spirits. I've hired people who write what the spirits say. I've seen a dozen women go into trances and speak in strange voices. I've seen tables lift, heard the clank of chains, and I've seen misty images that I was told were ghosts. But you know what?" He looked up at them. "They were all fakes. Every one of them."

He took a drink of his wine. "At first I was outraged at being duped, but after the first year I came to know so much about their tricks that I could have run a meta-physical house. I no longer got angry. I just pulled the cords that held the so-called ghosts, and I kicked out the posts that made the tables lift, then I left."

He looked from Jack to Darci. "Through all of this I've had to hear over and over how one person after another has seen my beloved wife in the house that was once ours. Even my daughters were seeing her. They weren't afraid of her, after all, she was their mother, but the nannies I hired were terrified. None of them would stay more than a month. In the end, I had to move from the house and leave the place where I'd known such happiness."

He closed his eyes for a moment. "But for all her appearances, my wife has never shown herself to *me*. I go to that house every day, sometimes three times a day. All I want is a chance to tell her how much I love her. You see . . ."

He looked at a painting on the wall for a moment, then back at Jack and Darci. Lavender seemed to be dozing in her seat, not quite aware of what was going on around her. "You see," Adam continued, "I wasn't a very good husband. I worked all the time and I was gone a lot. I think I wanted to prove to my relatives that I was as good at business as my father was. I felt guilty at inheriting so much, so to prove myself, I decided to double what he left me. I did that within five years after he died. It then seemed important to me to triple and qua-druple what he left me. After I met and married Diana, I told myself and her that I was working for her — not for me, but for her. She used to tell me that money didn't matter to her, that she'd be content to live in a farmhouse with me and our daughters. I knew it was true but I couldn't seem to stop working. I . . ."

He refilled his wineglass and drank half of it in a gulp. "I didn't know what I had until it was gone. Since Diana died, I haven't worked a day. I've spent my time with my daughters and in trying to bring back my wife for one moment so I can tell her . . . so I can tell her . . ."

"That you love her and that you're sorry for not realizing how important she was," Darci said.

"Yes," Adam said, looking at her. "Is that what you want to do with your hus-band?"

"No," Darci said seriously. "I want to rip

his clothes off and jump on his big, beautiful body."

For a moment Adam looked shocked, then he began to laugh and Jack joined him. "To the other Adam," Adam said, raising his glass. The three of them clinked glasses; Lavender tried to join in, but her glass missed theirs. When she tried to drink, she found the glass was empty. "Oh, all gone. More please."

"You give her more and I'll —" Darci began, glaring at Jack.

"What? Give me a headache? Paralyze me? You can't do that now, little sister, but then, you never could do that to me, could you?"

"Could she really do those things?" Adam asked.

"Not to me, but then Lavey was protecting me, weren't you, dear?"

"Always, my Jack," Lavender said, smiling at him in an idiotic way.

"I think you should put her to bed," Darci said sternly. "Alone. You hear me? I'm afraid of what you'll mess up if you touch her."

"You still think we're going to leave here?" Jack asked. "Look at the facts. In our century, my girlfriend had been killed and your husband was missing and probably dead. We had nothing there, but here —"

"No!" Darci said. "Adam isn't dead. I know that. *Knew* that, anyway. He was —"

"What?" Adam asked, with interest. "Where was your husband?"

"I don't know," Darci said, frustrated. "I felt as though some entity was keeping me from him, but I couldn't find out who. I know I was to find twelve magic objects and —"

"What?" Adam asked. "Magic objects? What do they do?"

"Don't get her started," Jack said, yawning. "We'll be here all night."

"I have nothing else to do," Adam said softly, looking at Darci.

"As far as I can tell, each object performs a specific function. I have a ball, not here but at home in my time, that heals people. I can use it by myself and it works on some things, but not on everything. It won't heal cancer, for instance. I can't make a person in a wheelchair able to walk, but I can make wounds heal faster and cleaner. I helped clear up the infection of a man who'd had a hand reattached."

"A hand reattached?" Adam said, incredulous. He picked up the little silver

225

box again and turned it about in his hands. "Your medicine must be marvelous. Do you think your little ball could repair a vessel in a person's heart?"

"It has, yes," Darci said softly.

"And this box has enabled you to travel through time, has it not?"

"Yes."

His gaze at her was intense. "If you could find the key to this box, do you think that you might be able to leave here, then return at another time? Perhaps with that ball that heals?"

Darci drew in her breath. "Go home, then come back when your wife is alive and heal her heart — if that was what was wrong with her, that is?"

"Yes, exactly," Adam said.

"You seem to trust a lot," Jack said. "If I were in your shoes, I wouldn't believe any of this. Who believes in time travel?"

"I don't have to believe," Adam said. "I just have to try it. If you're liars I lose nothing but some of the money that I have too much of. If you're telling the truth I have everything to gain."

"What money?" Jack asked. "Did I hear anyone ask you for money?" His voice was rising in anger.

"Don't pay any attention to him. His father is a billionaire so he's overly sensitive about money."

"A billionaire?" Adam asked, eyes wide. "I've never heard of such a thing."

"From a son's point of view, it's not great. I would've traded him for a chauffeur for a father. Actually, I did."

"None of it matters anyway," Darci said, "because we don't have a key to the box and I don't have my Touch of God, so —"

"Your what?" Adam asked.

"Touch of God. That's what the ball is." Adam looked at her as though he wanted her to explain further. "God gave the angels a touch from His fingertip, then each angel blew on the touch. They enclosed the touch and their breath in what looks to be glass, but it's quite indestructible."

"And how did you find this extraordinary object?" Adam asked.

"Finding it was easy. It was locked inside a ball of crystal and I felt its energy. The hard part was getting the ball out."

"And how did you do that?"

Darci looked down at her hands. "I passed a test." She looked back at him. "A woman had done a terrible thing to me and I knew it, but I saved her life anyway."

When Darci said no more, Adam looked at Jack and he shrugged. "I don't know anything about that," Jack said. "That happened before I met her, but I have seen her paralyze a room full of people. Pretty scary sight."

"I thought you didn't believe I did that," Darci said, teasing. "Greg said that you had a logical explanation for everything I did."

"Yeah, well, that was before I woke up in a land where they've never seen a computer or MTV."

"And what are these things?" Adam asked.

"If I stay here, I'll draw you pictures," Jack said. "In fact, maybe I'll invent them."

"MTV?" Darci asked. "Do you think any age really needs lewd videos?"

"They aren't all lewd and just because you're a virgin queen doesn't mean that the rest of us —"

"How about if you wake up tomorrow and Lavender is gone? Think you'll want to jump into bed with someone else right away?" Darci shot back at him.

"Who are you to judge me? I can see that you're lusting after Drayton here so hot that the silverware's about to melt," Jack said with rage in his voice.

Adam stood up so quickly that his chair almost turned over. "Sir! You will not speak that way at my table. You will apologize to Miss Marshall or I will throw you out!"

Jack stood up and glared at Adam. They were nearly the same height, but Adam was brawnier. "You think you can?" he spat at Adam.

"Jack!" Darci shouted.

Jack seemed to come to his senses and all the anger left him in an instant. "Sorry," he said to Adam. "I don't know what came over me." He ran his hand over his eyes. "For a minute there I felt like my old self." He looked back at Adam. "I really do apologize. I guess you know that Darci and I aren't really brother and sister, but we do sometimes fight like we are." When Adam said nothing, Jack turned to Darci. "I apologize for my words and for my attitude. I don't know what happened. It was like . . ."

He glanced at Lavender, sitting quietly, her head on her elbow and happily and silently watching the three of them, unaware of the content of what was being said.

"Apology accepted," Adam said. "Shall we sit back down? There's dessert yet to be eaten."

When Jack sat down, he looked at Darci in alarm. "I don't know what happened, but for a moment I felt that old anger, as though there was something inside of me that was telling me to give pain before someone hurt me. I don't understand it. Lavender's here. She's alive and in a body. Her spirit is anchored inside of her."

Darci said nothing, just looked at Jack in alarm. If only I had my powers, she thought. If only I could see and feel what was wrong! "Maybe it was temporary. Maybe it was just prewedding jitters. Or maybe you feel guilty for getting an innocent like Lavender drunk."

Truthfully, Darci knew what Jack was thinking because it was the same thing she was thinking. Earlier she'd said that maybe John had killed Lavender. Maybe John had been the one who pushed her off the building. It was true that the high school boy's paper had said that John was at the church when Lavender fell, but so much time had passed that maybe that fact was wrong. Jack had taken over John's spirit, but Darci knew that spirit was still inside him.

Reaching across the table, Darci took Jack's hand and gave it a reassuring squeeze. "If Lavender was being made to marry a man she doesn't want to marry, John is probably angry about that. Or maybe he's angry at you for taking over and making love to his girl."

"Yeah, maybe," Jack said, squeezing her hand back. "But I wish you could paralyze him. At least until after the wedding."

Darci smiled and leaned back in her chair. "Yeah, me, too."

"What do you think will happen to-morrow?" Adam asked as he handed around plates for the dessert. It had been natural to Darci to get up and help him. Adam started to protest, but then he'd smiled at her in a way that made her blush. That little smile had been so intimate that for a moment Darci was flustered. He's not your husband, she reminded herself yet again.

"What?" she asked when she felt both men staring at her, then she remembered Adam's question. "Don't ask me, I know nothing more than anyone else does. Jack, you know all that I do. Or, actually, you should know more than I do because you've been with Lavender all day. Have you spoken to her for even two sentences?"

"I'll tell what I know as soon as you tell me who Simone is."

Adam looked at Darci. "Did you go to Simone?" When Darci nodded, he said, "What did she tell you?"

"That I must return. Not that I should return, but that I *must.*"

"I should have guessed she was another psychic," Jack said. "I told you that I don't believe —"

The abrupt laughter of Darci and Adam cut him off, and when Jack got the joke, he looked a bit sheepish. "Okay," he said, smiling, laughing at himself. "So maybe now I do believe a little bit. Okay, so I believe a lot." He glanced at Lavender, saw that she had her head against the back of the seat, her eyes closed, giving a soft snore now. He turned back to Adam and lowered his voice. "The truth is that all we know is what we pried out of some high school kid who seemed to be in love with the beauty of Miss Lavender Shay. On her wedding day, she climbed to the top of a building and jumped off. Or was pushed."

"How did this affect the future?" Adam asked.

"It didn't," Jack said. "Not really."

"It affected Jack," Darci said. "You see, Lavender was so full of hate that she attached her spirit to him. He was the quintessential angry young man when I met him."

"As we just saw," Adam said, looking at Lavender, who was still sleeping. "Forgive

232

me for being naive, but I can't see her ever being full of hate. And if this event is to take place in less than twenty-four hours, how does she build up that much hatred?"

"A woman scorned," Jack said, lifting Lavender's hand and kissing it.

"I would never leave you, Jack," Lavender said abruptly, coming awake suddenly.

"Perhaps that's your answer," Adam said. "Perhaps she didn't leave you and her anger came from things that she saw you do later, in your time. You said you thought you were in love with another woman. Perhaps that set her off."

Darci was thinking about what Adam was saying. "The only thing that could make Lavender so very angry is if she were betrayed by Jack — not John, but Jack. She loves him and knows that he loves her, so if he —"

"If Jack harmed her —"

"That might make her angry enough to stick to him forever," Darci said.

"Wait a minute!" Jack said.

"You wouldn't betray me, would you, Jack?" Lavender said and began to cry.

"Now look what you've done," Jack said, his arms around Lavender protectively.

Darci gave a look at Adam and an unspoken agreement passed between them. In the next second she left the table and went upstairs to summon the nanny. The woman was in her nightgown and reading, and she was in a bad temper that she was being asked to do anything for anyone other than the children. No wonder the girls asked me to stay, Darci thought. She had to promise the woman extra pay to get her to come downstairs.

Thirty minutes later, the nanny and Darci had undressed Lavender and put her to bed. Grateful to get away from the bad-tempered nanny, Darci went downstairs.

"Give me a drink," she said as soon as she reached the library where Jack and Adam were sitting on comfortable chairs in front of the fireplace, both of them drinking glasses of port. "You have to get rid of that dreadful woman," Darci said to Adam. "You can't force your beautiful daughters to endure her."

"No one will stay because of the talk of a ghost," Adam said as he poured her a glass of port. "And don't tell me to move because I have to be near . . ." He looked away.

"Yes, I know," she said, accepting the drink.

"Now, about this key," Adam said.

"The key that I don't want to find," Jack added.

"Who said *you* have to return?" Darci snapped. "Maybe you stay and *I* go home." She wasn't about to tell him what Simone said.

"Okay," Jack said. "Point taken. Adam suggested that he and I get some lanterns and some men and go look for the key. We could search the ground where you and I first appeared."

"I doubt if it'll do any good," Darci said gloomily. "I figure that if the key wasn't in the box then it's lost. Or maybe it's gone back to its original container." She held up her glass and looked at the amber liquid. "Somewhere in this world is probably a cute little ceramic man sitting on a shelf. With my luck, he's probably in Istanbul — or somewhere where they're at war."

She turned to Adam. "You haven't seen a little ceramic man about four inches high, have you? He has on blue overalls, a brown cap, and great big ears. Sort of a gnome, or maybe a hobbit, only he has on thick-soled brown shoes."

When Adam didn't say anything, she looked at him harder, but his eyes were un-readable. "Excuse me a moment," he said, then left the room.

"Think he went to get your little man?" Jack asked.

"No," Darci said, frowning into the fireplace. "That would be too easy. If I've learned nothing else in my life, it's that I'm to be tested for absolutely everything."

"And if you win, what do you receive? Besides the great and glorious Adam Montgomery, that is?"

"I don't know and, to tell the truth, when I think about it, I get scared."

"Scared? You?"

"Oh yes. Very scared."

Adam entered the room carrying a black portfolio, sat down, and untied it to reveal an art kit. Inside was drawing paper and a dozen pencils. Curious, Darci watched as he took one of the pencils and began to sketch. Within minutes, he had drawn the little ceramic man exactly.

"Does he look like this?"

Eyes wide, Darci took the drawing from him. "Yes," she said. "That's him. But where . . . ? How . . . ? Do you have him?"

"No," Adam said, "but I know where he is."

"Let's go." When Adam didn't move, Darci sat back down with a sigh. "So tell me the whole horrible story. Where is it? Top of a mountain? A volcanic mountain?

With snakes covering the path?"

Adam looked at Jack. "Is this normal in your world?"

"That's just her — I think. I really have no idea. So where is this little man?"

"Locked in a safe," Adam said.

"Not so bad," Jack said. "I've dealt with safes before."

"The safe isn't as much of a problem as where it is. It's at the end of some tunnels and they . . ."

"Tunnels?" Darci asked, staring at Adam. "In Camwell? Tunnels in Camwell?" She whispered the last.

"Yes. You know of them?"

"I believe she killed some people in some tunnels in Camwell," Jack said smoothly. "At least I was told that she did."

"Are you all right?" Adam asked, reaching for Darci to steady her.

She leaned back against the chair and stared into the fire. So, at last, she was coming to the truth as to why she'd been sent back in time. Why had she been so naive as to think that Jack could have had anything to do with their return? He was merely the means so she could find the box. That an angry spirit had been hanging around him was secondary. After all, didn't millions of people have spirits hanging around them? Angry, jealous, insane, and/or whispering spirits were hovering over many people.

"Tell me everything," she said to Adam, her voice sounding as tired as she was beginning to feel.

"What do you know of Nokes garnets?" Adam asked.

"Never heard of them," Jack said, and Darci shook her head.

"Things in your world and mine are so different. Nokes garnets are what all the ladies want now. I wish we had time to talk about your time and mine," Adam said. "I wish I could spend the night here asking both of you questions, but it can't be. We must go tonight and get this little figure."

"Yes, of course," Darci said softly. "I was sent back in time to Camwell, Connecticut, so of course I'll have to go back into those tunnels. Why didn't I think of that in the first place?" She looked at Adam. "Is it possible that we could destroy those tunnels tonight? I'm not sure it will help the future, but we can try. I'm sure she'll just dig them out again. A backhoe can do in weeks what it takes men years to do."

She was aware that both men were looking at her in consternation, but she

didn't explain. "Tell me about these garnets," she said.

"Fontinbloom Nokes was — is — a man
who was always coming up with schemes
to get rich quickly. Do you have this type
of man in your time?"

"Unfortunately, yes," Jack said. "Too
many of them. But no Fontinblooms that I
know of."

"At one time Fonty worked for me and I
rather liked him. He was a bombastic liar,
but I found him entertaining, and I could
trust him with money. One time when he
was accused of stealing, I stood up for him
and helped find the real culprit. In the end,
everything turned out all right and I got
him released from prison, but I'm sorry to
say that the episode turned Fonty against
the whole town. He was already a man
who believed that people wished him ill,
but after that he became worse. But then
he found the little man."

"Where?" Darci asked.

"He was very secretive about that, would
tell no one, but he said it was a lucky object and it was going to give him a way to
get back at everybody who'd never believed
in him."

Adam took a drink of his port. "He
found silver, or at least what he thought

was silver, on a piece of land that belonged to his father. There was a falling-down old house on the property —"

"Built in 1727," Darci said.

Adam looked at her with one eyebrow raised. "Probably so. It looks to be that old, but how did you know? The place is little more than a fire hazard and ought to be torn down."

"It won't be," Darci said. "It will survive and become a bed-and-breakfast. What he found wasn't silver?"

"No," Adam said. "It was some worthless mineral that looked like silver, but what the assayer did find in the rubble was a boring little rock that contained a garnet that no one had ever seen before. It was named Nokes garnet after Fonty."

"Never heard of it," Darci said, "but until I watched the Gem Network I'd never heard of Tsavorite garnets or Mandarin garnets either."

"Gem Network?" Adam asked.

Darci waved her hand. She didn't have time to explain that now.

Getting up, Adam went to the hearth, picked up a little wooden box, opened it, and withdrew something that he handed to Darci. It was a gem, white and clear, but when she held it up to the light it had tones of blue and purple inside it. "It's beautiful," she said, handing it back to him, but Adam didn't take it. "Keep it. Perhaps when you leave you can take it with you. It belonged to my wife."

As Darci's hand closed over the gemstone, she couldn't look at Adam's face. "So this man dug the tunnels to get to the garnets."

"Yes," Adam said. "With heavily armed guards all around, he dug the tunnels, looking for the garnets. He's made a fortune as the garnets are in high demand now, and as far as anyone knows, they come only from here. In the past ten years Fonty has dug miles of tunnels."

He looked at Darci. "You seem to know these tunnels. What are they used for in your time?"

"Witches," Jack said quickly.

"But there is no such thing as a witch," Adam said. "Has your time gone back to burning them at the stake?"

"No, it was left to me to get rid of them," Darci said. "As for witches, evil exists, and in this case the woman owned the Mirror of Nostradamus, so whatever she was, she was truly evil." When Darci saw that both Adam and Jack were staring at her she said, "What?"

"The Mirror of Nostradamus?" Adam asked in a whisper. "Surely that's a myth. Like Aladdin's lamp."

"The mirror is no myth, and as for the lamp, I think that might be real, too," Darci said. "I'm not sure, but something someone said once made me think the lamp is on my list of twelve objects I'm supposed to obtain."

"Ah," Adam said, seeming to be at a loss for anything else to say. "Shall we go?" he said to Jack as he stood up.

"Ready when you are," Jack answered, standing up, also.

Darci put down her glass and stood, too. "I can't possibly wear this. I'd trip on the skirts." She smiled at Adam. "In my time, women wear trousers."

"Tight ones," Jack said, grinning. "Real tight."

Adam didn't smile. He looked Darci up and down. "You cannot possibly go with us," he said. "Jack and I will find the statue and bring it back here."

Adam seemed to assume that his decree was final, so he turned toward the stairs.

"Mr. Drayton?" Darci asked. "How many times have you been in the tunnels?"

He looked back at her. "Never." He knew about what she was hinting and smiled. "However, I do know the combination to the safe. I gave the safe to Fonty so we'll be able to open it when we find it."

"Great," Darci said as she sat back down in the chair. "You don't need to sneak into the tunnels and you don't need a guide through them. I can stay here by the fire and sleep. However, I'm curious about your plan. Since we're on a deadline and you don't want to waste time getting lost in that maze, maybe you'll go to your friend and tell him you need the little statue. What does it matter that he believes it has given him all his good fortune? Will you tell him you want to destroy it to get the key inside? Maybe you should tell him the truth, that you need the key so your new friends can go back to the twenty-first century. Oh well, I'm sure that you and Fonty are such good friends that he'll believe you and will happily hand over the statue to you. For old times' sake, of course."

Adam turned to Jack. "Do all the women of your time talk like this?"

"She's one of the nice ones," Jack said. "I had a girlfriend who turned a gun on me when I told her I was going somewhere without her. Of course, she was an FBI agent and outranked me and we were on assignment, but still . . ." He shrugged.

243

"What did you do?" Adam asked.

"Tied her to a chair and put tape across her mouth. She wouldn't go out with me again after that, though."

"Interesting," Adam said as he looked at Darci in speculation.

"Don't even think it." She smiled sweetly at Adam. "You want me to try to come back, don't you? If you leave me here tonight I promise that I won't even try."

Adam looked at Jack. "I don't envy you your time. Tell me where we went wrong that this has happened to women."

"Don't give them the vote, don't let them drive and, above all else, don't let them read romance novels. They start comparing you to some guy in a book. And, trust me on this, you'll never live up to the standards of Hawk and Ethan."

"Could you two stop with the male bonding and get me some pants to wear?" Darci said as she headed for the stairs. "If I'm going to be your guide, I need something besides fifty pounds of skirt swirling around my legs."

While Adam was shaking his head in disbelief, Jack said, "You wouldn't happen to have any firearms around here, would you? This isn't the time of the blunderbuss, is it?"

"It seems that what you have found in

machines you have lost in civility," Adam said.

Darci paused on the stairs. "Maybe we should have a talk about child labor in Victorian times," she said.

"You have nothing in your time that needs social reform?" Adam asked on the stairs behind her.

"While she gets dressed, let me tell you about terrorism," Jack said. "I think we males need to stick together."

Darci tried to smile, tried to tell herself that now was different from the last time she'd been in the Camwell tunnels. Now there was no woman with powers that she'd gathered from acts too heinous to think about. Now all that was there were men armed to the teeth with guns.

But the worst thing was that, this time, Darci would be going into the tunnels with no powers of her own. There'd be no more laughing and teasing as she'd done at the candy machines. She'd felt safe then because she'd known that no one was near them. This time she'd just have her eyes and ears, and her memory of what was where.

As Adam led them to the stairs to the attic, where he said they'd find trunks full of clothes, she offered up a prayer for protection.

Chapter Fourteen

"This is the most ridiculous situation I have ever encountered," Adam was muttering under his breath as he expertly handled the horses of the buggy. It was full night, with only a quarter moon, but both he and the horses knew the way to Camwell.

What he was complaining about was the fact that Lavender was in the backseat with Jack. She'd sobered considerably since dinner, but Adam was angry because she had on a costume that they'd found in a trunk in the attic. Jack had called it a "belly dancing costume," and he and Darci had come up with the idea of putting Lavender in it and using her as a diversion for the armed guards. Her lower face would be veiled to protect her identity. However, her extraordinary purple eyes would still show.

Adam had been horrified at the whole idea. There was little fabric in the costume and Lavey's midsection was bare. "She cannot possibly wear that," Adam said. "Her father would call me out. If I allowed this, any judge would order me hanged. Lavender Shay is a young woman of sterling repute."

"Until this afternoon," Lavender said, sleepy-eyed, still a bit tipsy, and grinning wickedly at Jack. She took the flimsy costume out of Adam's hands and declared that she'd like nothing better than to wear it. "And dance," she said.

The men had left the women alone in the attic for about thirty minutes while they dressed — or, in Lavender's case, undressed.

But Lavender had nearly chickened out. "I can't do this," she said, her hand over her bare belly. "I can't possibly . . ."

"You can't fool me," Darci said. "You love it! Good grief, but you look like a Victoria's Secret model."

"Do you mean Queen Victoria?"

"More or less. Queen of men's hearts, in this case. Lavey, you look great. Wearing those corsets all these years has given you abs modern women would kill for. Have you ever seen a belly dancer?"

Lavender blinked at Darci as though to say, You're kidding, aren't you?

At Darci's gym, she'd once taken a few

classes of belly dancing, so she showed Lavender a couple of moves. Within seconds, Lavender picked it up as though she'd been dancing for years. "This has to be a past life thing," Darci said, and again vowed that if she ever got her powers back, she was going to start looking into the past more.

Darci wrapped a long cape that looked like molting seal skin around Lavender's shoulders and they both went downstairs. In the library in front of the men, Lavender started to giggle. She thought Darci was more odd-looking than she was because Darci was dressed as a boy. She had on plaid wool trousers that reached to her knees, tall socks that disappeared under the trousers, and heavy shoes. On top she wore a white shirt with stiff collar and cuffs, and a pair of navy blue suspenders. She'd happily removed the artificial bun from the back of her head, combed out her hated ringlets, and tucked her hair up under a big newsboy cap. She felt the best she had since she'd arrived.

"Not a bad little tush there," Jack said when he saw Darci, making Adam frown in a way that reminded her completely of her husband.

Not to be outdone, Lavender dropped

the heavy cloak to the floor and stood before them in an outfit that was conservative to Jack and Darci's modern eyes, but Adam was shocked. Women of good repute did not wear flimsy garments that showed their bare middles.

"Shall I dance for you?" Lavender asked, her eyes lowered halfway.

"Yes!" Jack said.

"No!" Adam said as he picked up the cape and put it back around Lavender's shoulders.

Ten minutes later, they were all in the buggy and riding toward Camwell.

"I don't like this," Adam said. "I should have done this alone. I could have found the safe and brought the statue back on my own."

"Those tunnels are a labyrinth," Darci said. "I was taken from . . . room to . . . room." Her voice slowed as she remembered that horrible night in the tunnels.

"Did you actually kill people with your mind?" Adam asked softly so only she could hear.

"Yes, but I don't like to think about it, and I've never talked about it," she answered.

"Why have you been given such power?" he asked. "In my time there are people who would like nothing more than to have the ability to kill with their minds. In the wrong hands . . ." He gave her a sidelong look.

"Yes," she said. "In the wrong hands an ability such as mine could do much evil — which is why I'm glad I have it and not someone else." She was trying to make a joke, but Adam didn't smile. Like my Adam, she thought. He always had the ability to see to the very core of a matter.

"Why was this ability given to you?" Adam asked again. "And what are you to *do* with your such power?"

She thought for a moment. "Only in the last months have I begun to ask myself that. When I was growing up all I wanted was love, and as an adult I wanted the same thing. When I had my husband and my daughter and all my family near me, I was content. I wanted nothing else. I was even trying to learn to cook!"

"But what about this talent that God has given you?"

"I did some work for the FBI — to help the government — and I visited hospitals, but nothing much. Adam didn't like for me to do much because I tend to jump into danger."

"Like now," he said as he turned a curve.

"Yes, but then my husband was always walking into danger. He and my father would use the mirror —"

"The Mirror of Nostradamus?"

"Yes, that one. They'd find problems in the world and fly somewhere to right them."

"And that's what he was doing the day he disappeared?"

"I guess so. He was never able to keep me from knowing what he was doing, but he did that day. And now I don't know where he is or how to find him. I know he's alive, but he's in a coma, I guess you'd call it. Not asleep, not awake. Suspended animation. And for all that I've searched, I've come no closer to finding him."

"Perhaps it's the journey itself that has been the goal. Have you learned anything while on your search?"

Darci looked at him, wide-eyed. "I couldn't begin to tell all that I've learned." She thought about her time in Alabama with Linc and what she'd seen and done there. And she thought of the last days with Jack. "I think what I've learned most is that my ability *is* a gift. I have always hated it. I've used it as little as I could because I hated being a freak, and hated being . . ." She took a breath and made herself say the words. "The Hillbilly Honey."

"The what?"

"It's a name the papers gave me. They hinted that I killed my rich husband and his sister for money."

"But money isn't your problem, is it?"

Darci smiled. "No. My father made experiments to see if I could pick stocks that would make money. I could, and easily. The irony of that is that I met my husband because I desperately needed money. Had I known that I could merely run my finger down a stock market sheet and make thousands upon thousands, I never would have met him."

Adam was quiet for a few minutes. "This is new to me and it's difficult for me to actually believe all that you tell me, but if any of it is true, then I think there's been a reason for your husband's disappearance. You say you've learned much in your search for him. Perhaps you needed to learn these things." He sighed. "I wish I could find the reason for my wife's death, and I wish I could find out why her spirit appears to others but not to me."

"Your grief probably won't let her leave the earth," Darci said. "If you could release her, she might be able to leave this plane."

"And perhaps if you stopped searching for your husband he could die," he shot back.

They sat in silence for a moment, then Darci looked at Adam in the moonlight and they smiled at each other. Neither was going to give up holding onto the person they loved so much.

Minutes later, Adam stopped the carriage and Darci knew where they were. Not far down the road was what would someday be known as the Grove. It would become an expensive resort, but now it was just a collection of derelict old buildings that looked as though they were about to fall down. She wondered if Fontinbloom Nokes used the money he made from the garnets to restore the buildings.

Adam got down and helped Darci to the ground, while Jack got Lavender out. She'd sobered up more and from her swollen lips, it looked as though she and Jack had done a lot of kissing while in the back of the buggy.

"I was thinking," Jack said quietly, knowing the sound of his voice would carry in the still night air. "I should stay with Lavey. I can't leave her alone with a bunch of men with hands and guns."

"I don't think you should do this at all,"

Adam said sternly. "I think you two should stay here while Miss Marshall and I go into the tunnels and search for the safe as quickly as possible. Truthfully, I think I should go in alone."

"No," Jack said firmly. "You two need us. Lavey and I'll make so much noise that the attention of the guards will be on us. Do you have a plan of how you're going to get in? You can't very well walk in through the front door."

"There's another entrance," Adam said.

"Through the floor of the icehouse," Darci said quickly and was rewarded by a little smile from Adam.

"Yes. You used it before?"

"No. It was used only for storage when I was here, but I felt that there had once been a connection to the tunnels."

Jack pulled a rifle from the back of the buggy and handed it to Adam. "Breech loading," he said to Darci. "Hot off the assembly line — except that I don't think assembly lines have been invented yet." He looked at Adam. "When we get out of this I can tell you a few things that could make you a fortune."

"No thanks," Adam and Darci said in unison.

"The men work night and day in the

tunnels so they'll be lit, but as we make our way across the fields to the icehouse we'll be in the dark. Will you be all right?" Adam asked Darci.

"Yes," she answered, then looked at Jack. At the moment he felt like the brother she'd never had. "You'll make lots of noise, won't you?"

"Lots and lots," he said softly. "I wish I could go with you, or that you could stay with Lavey and I could go in your place."

"Are you getting soft on me?" Darci asked. "Wait until I tell Greg!"

"I'm staying here in this time, re-member?" Jack said, grinning at her, then he gave Darci a sisterly hug and a kiss on the cheek. "You're a real pain, you know that?"

"Yeah, sure," she said, then Adam turned and she followed him into the dark-ness. She said nothing as they moved through the underbrush in the direction of the old houses. When she'd been with her Adam and had had her powers, she'd talked and made noises. She knew when there was danger close by. But not now. Now she followed Adam as closely as pos-sible. Neither Adam nor Jack had men-tioned giving Darci a rifle, but in the attic, in the bottom of an old trunk, she'd found a dagger. It was small and sharp, and the hilt had been decorated with jewels — fake or real, she didn't know. She'd shoved it in its scabbard inside her pocket. With every step she took, she could feel the stiff case against her leg.

After a while they reached a clearing, and Adam held his arm out to keep her from moving out of the brush. He listened and when he gave the signal, they both ran toward an old building and pulled open the creaking door. Once inside, they leaned against the wall and waited to see if anyone had heard the door.

As she stood there, Darci's eyes adjusted to the interior darkness, and she was glad she had no power. This building would someday be converted into a guest house where she and her Adam would stay. If she had power now, she knew that she'd be feeling him and she couldn't risk that right now. The man was too much like her husband, too much of a temptation.

She stayed still when Adam began to move about the room. She could barely see his outline, but she knew that he was inching along, trying to find what was left of the trap door. "Careful!" she whispered. What if the door had rotted away and he fell through the hole?

After a minute, she felt his hand reaching for hers. When she took his hand, a feeling of safety came over her, and she clasped it as though it were a life jacket.

"I'll go down first, but stay close to me," he whispered into her ear and she nodded.

It was difficult for her to let go of his hand, but she had to. She could feel more than see as he started down a ladder. Maybe it's a rotten ladder, she thought, but when it didn't break under his weight, she let out her breath. When Adam was partway down, he put his hand on her ankle and tugged to let her know she was to start down the ladder.

All the way down he covered her body with his. He was much taller than she was so he tested each rung before he allowed her to step on it, and he protectively surrounded her each step of the way.

Darci tried not to think of the closeness of their bodies. It had been so very long since she'd been this near to a man. Temptation, she thought. That's all this man is. He's temptation. He's not real, just someone to tempt me. Who is doing this to me? she wondered. And why?

When Adam's feet touched the ground, he reached up, took her by the waist, and lifted her down. Unnecessarily, he motioned that she was to follow him. When her foot touched water, he grabbed her hand.

"There's an underground stream here," he whispered, "so stay as far against the wall as possible. I see a light ahead."

She nodded and he took his hand away, then he began inching his way along the dirt wall. Darci kept her hands on the wall, feeling the rocks that protruded, now and then feeling a creepy-crawly thing, and she had to suppress her revulsion.

When they came to the end of that branch of the tunnel, Adam flattened against the wall, his arm across her upper chest as he held her pinned against the wall.

Darci listened but heard no one and nothing. The silence was as deep as only being underground could make it. As her eyes adjusted, she saw that the little stream went to the left, around the outer wall of the open area in front of them.

It took her a moment before she realized they were looking into the room that would someday have vending machines in it. The room would be much larger in her time, but she knew it was the same room. Someday, the tunnel they were in would be closed off, and she was sure there hadn't been a flowing stream along the back. Perhaps the stream had dried up, so they'd closed off the passage that led up to the icehouse. It had certainly been sealed off when she and her Adam had been there.

On the far wall were the three tunnel openings and for a moment Darci visualized Adam kneeling there and searching for footprints.

Cautiously, Adam Drayton stepped into the room, then motioned for Darci to follow him. After the darkness of the tunnel, the room with its four lanterns hanging from the walls was almost bright.

She had no idea where Nokes put his safe, but she knew where there were some rooms in the tunnels. She motioned for Adam to follow her, but he caught her arm and pulled her back, shaking his head no. He pointed to the three openings with a question on his face. She pointed to the one on the far right, then Adam got in front of her, his rifle at hip level and ready.

They tiptoed along silently, but it was all Darci could do to hold back tears. She vividly remembered the first time she'd followed Adam into this tunnel and how joyous she'd been! No one on earth had been happier than she was that day. She'd sensed that, eventually, Adam would come to love her, and she'd been anxious to get started.

Now she was in another time, with another man who looked and acted like the man she loved, and Darci had to constantly remind herself that this man wasn't *her* man.

Suddenly, Adam stopped walking and flattened himself against the wall, again pushing Darci back. Déjà vu, she thought, because, just like the first time, she heard men's voices coming from down the tunnel.

"Dancing?" a man said. "Are you crazy? Who'd come here to dance?"

"Anybody that wants money," another man said.

"What if Nokes finds out about this?"

"What's he gonna do? Fire us?"

The men laughed together and Darci could hear their feet hurrying across the dirt floor. She knew that there was a staircase at that end of the tunnel. The night the witch had taken her, Darci had walked down those stairs.

She cried to blank that image out of her mind but couldn't. She'd been wearing a white gown that night and she knew that she was being led to a chamber of sacrifice. Her only solace had been her hope that

Adam may have escaped. She'd been concentrating so hard that she didn't know he was chained to a wall only a few feet away.

When it was silent again, Darci motioned to Adam that just ahead, on the left, was a cutout in the wall. It was where she and Adam had nearly been caught, where Adam had cut her hair with a dagger that turned out to be used for the sacrifices. Looking back on it, she wondered if the witch had put such a valuable knife in a place used to store cups and plates as a lure to her, to Darci, who the witch wanted so much. The mirror had told the witch that a young woman with nine moles on her hand was going to kill her. Several young women had been killed before the witch found Darci.

Inching along, Adam soon saw the room with the iron gate. It hadn't changed since Darci had seen it last. Inside were shelves loaded with boxes of what looked to be supplies. This time, though, there was no tantalizing dagger lying on a shelf just out of their reach.

Darci let out a sigh. She'd been hoping that the safe would be here, in this easiest place to reach, but it wasn't.

She looked down the corridor and decided not to go that way. There could be a guard sitting there, a rifle across his lap. Besides, it was her guess that a man like Nokes seemed to be wouldn't keep his safe in a place where his workmen congregated.

She motioned for Adam to follow her, then went back the way they came, to the big room that would someday be enlarged with a Bobcat.

"I know of two big rooms," she whispered to Adam as he bent down to hear her. Darci wasn't going to tell him that she'd never actually been to either of the rooms, but she'd heard her father tell of every second he and Adam and Bo had searched for Darci. He'd said that he wanted to remember and record everything so he'd had Bo draw a map to the tunnels.

"One has an oak door," Darci said. "At least it did in my time, so I don't know if it's there now or not."

"A carved door, with a secret way to open it?" Adam asked.

"Yes! Is it there?"

"Yes. Nokes told me of it. He traded a sack of gems for it, and said that if you don't know how to open it, there's a trap. A deathly trap."

"I know how to open it," Darci said as she turned away from him so he couldn't see her face. She knew it was three things that she had to push. Animals? Leaves? Or was it a tree trunk that she had to push? And in what order? What was it that Bo had said about opening the door? It was a rhyme, or maybe a word.

She tried to remember back to the day when Bo had been telling her father so he could record the information. By that time the door had been destroyed, along with the tunnels, and everything that had been in them. There were some stolen first-century panels that had gone to museums. Adam said that he didn't care if the sacrificial altar had historical significance or not. He had it blown into tiny pieces.

"Come," she said over her shoulder, then hurried down the smallest of the three tunnels. After several minutes, she turned right; Adam caught her shoulder, and pointed. The tunnel in front of them widened, and there was more light farther down.

She couldn't help smiling at him as it looked as though she'd guessed right. This seemed to be the hub of the underground operation.

Adam moved in front of her, stepping slowly and quietly, looking about at every moment. Once they had to stop when they heard male laughter.

"Never seen anything like it," they heard.

"I threw last month's pay at her," said another male voice.

"So what's that? Nokes give you more than six cents?"

"All the fancy stones I could steal," said the first man. Their laughter faded as the men moved away.

Adam and Darci stayed still until it was quiet again, then Adam started moving. Minutes later, they were standing in front of a door that was carved to represent a jungle. From the look of it, she thought the door must have been made in South America.

Looking at the door, she tried to remember all that her sister-in-law had said. What was it Bo had said that day? Eliminate. Boadicea had said in her awkward cadence, "Eliminate. E.L.M. Eye, leaf, medallion. You only have to remember that it is the most large leaf."

Darci blinked a couple of times, drew in her breath, then pushed the eye of a funny-looking little animal, the biggest leaf, then the medallion in the corner.

When the door opened, Adam gave her a grin of such praise that she felt as though she could have floated into the room — if her legs hadn't been rubbery from her fear of not getting it right the first time, that is.

He didn't hesitate as he pushed the door open, entered the room, then closed the well-oiled door behind them. The only things in the room were a big, carved bed, a bedside table with a wash set on it, and a safe. Did the man Nokes sleep here? Darci wondered. With his money? If he did, then they'd better get out of here soon or he'd find them there.

Adam saw her looking at the bed and knew what she was thinking. "We should have time," he said. "Fonty will see Jack and Lavender first. It'll take him some time to get rid of them. He'll be furious that his men aren't working every minute. I'll get this open and we'll be out of here in no time."

Darci stood by the door, her heart in her throat, and watched him turn the knob on the safe. True to his word, the door swung open seconds later. As he opened the heavy door, Darci peered around Adam and looked inside. There were stacks of cash, and many red leather pouches that she figured were full of the Nokes garnets. Money and gems seemed to be all that were in the safe.

Quickly, Adam began moving the stacks of bills around, searching behind them. At last he pulled out the little man.

"Yes!" Darci said as she made a fist and moved her arm downward.

Adam laughed at her gesture, then imitated it. "Yes!"

Smiling, he closed the door to the safe, slipped the little man into his pocket, then motioned for Darci to go ahead of him to the door.

In the next second their triumph was shattered as they heard a noise outside the door, not exactly as though someone was knocking, but he was definitely doing something to the door.

"It's Fonty," Adam said. "He's the only one who knows how to open the door. Quick! Get under the bed."

Before Darci could think, Adam had pushed her onto the floor and was scooting under the bed beside her, his rifle at his side. The floor was damp and it was dusty under the bed; she had to hold her nose to keep from sneezing.

In silence, they watched the feet of the man enter the room. If I had my power now, Darci thought, I could put him to sleep and we could leave. But she had no power.

The feet walked so close to the bed that Darci drew in her breath. The man was going to bend down and look under the bed! If he was so paranoid that he slept with his money, then he was the type to check under the bed every night.

Adam moved a bit closer to her, using his body to protect her. She knew that he was ready to leap. If this man Fonty started to look, Adam was going to do what he could to keep Darci hidden.

But the man didn't bend down. Instead his pants fell to the floor and they could see his long underwear and his boots. He waddled over to the bed, his pants around his ankles, and sat down. The old bed, with its feather-filled mattress, sagged under his weight so that Darci had to roll closer to Adam to keep from being hit by the mattress. She looked up in alarm. If the man lay down on the bed, they'd have no hiding space.

Lifting his arm, Adam made a motion that she needed to be ready to roll his way when the mattress sank farther. Seconds later, they heard the boots hit the floor, followed by the man yawning and scratching, then he fell down into the center of the bed.

Darci rolled to her right, jamming close

to Adam's body. He had moved to the edge of the bed, and he put his arm out to hold her, to keep her closer to him and away from the sag in the mattress.

For a moment Darci closed her eyes. What if this were her Adam? she thought. What if right now she had the right to turn in his arms and kiss him?

She didn't move. It took all her willpower, all her courage, but she didn't move. Unfortunately, Adam did move. He touched the hair at her temple, caressed it, then tucked a strand behind her ear.

Please, she prayed. Help me resist this.

She didn't know if she was praying to God or maybe to the spirit of her husband. Please, Adam, she thought, if you're anywhere that you can hear me, help me now.

Adam Drayton's hand moved to her cheek. She could feel his heart beating against her back. She could feel . . . she could feel that he wanted her.

She closed her eyes again. It had been a long time since she'd been with a man. Already, overhead, they could hear Nokes's snores. The man was asleep, and by the sound of the snores, she didn't think he would hear them if they slipped out of the room. He probably wouldn't hear them if they rolled out from under the bed and made quiet love on the floor.

How long? Darci thought. How very, very long had it been since she'd felt a man's touch?

Adam's hand was on her neck now and she could feel his rampant desire. God would forgive us, wouldn't He? she thought. They were two extremely lonely people in unusual circumstances.

Darci tried to think of *her* Adam, of the man she'd vowed to love forever, but she also felt this other man's hands on her shoulder, traveling downward.

Above them, Nokes rolled over and the mattress sagged in another place.

And it was then that Darci felt a tiny spark run through her. It was a spark of . . . feeling. Her old feeling. It wasn't what she'd come to call power — and thought of privately as Power — but it was something.

She could feel the pull of the little ceramic man in Adam's pocket. She knew exactly where the man was because it was humming. Like the key had hummed at the FBI agency. She'd followed that hum as it got louder and it had led her to Jack, who'd led her to the box that fit the key.

The little man's humming was sending a signal to something else that was also humming. It was as though she and Adam were caught between two night creatures that were calling to each other.

When Adam's hand abruptly stopped moving, she turned her head enough to see his eyes and looked at him in question. Did he feel it, too? she wanted to ask him. From the expression on his face, he did.

Slowly, he managed to inch his hand down to his pocket. He halted once when Nokes stopped snoring. They held their breath and waited until the snoring started again.

Adam managed to remove the little man from his pocket and put it in Darci's hand, for the direction of the humming was on the other side of her. Taking the man, she held him out as far as her arm could reach.

Nokes rolled over again, the snoring stopped, and they had to wait while he moved around before he settled down again. Adam and Darci held still, their breaths held until he was snoring loudly again.

Lifting her arm, Darci stretched it out. She could feel vibrations in the little statue now, and they got stronger when her arm went to the left, toward the bulge that was Nokes.

She glanced back at Adam to tell him

that she was going to slide on her stomach and try to find what was pulling at her. He shook his head no as vigorously as possible, considering the way he was pinned, but Darci nodded yes.

Rolling to her stomach, she tried to make herself as small as she could. She'd gained weight since she'd first met Adam. She'd eaten a lot and had had a baby, both of which had filled her out. She wasn't fat, but she was no longer the waif she had once been.

It was difficult trying to move under the hanging-down bulk of Nokes without touching the mattress. She couldn't lift her head, couldn't use her elbows to move herself. She had to scoot and wiggle. The floor was damp dirt and there were rocks sticking out of it, and the rocks seemed to know just where her ribs were. Twice she had to work to keep from crying out when a rib was bruised.

After a long while and a lot of work, she felt the little man in her hand vibrate so hard she almost dropped him. Whatever had set it off was just over her head.

With her heart pounding, she rolled out from under the bed — just as Nokes's arm dropped. In an instant, she had to combat fear and loathing as a fat, dirty hand flopped down onto her face. She lay still and waited. Would he feel her face and wake? As she lay there, she looked up to see a pistol barrel protruding over the side of the bedside table. If he woke, there would be bullets exchanged between him and Adam, and someone would die.

After what seemed like hours, she was sure that Nokes wasn't going to awaken, so she slowly shuffled back under the bed, this time faceup. She glanced at Adam, and saw that he'd moved his rifle to the near side of him. If he had to shoot Nokes he would be shooting a man who was his friend. And all for a woman he barely knew.

Darci looked back at the underside of the bed, but saw nothing that could make the little man hum. For one horrific second she thought maybe it was Nokes himself. Was he so attached to the little ceramic man that it would call out to him if it were being stolen?

She looked back up at the bed again and this time she thought she saw something shiny. The underside was all ropes and old boards, but maybe what she was seeing was a nail.

Darci stretched her arm out, holding the statue up as high as she could, and when it got within a couple of inches of the shiny thing, she felt a . . . a "joining of voices" is the only way she could describe it. The two objects were in perfect harmony.

She glanced at Adam and again he was shaking his head no, that he didn't want her to do whatever she was planning to do. Darci nodded, then began to move her arm down to her trouser's pocket. It took some fiddling, but she managed to get the little dagger out of its sheath and into her hand. She had to do more scooting and had to put her arm next to the bulge of Nokes, but she managed to get the knife tip onto the shiny object.

A few minutes later, it popped out and Darci almost dropped it. She had no time to look at it before she jammed it down the front of her shirt, into the two layers of underwear that kept her shirt from being transparent.

Triumphant, she flattened her body to look at Adam. He was glaring at her, his eyes telling her that they had to get out immediately.

When she nodded to him, he motioned for her to back out. Nokes was snoring loudly as she scooted out from under the bed, belly up, head first. This time Nokes's dirty foot was hanging off the bed and

Darci turned away when her face got too close. Minutes later, she was completely out. Adam was waiting for her by the door, and had silently opened it.

She could tell that he was angry when he half pushed her through the door and out into the tunnel, closing the big, carved door behind them.

"I hope you obey your husband better than that," Adam said through clenched teeth as soon as they were a few feet from the door.

"Much less," she said, feeling good that they were now out from under the bed. But, best of all, she felt that someone had helped her. She had asked for help and she'd received it. For the first time in a long while she didn't feel *alone*.

"I never obey him," she said happily. "Never, never, never."

Adam led them out of the tunnels. Expertly, he made all the correct turns, and once they were in the big room he hurried to the small opening in the far wall, the one that followed the stream out. Darci kept close behind him, and they said nothing until they'd reached the icehouse and climbed up the ladder. At the top in the icehouse, Adam helped Darci up. When they stood together in the blackness inside the old building, he said, "I want to apologize for my behavior back there. I mean, what I did while we were under the bed. I think it was the moment and the situation."

"It's all right," she answered, feeling his embarrassment. "I know how it feels to be alone."

"Yes, I think that's part of my attraction to you. Darci," he said softly, "I've known you but hours, yet I feel a kinship with you. If you were to stay here —"

Reaching up, she put her fingertips over his lips. "I know. I've always known. You and I could . . . we could come to mean something to each other. But no, I can't stay. You're not my Adam and your daughters aren't my children. I'm sure I could come to love all of you, but there's . . ." She hesitated.

"Yes, I understand. We would be substitutes for other people," Adam said after a moment, then he stepped away from her. "But if you find that you can't return, you'll always have a home with us, and it will be on any terms you want."

"Thank you," she whispered. In the next instant the door to the icehouse flew open and the moment was broken.

"Ready?" Jack asked. "I think we should

go before Nokes shows up. From what his workmen said about him, he sounds like someone I don't want to meet. What?!" he said when Darci and Adam started laughing.

Chapter Fifteen

‹‹ ››

"I had a wonderful time tonight," Lavender said, closing her eyes for a moment in memory. "The miners sang songs and I danced to the music." She was back in her tight clothes again, her waist corseted, her legs hidden under pounds of fabric. If it had been left to her and Jack, she would have stayed in her costume, but Adam was so uncomfortable with her near nudity that she'd given in and put her clothes back on.

As for Darci, she'd refused to remove her trousers and put that dreadful corset back on. Between the comfortable clothes and their success in the tunnels, she was feeling wonderful. With each passing moment, she seemed to be becoming clearer about who she was and who this man sitting near her was. He was *not* her husband. For a while there, under the bed, she'd wavered, but someone somewhere had helped her. That she wasn't alone had given her new confidence and new energy.

"I wish I could have seen you dance," she said to Lavender, smiling, but her smile hid what she was thinking. Now what happens? she wondered. What happens to Lavender? Had tonight's adventure been the real reason that Lavender's spirit had followed Jack's into the twentieth century?

Darci had a thought that made her draw in her breath sharply. What if it was Jack's leaving that made Lavender jump off the roof? What if she'd spent an exciting evening with Jack, then after he left to go back to his own time, Lavender was faced with a lifetime of living with John Marshall, a man she had been intending to break away from?

"Did someone walk over your grave?" Lavender asked when Darci shuddered.

"No, just thinking. Tell me what you didn't like about John before yesterday."

"Dull," Lavender said, looking at Jack with adoring eyes. "He was so dull. Nothing in the least adventurous about him. So very proper at all times." She was sipping black tea while the rest of them had glasses of champagne. That Adam had refused to allow Lavender more booze was another thing that made Darci realize that this man wasn't her Adam. Her Adam had a wicked sense of humor. And he knew when to relax and have fun. And he would never have taken away a person's happiness in achievement as this Adam was doing to Lavender.

You're welcome to him, Diana, Darci said to herself an hour after they returned.

"How could any man be dull around you?" Jack asked, his eyes glittering for a moment, then he gave a fake yawn. "I don't know about the rest of you, but I think I need to get some rest. It'll be dawn in a few hours."

Darci knew that if the house were quiet, Jack and Lavender would be in the same bed within seconds. After all, they thought this was to be their wedding day, so why not spend the night together?

She searched her mind for a reason why they should all stay awake. "But we can't go to bed now. Jack, did you forget that this is not only Lavender's wedding day but it's also her birthday? We must celebrate."

When Jack looked blank, she glared at him, willing him to remember that when Lavender was in Chrissy's body, she'd said she was being married on her birthday.

"Oh, right," Jack said. "I forgot completely. And I don't have a present for you."

Lavender looked from Darci to Jack, then to Adam. "Tell me, Mr. Drayton, what do you think of a husband and a sister-in-law-to-be who can't remember your birthday?"

"I'd say that you should be able to choose your own gift. I have some lovely horses that would be very nice for a young lady. Shall I charge him double for them?"

All four of them were smiling. "Perhaps a trip," Lavender said. "To somewhere divinely exotic. New Zealand, maybe."

"Yes, that sounds nice," Jack said. "What about you, little sister? Like to go to New Zealand?"

Part of Darci wanted to play the game, but another part wanted to remind Jack that they had to return to their own time. Giving enjoyment won out. "New Zealand sounds heavenly. A Victorian world that hasn't been explored. No fast food. No WMDs that no one can find."

"Just head hunters," Jack said. "And diseases we haven't known for centuries."

"Actually," Adam said, "I'd like to talk to you two about some things. Perhaps you could tell me of this assembly machine."

"Assembly line," Jack said. "It's a simple process, really. It just means that —"

Lavender sat up straighter in her seat

and said loudly, "I'd like to talk about the fact that today is *not* my birthday." There was some petulance in her tone. It was obvious that she wasn't going to give up her time with Jack to let him talk about an "assembly machine."

"Not — ?" Darci began.

"Not — ?" Jack began.

"Is this significant?" Adam asked.

Darci and Jack looked at each other with wide eyes. "Whose birthday *is* today?" Darci asked, looking intently at Lavender. Her voice rose. "Who has a birthday on the twelfth of June?"

"I have no idea," Lavender answered. "No one I know. I wouldn't have scheduled my wedding on the birthday of anyone close to me. In fact, we wanted to be married last week, but my cousin's birthday was that week so we changed the date. As for my birthday, it's in April. Jack, don't you remember what you gave me this year?" Her eyes were teasing. "You haven't mixed me up with one of your other girls, have you?"

Both Jack and Darci blinked at her, unable to understand what they were hearing. They had a great deal to say to each other, but they knew they could say nothing in front of Lavender.

Adam looked from one to the other and seemed to understand their dilemma. "If Miss Shay and I are no longer needed, I think we should be off to bed. Besides, a bride shouldn't see so much of the groom on her wedding day. You'll be tired of each other before the honeymoon begins."

"I could never get tired of Jack," Lavender said as she suppressed a yawn. "But I must admit that I'm exhausted. Drinking for the first time in my life, then dancing while standing on top of a buckboard . . . truly an incredible day. By the way, Jack, my dearest, how much money did we collect?"

"Nearly two hundred dollars and half a shoebox full of garnets."

"How wonderful," Lavender said, her eyes sleepy. "Good night, Mr. Drayton. Good night, my dear sister. Good night, my beloved Jack, my almost husband."

There were murmurs of undying love from Jack, and courteous responses from Adam as Lavender went up the stairs.

"Yes, good night," Darci said distractedly. She was still thinking about what she'd heard. She'd never missed her powers as much as she did now. If she had her abilities she could have figured out what was going on a long time ago.

"Mrs. Montgomery," Adam said formally, "may I see you for a moment?"

"Don't you leave," Darci said under her breath to Jack. "Don't move an inch and do *not* slip upstairs and get in bed with Lavender." Louder, she said, "Jack, you and I need to brainstorm and figure out what's going on here."

"Brainstorm," Adam said, turning the word over in his mouth. "What an excellent word, and I think I can guess its meaning."

As Darci followed Adam into the library, her mind was on other things. How could they have been so stupid as to assume they knew what had gone on after Lavender died? And what did it mean that Lavender's birthday wasn't today? The angry spirit that had been around Jack had said her birthday was on her wedding day.

"Darci," Adam said, his voice low and familiar, all formality gone. "I want to say . . ." Looking down at her, he smiled. "You're thinking of your mystery, aren't you?"

"Yes. You see, I think Lavender might die on her wedding day."

"Ah, I see. If Jack leaves her, she will die. If not all at once, then slowly. Like you and me."

He had her attention now. "Like us," she said. "Without . . ."

"The other half of us," he said softly. "You and I aren't whole people." He lifted his hand as though he might tuck a strand of hair behind her ear, but he didn't. Instead, he straightened his back. "I'm not sure I'll see you in the morning. I don't know that I can bear to say good-bye. You remind me too much of what I've lost. But now I have a question to ask you."

"Yes?"

"What did you pry out of Fonty's bed?"

Smiling, she reached down inside her shirt to pull it out. She could feel Adam's eyes on her, feel his blush, but she could also feel his interest.

Holding out her hand, she slowly opened her fist to show him what she'd found. In the carriage ride back, she'd felt the object through her clothes so she knew what it was, but she hadn't yet looked at it. She'd planned to do that when she was alone. But Adam had been with her, had risked his life to find the object, so he deserved to see it.

In the palm of her hand was a crucifix. But as prepared as she thought she was, she still drew in her breath. It was exquisite — and old. Maybe even very, very old.

The suffering figure of Christ was so detailed she could see the veins on his forehead even though the whole crucifix was only about an inch and a half tall.

"May I?" Adam asked and Darci handed it to him. He took it to the fireplace where the light was better and stared at it, then he withdrew a magnifying glass from a desk drawer and studied it. "Exquisite," he whispered. "I don't think Nokes put it in the bed frame, so it must have been put there by someone else."

"For me to find," Darci said softly. "And so it won't be found many years from now by a woman of great evil. At least I assume it was one of the objects she had. I was told she had many." Reaching into her pocket, she withdrew the little ceramic man and handed it to Adam.

Holding the objects, one in each hand, he said, "They still vibrate, but not as strongly as they did when we were under the bed together."

"Maybe they were just so glad to see each other that they became very excited," Darci said.

"Maybe so," Adam answered, chuckling. "So what do you plan to do with them? Can you take them back with you?"

"If I go," she said. "If everything isn't

messed up because we thought someone was Lavender who isn't, that is." She shrugged. "I don't know what will happen. When, if, I don't know. But I plan to carry the box and the key that's inside that man with me every second today. If it looks like things are going wrong, I'll open the box and maybe Jack and I will go back to our own time. Or maybe we'll go back to the year 601. Maybe we'll be trampled by dinosaurs. Or maybe we'll find ourselves on a spaceship."

Adam was grinning at her. "Pardon my selfishness, but, if for no other reason, I wish you could stay so I could hear every word about your world."

"I'd like to hear about yours, too," she said wistfully, then recovered herself. "Do you mind if I get the key out now?"

"Shall I break him for you?"

Darci eyes twinkled. "Be my guest."

Adam put the little ceramic man on the stone hearth and gently tapped it with the iron poker. It didn't break. He hit it again, this time harder. It didn't so much as chip. Adam whacked the man with enough force to shatter it — but it didn't hurt it in any way.

He looked at Darci in astonishment.

"I know," she said, laughing. "My father and I tried everything before he decided to wash the little man." There was a vase of flowers on a side table. She removed the flowers, then dropped the man into the water. There was a sizzle and the outer covering vanished, leaving in the vase a very ordinary-looking key.

Adam laughed. "Nokes could have owned the man for a century and never found out what was inside it. To my knowledge he's never washed himself nor anything around him."

"I'll never forget those feet," she said. Putting her hand on Adam's arm, she was suddenly serious. "There's no way he could find out that *you* were the one who took his good luck piece, is there?"

"I don't think so."

"But he must know that you know the combination to the safe."

"Even in our time we have people who make a profession of opening safes," Adam said, amused. "I have an honorable reputation so I don't think he'll suspect me."

"Are you sure?"

"And if I'm not, what will you do?"

"I'll —" There was nothing she could do. She was merely a small woman without any extraordinary powers of any kind. "I don't know what I could do," she said at last.

Darci took the key out of the water and dried it on her shirttail. "I think I'll keep this with me. You don't have a cord that I could use to tie it around my neck, do you?"

"I'll find something and I'll send it to you in the morning," he said, taking the key from her. "What do I do with this?" He held up the beautiful little crucifix to the light. "I think it's Italian, no later than the fourteenth century. It's quite the finest workmanship I've ever seen."

"Simone's son, Tom, works for Jack, and Tom's going to bury something Simone gave me by a church that I know survives the Civil War. Could you get Tom to show you where he buried the egg? I'll find both things after I return to my own time. If I get back, that is." She glanced toward the door, wanting to talk to Jack about what they were going to do next.

"Yes, of course," Adam said, staring at her as though he meant to memorize her face. He stepped away from her. "I'll bid you good night, then. It'll be dawn soon and I know you'll leave. I want to say, Mrs. Montgomery, that tonight has been . . ." He seemed to run out of words.

Darci turned away from his intense stare. She didn't want to do the same thing to him.

After a moment, she looked back at him. "Me, too. I was frightened every minute we were in the tunnels, but in the end it worked out well. I don't know how to thank you, and I will always remember what you've done."

He seemed to have recovered himself as he smiled. "I ask two things of you. One is that if you do return, I want you to explore what that box and key can do, and, if you can, I ask that you use that . . . what was it? That healing ball?"

"Touch of God."

"Yes, if it exists — please excuse my cynicism — but if it exists, and if you have powers, and if —" He waved his hand. "If it is possible, please let me see my wife again. You have revived my memories of her to the point of pain."

"Yes, I understand," she said, stepping away from him. She feared that he might try to pull her into his arms. "And the second request?"

"Only that you remember that if you should find yourself stranded here, my door is always open to you."

"Thank you," she said, then stood stiffly while they struggled with what else there was to say to each other. In the end, Adam said nothing, nor did she. He gave her a little bow from the neck, then quickly left the room.

Darci stood alone in the beautiful library and told herself that she would not cry. Adam Drayton had made her feel closer to her husband than she had since he'd disappeared.

Squaring her shoulders, she went back to the parlor where Jack awaited her. "Lavender?" she asked.

"In bed. Alone," Jack said with great regret in his voice, then he turned to business. "Any idea of what's going on?"

Darci sat down hard on a wing chair and stared at the fire. "None at all. When we talked to that angry spirit around you, she said she was Lavender Shay and that you two were going to get married, on the twelfth of June, 1843. So that's today. She also said it was her birthday."

"And that her father was ill."

"Oh, right. You had to wait for something because her father was so ill."

"The honeymoon," Jack said. "She said we had to postpone the honeymoon because her father was ill."

"But Lavender's father is fine," Darci said. "I don't understand what's going on, do you?" When she looked at Jack, she saw that his face was as puzzled as she felt.

"No idea whatever. Unless she was lying."

"Which one?"

"The spirit. Do they lie? Can they lie?" Jack asked.

"Sure. They're just people without bodies. Just because they get rid of their earthly flesh doesn't make them angels."

"If this weren't so serious I'd laugh at that." Putting his hand on the mantel, he stared into the fire. "How can I protect Lavender if I don't know what's going on?"

"Is there another woman who thinks she has a right to marry you?"

"Every one I've ever been to bed with," Jack said with cockiness.

Darci narrowed her eyes at him. "We can do without Jack the Smart Alec, that jerk I met in Greg's office."

"He's still in here, along with John Marshall. It's getting a little crowded, though. There's the haunted Jack who hates his father, the Jack who's in love with Lavender, and John who's dull and boring but who is also desperately in love with Lavender." He looked at Darci. "You know, it's odd about Lavender calling Marshall dull. He's inside me and he doesn't feel dull at all. In fact, he's done some pretty rowdy things."

"Maybe he's afraid to let her see that

side of him. Maybe he thinks Lavender's a woman of such virtue that all she wants to do is have tea parties. I doubt if he'd believe that she wanted to dance half naked in front of a bunch of miners."

Jack gave a one-sided grin. "You should have seen her. She was magnificent. If I didn't know better I would have thought she was Arabic. I tell you that I got so jealous of those men looking at her that I . . . I . . ." He rubbed his palms on his trouser's legs.

"You are John and John is you," Darci said. "You're separated by a few hundred years but you're the same."

"Maybe not. Maybe I'm just occupying his body. And keeping it. I'm not leaving Lavender."

Darci put her fingertips to her temples. "This thinking is hard work," she said. "It's much easier to go into a trance and come out with the answer." When she looked at Jack, he was shaking his head in disbelief, but she ignored him. "What if the spirit lied to us and she wasn't Lavender Shay? Maybe she wanted to be Lavey so much she thought she was her. What if she thought you were going to marry *her?* Maybe she thought that if she pushed Lavey off a building you'd marry her instead."

"Maybe John did kill Lavey," Jack said quietly. "Remember that the paper said he married someone else after Lavey's death."

"Or maybe he didn't know that Lavender had been murdered. Do you think he married the murderer? Okay, what we need to know first is who John Marshall had been to bed with."

At that, Jack became conspicuously silent.

"What is it that you don't want to tell me?"

Jack ran his hand along the mantel. "I told you that neither John nor I were saints or angels. Only I had a reason for what I did, while he —"

"Yeah, I know," Darci said impatiently. "You were the poor little rich boy who didn't get enough love. You got enough food and you had a best friend and, oh yeah, you had his parents who loved you madly, but your daddy didn't praise you enough, so you turned to drugs and bad ways."

"How has anyone let you live this long?" Jack said with clenched teeth. He stared at Darci and she stared back.

"Okay," Jack said at last. "What's different in John's case is that it was 'like father, like son.' His father likes floozies and his son did, too."

"Like you," Darci said.

"No, there you're wrong. I like my women smart and beautiful and talented. I like a woman who gives me a run for my money." At that, he looked Darci up and down in the manner of the old Jack, but she ignored him.

"No, I mean, 'like father, like son.' You're just like your father."

"I'm what?!" Jack half yelled, then lowered his voice. "I'm not at all like my father."

"Right," Darci said, sarcastic. "Let's see. Your father is cold; you've always been cold to people. Your father is obsessed with money; you get upset at the mention of money. Your father has been doing something undercover, evidenced by the items in his secret room, and you do nothing but undercover work. The world thinks your father is a good, kind man but he's not, and you aren't what you appear to be, either. So what's different between you two?"

Jack's face was white, and he looked as though he'd been hit with something. His mouth was open, as though trying to get his breath. "You know, I think I liked it better when that angry spirit was hanging around me. Then I was so angry that

294

nothing anyone said got to me."

"Who *is* that angry spirit?" Darci asked. "Who thinks you're going to marry her? Whose birthday is today and who has a sick father? What woman have you bedded and made her think that there was going to be more?"

"Not me. John Marshall, remember? I'm the one who had it all and wanted more."

"Who have you angered enough that she followed you into the next life — or probably next lives, since it's been so long. Who has worked to make your life miserable?"

"Just one woman?"

At that Darci stood up. "I'm going upstairs to get a couple hours of sleep. You should stay here and think about this."

"Okay," Jack said calmly. "The truth is that I don't know. I told you that this Marshall character is fading inside me. Or maybe it's that I'm fading inside myself. Whatever is happening, with every hour I seem to feel him less. Maybe having spent a lifetime surrounded by an angry spirit has made me stronger, or made me more greedy so that I'm taking more than my share. I don't know. I know that when I woke up in his body, I could feel him and remember what he did, but gradually that's changed. Now it's ninety percent me in here and only ten percent him." He grinned at Darci. "Maybe I should be hypnotized to bring him out."

Jack had been making a joke, but as he looked at Darci, his eyes widened. "Can you ride a horse?"

"Not at all. I fall off the side the minute the creature takes a step. Why do you want me to ride a horse?"

"This woman you went to, this Simone, the one you've tried to keep secret from me. Do you think that she might be able to find out who this person is?"

"I don't know. I think she has more power than she thinks she does, but I don't think she has much." Darci's head came up. "Do you think that she might be able to tell us what *did* happen?"

"Did, as in hasn't happened, yet what could happen this afternoon?"

"Exactly," Darci said. "You know what I'm wondering? That paper said that Jack married after Lavender died, and he died when his house burned down. Wonder if it was an accident?"

For a moment, Jack and Darci looked at each other in silence.

"I'm going to pack my Victorian clothes," she said. "I don't want to shock anyone in my plus fours. While I'm packing, I want you to go to Adam and get the key and the crucifix, and ask him if we can borrow a horse. Can you ride a fast horse?"

"I can ride a bucking bronco if I have to. What crucifix?"

"I'll tell you on the way to Simone's house — if I can find it in the dark. How long before it's daylight?"

"No more than three hours, I'd think."

"What do we do about Lavender?" Darci asked.

"How about if we leave her here under Drayton's care? Think he can guard her for us?"

"I think he can do anything," Darci said, then saw Jack's look of speculation. "Don't start making up things."

"I want you to tell me everything that happened tonight." He gave a little grin. "Maybe you'll want to stay here, too. Maybe there'll be a double wedding this afternoon."

"No," Darci said softly. "If at all possible, I'm going home to my family."

"You'll probably get there in another hundred and some years." Jack was grinning, laughing, but she wasn't. She wasn't going to tell him what Simone had said about Darci having only one life and needing to return to the twenty-first century. Nor was she going to tell him that Simone had told her that if a spirit had power, it always had power. When she'd been with Adam under that man's bed, she'd felt the vibrations between the two objects. Maybe some of her power was coming back to her. Or being released, she thought with a grimace. Maybe whoever had hidden her power was beginning to release it.

She did, however, tell him in detail about the hiding place where Tom was going to put the magic objects. Jack listened and nodded, liking her plan. "Now go ask Adam to take care of Lavender," she said. She wasn't going to tell Jack that the last thing on earth she needed was to see Adam Drayton in bed. "I'll meet you back here in ten minutes."

As soon as Jack left the room, Darci turned toward the stairs to get her clothes, but, yet again, she had that feeling that she was being watched. She rubbed at her forearms to settle the hairs that were standing on end. A glance at the windows showed that it was still black outside, and she could see nothing.

Turning, she started up the stairs, but stopped again and looked back quickly.

Nothing. For what had to be the thousandth time, she wished she had her powers. If she did, she would know if there was someone outside, how many, and what sex. She might even know what he wanted. If she saw the person, she'd know by his aura whether his motives were good or bad.

She closed her eyes for a moment and concentrated. If she had her powers now she could paralyze whoever was outside, and she'd be able to find out what had happened and what was happening.

But she could tell nothing. She shivered once, then ran the rest of the way up the stairs. Right now she wanted to be near Jack or Adam, and a rifle.

Chapter Sixteen

"Lord a mercy, child," Simone said, "I can't do that. Even my grandmother would have been hard put to do what you're asking."

"I want you to see if you can tell us what's going to happen today, and who's involved. It's not difficult."

"Maybe not for someone with your power, but it's impossible for me."

Darci narrowed her eyes at the old woman. "What is it you don't want to do?"

"Change things," Simone said quickly. "That's not my place. Maybe that girl is supposed to die today. What right do I have to try to change God's plan?"

Darci threw up her hands and looked at Jack, who was lounging half asleep in an easy chair in Simone's tiny parlor.

Leaning forward, Simone took Darci's hand and held it. "You have the box and the key now, don't you? You should use it to go home. Go now. Hold onto him, open the box, and leave here."

"But what about Lavender? You told me that the three of us who came here had to leave *together.*"

Simone looked at Jack to make sure he wasn't listening, then leaned closer to Darci. "There's a spirit around him now and I don't think it's someone who loves him. Who hates him?"

"I don't know," Darci said. "We've been trying to find out. I think he must have made some woman think he was going to marry her. She's very angry, so angry that she follows him into the future."

Simone leaned back in her chair. "My daughter knows which women hate which men."

Darci's eyes widened. "Abortion," she said softly. Of course. Unwanted children. Out of wedlock. She looked at Simone. "Where does your daughter live?"

"In town." She smiled. "But right now she happens to be asleep in my bedroom. Perhaps we can wake her up and ask her who hates John Marshall enough to haunt him forever."

"Yes, let's do that," Darci said.

"There are seven women on this list!" Darci shouted at Jack over the pounding hooves of the horses. "Seven! You either —"

"Not me. John Marshall."

"Same spirit; different body," Darci said. "You either impregnated them or they were buying love potions to make you fall for them. What in the world was your appeal? And you said John *loved* Lavey. So why all the other women?"

"Ever hear of sex?"

"I vaguely remember it," Darci answered.

"Lavender is a good girl. I couldn't touch her and there were all those other women offering themselves to me. What was I . . . he supposed to do? Say no?"

"But the abortions."

"It's a different time. All that's a woman's responsibility, not a man's."

Darci grimaced. "The irony is that Lavey was bored by you, by John. You were treating her like a piece of porcelain rather than like a real woman. All in all, you were a real jerk, you know that?"

Jack gave a snort of laughter. "It's a good thing my ego is intact or I'd be hurt by your words. As it is, I'm shedding tears."

"It's the wind," Darci said. She was holding onto him tightly, trying not to fall off the horse as they rode back to Camwell, and she was thinking of the task in front of them. How did they find all these women in the few hours they had before the wedding? Jack had said it would be simple. All they had to do was ask for birth dates. "And she'll tell the truth?" Darci said. "A woman who is so full of hatred is going to tell the truth?"

"Why should she lie about her birth date? The twelfth of June. Simple. Find out whose birthday it is, then we have her."

"Then what?" Darci asked.

"Tie her in the cellar until Lavender and I are married."

"And history changes to Lavender dying after her marriage instead of on the day. Wow! That helps a lot."

"You could always open your little box and go back now," Jack said over his shoulder. "But no! You need Lavey and me, don't you?"

"You were listening!"

"To every word. I wouldn't have missed it for the world. So what's your plan, Little Miss Boss of the World?"

"I'm not — Okay, so maybe I've been called that before. But it was because I used to *know* what to do. I could look into the future, into people's hearts, and I could —"

"Yeah, yeah. I've heard it all before.

303

What's your plan now?"

"Beats me," Darci said.

"Good," Jack answered. "If you don't know what to do, maybe you'll listen. I'm going to go to each of these women and talk to them."

"You're what?! You can't do that. One of them hates you."

"Or loves me."

"Same thing. She wants you either in this century or in the next, or the next, and she means to have you. I don't know that I've ever seen such a powerful hatred. You can't —"

At that, Jack pulled the horse to a halt. "You either go along with my plan or I let you off here."

"Here" was nowhere, as only the country before cars could be. All Darci could see for a mile down the road in either direction was trees. There weren't even any farmhouses in sight. Not that a farmhouse would help without a telephone.

"Okay," she said, her lips tight. "I'll do it, but I don't like it."

"That's all I ask," Jack said as he nudged the horse forward. "All I want you to do is stay with Lavey all day. She goes to the outhouse, you go with her. Got it? No running off to see any psychics, no playing detective. If you stay with Lavender and never leave her alone, that in itself will change history. Have I made myself clear?"

"Absolutely," Darci said, then was silent for a while. "Jack?"

"Yes?"

"If we go back to our own time and we've succeeded in getting that angry spirit away from you so my powers can reach you, you know what I'm going to do?"

"No, what?"

"Cause you real pain."

Laughing, Jack kicked the horse to go faster. When Darci had to grab him tighter to keep from falling off the back, he laughed harder.

"Darci, you're a dear sister," Lavender was saying, "but I do need some air. I'll be back in a few minutes."

Darci decided to count to ten, but only got to two. "You can't see Jack. You can't leave this room. In one hour you're going to be married and until that time you're to stay here and wait."

They were sitting in Lavender's bedroom and she was dressed in the most elaborate white dress that Darci had ever seen. It must have a hundred yards of white silk in the skirt alone. It had taken Lavender's aunts three hours to get her into the concoction. And once she was dressed, they'd ordered her to stay and sit. She wasn't to move until someone came for her and told her she was to go to the church.

Darci was sure the aunts were punishing Lavender for being out all night. Chaperoned or not, Lavender should have been at home on the night before her wedding.

As for Darci, the aunts were so angry at her that they weren't speaking to her. They merely looked at Darci, stabbed her with their eyes, then turned away and did something more to Lavey's dress.

But the second the aunts were gone and Lavender and Darci were alone in the room, Lavender wanted to slip down the back stairs and see Jack.

"I know it makes no sense," Lavender said, "but I must see him. I want to ask him something."

No doubt she wants to ask him if he still loves her, Darci thought. She was back in her corset and she was too hot and tired from a night of no sleep to put up with Lavender's love needs. Her own maid, Millie, had come to the Shay house to jam Darci into a frothy, hot, stiff, itchy dress of — what else? — lavender silk, and Darci was to sit as still as Lavender was. The only good thing about the dress was that she could easily conceal the silver box in a pocket. And maybe an anvil or two, she thought.

Darci toyed with the gold chain necklace about her neck. When she and Jack had returned from Simone's house, a young man was waiting for them on the porch. He had a package from Adam Drayton. Inside was a beautiful gold chain and the key they'd found in the little statue. There was a note with it.

I thought about going to the wedding, but I could not bear it. The necklace belonged to my wife. Please keep it as a remembrance of our adventure. I will bury the crucifix and the garnets from the miners with the egg you mentioned. Please don't forget our bargain.

Adam

"We can't go outside," Darci said for the thousandth time as she slipped the chain and key back inside her dress. Lavender was being such a pest that Darci was sorely tempted to tell her that someone wanted to kill her within the next hour. Darci felt the injustice of it all. Not only had she traveled through time to help this woman, she was now slowly roasting inside fifty pounds of silk.

Opening her mouth to say something, Darci looked up at a knock on the door. It was her maid, Millie.

"I have a note for you, Miss," Millie said, holding out a folded paper.

"It's from Jack," Lavender said as she made a lunge for the paper.

But Millie pulled it back. "It's for Miss Darci," she said, then stepped into the room to hand the paper to her. Darci opened it.

I know everything. Meet me at the usual place.

Jack

Usual place? Darci thought. What does that mean? Where is that?

"It's from Jack, isn't it?" Lavender said, again reaching for the note, but Darci handed it back to Millie. "Tell him I'll be there," she said, then the girl left the room.

Darci was smaller than Lavender, but she was strong. She put her hands on Lavender's shoulders, pushed her to sit on a hard little chair, and looked into her eyes. "Listen to me. We've been careful not to tell you about this, but someone wants you dead. Do you understand me? Dead. Jack and I've been protecting you and trying our best to find out who's trying to kill you."

"That's ridiculous. Who would want me dead?"

"The women John Marshall slept with and promised to marry. Two of them were going to have his children but John paid for the abortions. The other five . . . The truth is that we don't know about them, but Jack's trying to find out. Now it looks like he's found out something and I have to go to him to hear what it is. *You* are to stay here in this room. Do you understand me?"

"You talk about John and Jack as though they're two different people."

"They are. Sort of. Lavey, did you listen to anything I said?"

"Yes, and I've heard it all before, but I don't believe a word of any of it. I did, but I don't now. John has changed into Jack, and no matter what he calls himself, he *is* extremely attractive to women. Darci, dearest, you always were so dramatic."

"You never met me before yesterday," she said, frustrated, but Lavender just laughed at her.

Straightening, Darci looked down at

Lavender and knew that she'd not stay in the room. She was a woman in love and nothing was going to hold her. Darci tried to be understanding. If she'd been told that Adam was outside, could she have voluntarily stayed a prisoner in a room?

Opening the door, Darci looked in the hallway and saw her maid. "Would you do something for me, Millie?" she asked, then told her that she wanted her to stay with Lavender. "If she tries to leave the room, go get the aunts."

"Yes, Miss," Millie said. "You look beautiful."

Darci didn't smile at the compliment. On the back of her head was a bun of real hair — probably bought from some immigrant, she thought in disgust — that had to weigh six pounds. Beside her face were ringlets plastered into place with something that made steel seem soft. Under her corset her ribs itched, and she was having trouble breathing. I should stay here and become the first Coco Chanel, she thought to herself. I could beat her to liberating women from the corset.

"I'll be back as soon as I can," she said to Millie, then Darci did her best to run down the back stairs. She had to stop twice to catch her breath before she could start running again. She had to run through the kitchen and a few people called to her, but they were so busy with the wedding preparations that they could pay no further attention to Darci.

Where could Jack have meant by "the usual place"? she wondered. Outside, it wasn't a lot cooler than it had been in the house. Picking up her skirts and knowing she would be causing a scandal by showing her ankles, she began to hurry down the street toward the house of John Marshall.

When she opened the front door of the empty house, she looked into the barrel of a pistol held by a large, red-haired man. From the look of his slack lower lip with the drop of saliva, and the dull gleam in his eyes, he wasn't very intelligent.

"Sis said you'd come here," he said. "She told me you'd do what she wanted you to."

Darci backed up to the door, her hand on the handle.

"You can't leave this house," he said. "Mr. John is going to marry my sister and not that other girl."

"And who is your sister?" Darci asked, trying to inch her way around the door so she could make a run for it.

The man looked at Darci blankly. "You don't know Millie?" he asked after a while.

It hit Darci then that this man with his red hair was the brother of Millie, her red-haired maid. Millie hadn't been on the list that Tula had given them. But then, what did Millie need with love potions? She lived with John Marshall.

For a second all that Darci had heard went 'round in her head. Millie had been angry because she wasn't going to get to go to Lavender's house to work. She was being left behind. There was the time on the stairs when Darci thought someone was watching her and it had made her hair stand on end. Even without ESP she'd felt the malevolence emanating from Millie.

She looked at the man, at his slack-jawed face, and she could feel the love he had for his sister. What had Millie told him about Lavender? About Darci?

"My brother is the lowest snake to ever have lived!" Darci said. "Scum of the earth. Maggots would gag if they fell on his skin."

The man opened his eyes wide and the gun lowered. "Millie doesn't think that. She says that women lead him astray."

"Did you know that Lavender knows about Millie and plans to harm her? Lavender wants John all to herself."

"Miss Shay wouldn't hurt anybody," the

man said, raising the gun again. He looked confused. "Millie told me you'd be on Mr. John's side."

"But I'm not. I wish he was going to marry Millie."

"How could somebody like Mr. John marry Millie? She's the maid."

Darci wanted to yell, Then what does Millie want? but she couldn't think how to put it politely. All she knew for sure was that whatever was going to happen would occur within the hour. She *had* to get to the roof of Lavender's house. With or without this man, she had to get there and stop what was about to happen.

"You don't know my brother like I do. Where is he now?"

"He's all right. He's in the stables, all tied up. When he doesn't go to the wedding, Miss Lavender won't marry him. He'll take my sister away then. He'll live with her like Mr. John's dad lives with that woman."

"Ah, I see," Darci said. "What a clever plan. Millie is always very clever, isn't she?"

"Yes," the man said proudly.

"But sometimes bad people can be more clever than good people."

"Huh?"

"I think that Lavender is more bad than your sister can handle. I think Lavender means to get your sister to the roof of her house and throw her off."

The man stood there blinking for a few seconds and the pistol lowered. He didn't seem to know what to do.

Straightening her shoulders, Darci pulled herself up to her full height — which meant she was about half the size of the man. "I want you to go to the barn and let Mr. John out. He needs to face what he's done. We'll turn him over to the sheriff right after we save your sister from death. Meet me at the church. That's where they'll be."

She saw that she'd completely confused the man, which gave her a few seconds to act. Cursing the giant skirt of the dress, she grabbed handfuls of it, pulled it up, glad for the crinoline underneath, and slipped out the front door. She didn't know if the man would obey her or shoot her, but she had to brazen it out. As she ran, the skirt now up to her knees — which were hidden by knee-length cotton drawers covered in ruffles — she expected a bullet to enter her back.

But she heard nothing as she ran. The streets were nearly empty, most of the people in town now at the church awaiting what was to be the event of the season.

"Please release Jack," she chanted to herself and wondered if she should have made sure the man untied Jack before she took off. But she'd had no time to lose. It couldn't be more than forty-five minutes before the wedding.

She reached the back of the house, saw that the kitchen was packed with people, and had no doubt that if she were seen, someone, probably an ancient aunt, would grab Darci and lock her in a room. No one was going to believe that the bride was about to be killed.

Keeping out of sight, Darci ran behind the stables, her skirt dragging through half a dozen fresh piles of horse manure, as she went to the side of the house and the biggest open window. She had to jump three times before she caught the windowsill, then, fighting skirt, petticoats, and crinoline, she tried to heave her legs up. It took all her strength, but she made it to fall into the bedroom of Lavender's father. Her skirt plopped down over her head and she wasted several minutes fighting the thing down.

As quickly as she could, she righted herself and ran to the door. She could hear people talking downstairs and she didn't know whether to call out to them or not. Would they believe her? If they did, would they help or hinder? If Millie saw a lot of people running toward her, would she panic and push Lavender off the roof?

Outside the door, Darci ran up the stairs to the second floor, then down the hall, looking for the stairs to the roof. No stairs. No panel in the ceiling that could be pulled down.

Frustrated, she made fists and hit her huge purple skirt. Where? she thought. Where could the stairs be? How did she get to the roof? Help me please, she prayed.

Suddenly, she knew. Again, she felt as though someone was helping her. Turning, she ran back down the hall and opened a door she'd opened before. It led into a small bedroom that was probably for a servant. Behind the door was another door and when Darci opened it, she saw the very narrow stairs that led up to the roof.

She had to lift her skirt so high that it was nearly in her mouth, and she could barely see over it.

She opened the door that led onto the widow's walk that surrounded the top of the tall house, and there Darci saw what

316

she had hoped not to see. Millie was standing in the shadows of the stair housing, a gun aimed at Lavender, who was pressed up against the short railing around the edge of the roof.

"She took what was mine," Millie said matter-of-factly, seeming not to be surprised that Darci had arrived. "Now I'll take what she wants."

"Millie, my love," came a smooth voice from behind Darci. It was Jack and he must have been just a few feet behind Darci.

"Jack?" Lavender said, her face beginning to glow. In spite of the situation, all she seemed to think of was Jack.

Jack kept his eyes on Millie, not daring to look at Lavender. "She's not worth it," Jack said, charm oozing from him. "Don't you know the truth about why I'm marrying her?" He was walking toward Millie, past Darci. She could see the raw places on his wrists where he'd been tied, and his knuckles were bloody, so she guessed that he'd fought Millie's brother.

"Don't you know that I *have* to marry her?" Jack said, his eyes on Millie's. "Old Man Shay is blackmailing me. He's going to pay off my debts if I marry his daughter."

Jack was walking slowly but steadily toward Millie, and Darci almost smiled. He'd get the gun from her and everything would be all right.

But a sound from Lavender made Darci look at her. Lavender, tears of pain in her eyes, had her fist to her mouth. She was *believing* Jack!

Darci tried to get Lavender's attention to tell her that what Jack was saying wasn't true, but her movement made Millie glance at her.

"Is this true?" Millie asked.

Darci wanted to tell Millie the biggest lie she could think of, but she knew she had to reassure Lavender, too. "I'm afraid of heights," Darci said aggressively. "Make her get away from that edge."

The bravado had worked with her brother, but it didn't work with Millie. She stepped farther back from Jack, waving the gun. "You stay there," she said to Lavender, then pointed the gun at Darci. "Why was he marrying her?"

"Because he had to," Darci said. "Because our dreadful father has run up bills and they have to be paid off. If they aren't we'll lose the house and everything else. Mr. Shay wants John to work for him, but my brother doesn't want to, so Mr. Shay said he'd pay John if he married his daughter."

As soon as she finished this speech of lies, Darci looked at Lavender and saw that she was believing every word — and she was devastated.

"I saw you last night," Millie said. "I was outside that man's house in Drayton Falls. I saw all of you in there laughing and having a good time. You didn't look like you were being made to marry her."

"I'm a good actor," Jack said, smiling at Millie. "Didn't I keep you in my house so I can visit you whenever I can? As soon as I get this over today I was going to go to you. You know that I love you and always have."

Hearing the man she loved say he loved another was more than Lavender could bear. With her eyes full of tears, her heart full of agony, she turned sharply away from Jack. When her leg hit the little rail around the roof, the wood broke.

For a moment, Lavender floundered, clutching at the air as she tried to get her balance.

Heedless of the gun aimed at him, Jack leaped to save her, but Lavender pushed him away. Throwing his arms wide, he grabbed her as she fell.

Lavender and Jack went over the roof together, side by side, holding each other.

In shock, Millie dropped the gun to the roof and froze in place.

Darci knew she had no time to hesitate. She ran through the door to the stairs, then went down them as fast as she could. By the time she reached the outside, there were many people running, and a circle had formed around the two people on the ground.

She pushed her way through them to see Jack and Lavender lying on the ground, their young, beautiful bodies broken and bleeding — and intertwined.

When Lavender, lying in a pool of blood that was rapidly saturating the ground, moved her eyelashes, Darci went to her and took her beautiful head onto her lap. There was no need to not move the patient; no nineteenth-century medicine was going to save these two.

"He didn't mean it," Darci said to Lavender. "Jack loves you and only you."

"Yes," Lavender managed to whisper. "He died for me." She moved her hand as though she were seeking something.

Reaching out, Darci picked up Jack's hand and put it in Lavender's. She didn't know if he was dead or alive.

There was shouting and Darci looked up through the crowd. The people parted a bit and she saw a man holding Millie's arms behind her back. Darci knew what was ahead for the girl: a trial and a hanging. She well deserved it! Darci thought, but in the next second, she yelled, "No!" The man holding Millie stopped. "You have it wrong," Darci said loudly. "Millie was trying to save Lavender. The two of them fell. It was an accident."

"But the gun?" the man said. "She had a gun."

"It was Jack's — John's gun. He always carries it. Millie is a heroine. She almost fell with them when she tried to save them."

Darci watched Millie's eyes change from rage to tears. The man dropped his hold on her, then held out his arm for Millie to lean on. The crowd closed back around the people on the ground.

"The doctor's coming," Darci heard someone say, then she heard the noise of many people running and shouting. She knew it was the people who'd been in church waiting for this happy couple to walk down the aisle.

Darci knew she had no time to lose.

"What are you doing?" she heard

someone ask as Darci pulled the little silver box from inside her skirt pocket and remove the gold chain from around her neck.

"The doctor's here, let him through," someone shouted.

"Here! Stop that!" someone else said to Darci, but she ignored all of them.

Lavender and Jack's hands were clasped on Darci's lap. Simone had said that all three spirits would need to return together. That meant Jack, Darci, and Millie, who had lied and said she was Lavender. But Darci knew those three spirits were never going to be together. Life was flowing out of Jack and Darci had no more time. Perhaps Lavender's love could replace Millie's hate.

She put the key in the box, put her hand atop Jack and Lavender's hands, then turned the key.

Part Three

2004

Chapter Seventeen

After Darci stopped falling through the void, it took her a long time before she could open her eyes — and even when she did, all she could see were the bodies of Jack and Lavender, intertwined and bleeding on the ground. Her tears started slowly, rolling down her cheeks in silence, then they began in earnest, shaking her body with her sobs.

"Hush," came a familiar voice in her ear, then arms surrounded her, pulling her close. It was Jack and they were on the bed in the blue bedroom in his father's house, the place they'd been when they'd left. Everything was the same — except that everything had changed.

Jack held Darci while she cried, and she felt his tears on her neck.

"She was so sweet," Darci said between sobs. "So innocent. She loved you — and me — so much. She asked nothing of anyone. She . . ."

"Quiet," Jack said, smoothing Darci's hair back from her face. "It's over now. It was over a long time ago."

She pulled back to look at his face, seeing the deep circles of grief under his eyes, but he was alive. "You're home now and safe." She took a deep breath. "When you fell off the roof, did you die?" she asked softly.

"No, I was just in such pain that I couldn't speak or even open my eyes. I think most of the bones in my body were broken, but I knew what was going on. I knew that Lavey . . ." Closing his eyes, he turned away from her.

"How are you now?"

"Fine," he said, moving away so he was no longer touching her. He lifted his arm and turned his hand around in circles. "See, nothing broken. How about you? How are you?"

Lifting up on her elbows, she looked about the room, which seemed familiar and strange at the same time. Everything in the room seemed too bright, too garish. She had on trousers and a shirt and they seemed almost indecent. Lavender, Lavender, her mind kept saying. She'd wanted to prevent the young woman's death, but hadn't been able to.

"I'm fine," Darci said, "but then I didn't fall. I was — Oh!" she said, sitting up straighter. "Oh. I can feel things. I *know* things." She sat up, her eyes wide. "That table over there? A woman used to sit at it and sew and cry for the man she loved. He was killed in a war. See that lamp? It was made by a man who was stealing from the company. See that —"

"I get the picture," Jack said, still on the bed. "If you have your powers back, can we talk to each other with our minds?"

Turning to look at him, Darci sent him thoughts about how heroic she thought he'd been when he'd leaped after Lavender. Jack had made it up to her for all the scoundrel things that John Marshall had done to her.

"Nothing," Jack said. "I hear nothing."

"Then the angry spirit that was around you is gone."

"Both of them are gone," Jack said and looked as though he might cry again. "Lavender's gone from my life and Millie's spirit no longer haunts me. I no longer feel that anger inside of me."

Darci moved a pillow behind her head and leaned back. Before what they'd been through she would never have allowed Jack to stretch out on the bed beside her, but now it seemed natural. Now it seemed like he was the older brother she'd always wanted. "I guess Millie so wanted to be the woman that you were marrying that she believed she *was* Lavender. That's why her spirit lied to us."

"Yeah, I guess."

Darci felt as tired and sad as Jack looked and sounded, but one of them had to be the person who did the cheering up. "Your aura has changed," she said, and tried to keep the joy she was feeling out of her voice. Once again, there was color surrounding him — and she could see it! When she'd first met Jack, his aura had been mostly red, the color of anger, and the more he was around Darci the redder his aura became. But now the anger was gone. Now, in spite of his depression about Lavender, his aura was a lovely blue.

"I'll find Lavey's spirit for you," Darci said, putting her hand on his forearm. "I promise that I'll do whatever I can to find her."

"Before or after you find my father and your husband?" he asked nastily.

"You know, don't you, that now I can give you a killer of a headache?"

Jack didn't smile. Instead, he got off the bed and stood up. "If you make my head hurt, will it take away my thoughts? My memories?" He ran his hand over his eyes. "Love stinks!"

"You're not the first person to say that," Darci said, smiling.

He glared at her. "You had a chance with Drayton. Why didn't you take it?"

"Why did you love Lavender and not any of the many other women in your life?"

"I don't know," Jack said, sitting down on a chair across from the bed. "How long has it been since we had any sleep?"

"Seems like a month or two," Darci said, yawning. "How about if we sleep now and tomorrow we do what we were sent to this house to do?"

"Sounds great to me." He walked to the door, then paused. "Darci?"

"Yes?"

"Do you think you really could find Lavey? Do you think her spirit has been put into another body?"

"Probably," she said, trying to keep her smile intact. She wasn't going to tell him that it was possible that Lavender's spirit could have been put into a man's body or that Lavey was now a cross-dresser, dancing in a gay revue in Vegas. Or maybe she was three years old. Or ninety. "We'll find her wherever she is."

Giving her a smile, Jack left the room.

When she was alone, Darci lay back against the pillows and thought that she'd make a short trip downstairs to Jack's father's bedroom and have another look at those objects hidden in that room. Maybe there was more energy in them than she'd at first thought.

But the exhaustion of the past two days overwhelmed her and she didn't wake until Jack drew the curtains back and sunlight hit her face.

"What time is it?" Darci asked, struggling to sit up, then fell back down when she saw Jack. "I think I need some more sleep, and I know I need some food."

"How about this?" Jack asked, holding a large glass of freshly squeezed orange juice under her nose.

"Mmmm," she said sitting up, reaching for the glass.

But Jack held it back from her. "Or would you rather have this?"

Extending his hand, he held out the iron egg that Simone had given her. The energy Darci felt coming from the egg was like nothing she'd ever felt before. "Gimme," she said, and Jack had to catch the full glass before her enthusiasm made him drop it on the bed.

He sat on the end of the bed and watched her hold the egg, turning it over in her hands, and helped himself to the food on the tray he'd placed on the side of the bed. "Like it?"

"How? Where?" she asked in awe as she took the juice from him. "Tom was supposed to have hidden this. Did you bring it back with you?"

At that, she clutched at her neck and instantly felt that the gold necklace with the key on it was gone.

"Drayton's chain isn't there but the key's in the box." Jack nodded toward the silver box on the bedside table. The key was sticking out of it.

Darci set the juice down, grabbed the box, and removed the key so fast that Jack laughed at her. She looked at him suspiciously. He was fresh out of a shower, had on clean, ironed clothing, and shiny shoes. "What's up with you?" she asked. "Why are you up so early? Where did these things come from and who made breakfast and why do you look *happy?*"

"Dear, dear little sister," Jack said, pushing the tray toward her, and laughing when she held the iron egg in one hand and ate with the other. "First of all, it's two o'clock in the afternoon, and although we think it's been centuries since we were last here, we were actually away only one night. The spell you put on my lazy relatives is still holding. Who would have thought they would make such splendid servants? They've cleaned every corner of this house and have cooked enough food to feed half the neighborhood. If we had neighbors, that is. Dear ol' dad couldn't bear people close to him so he bought everything within a mile of his ugly old mansion."

Jack broke off half of one of Darci's blueberry muffins and ate it. "Homemade," he said. "Who would have thought? I sent my relatives and the food to a homeless shelter."

"Great idea," Darci said, eating strawberries floating in cream. She still hadn't let go of the iron egg. "What about this?" she asked, holding up the egg. "Where'd you get it?"

"Ah. That. Did you forget that under this lady-killer exterior I'm an FBI agent?"

"The question is whether or not the FBI remembers. What did you do?"

"An old-fashioned fax." He paused, smiling. "Funny to think of a facsimile machine as old-fashioned, isn't it? What did you miss the most?"

"My daughter and flush toilets," Darci

said quickly. "Could you stop with the foreplay and tell me where you got the egg?"

"I sent a fax to Greg's home number and told him to send someone out to the church in Camwell and dig up some items."

Darci paused with a bite of quiche to her lips.

"Don't give me that look. It's the FBI, remember? They're used to secrets and the weird and strange."

"Not quite as strange as what you and I've been through."

"Yeah," Jack said, starting to take another muffin, but Darci aimed her fork at his hand. "Actually, I thought there would be two things hidden away, the egg and that crucifix you and Drayton found. I didn't know there'd be more."

"More?" Darci asked, wide-eyed.

"No, just eat. It can wait."

"What can wait? Your headache? Or should I paralyze you?"

"Like you did to Greg?" he asked, smiling. "At the time I was pretty angry, but now it seems funny. His legs were . . ." Jack leaned back on the bed, bent his legs, and drew them up. "Funny, huh?"

"I'll give you to the count of three,"

Darci said, her lips in a tight line.

"Be my guest," Jack said, holding out both hands to indicate the big metal box on top of the table on the far side of the room.

Darci was out of bed in a second. She was wearing her clothes of the day before, having collapsed into bed without bothering to change. There was a mirror over the table and she saw that her hair was sticking up straight, but she smiled when she ran her hand over it. It felt soft and clean, something that she'd dearly missed when she was in 1843.

She looked down at the box in wonder. It was an old accounting box, the kind you still saw in antique stores. This one wouldn't have fetched much money because it was rusty and dented, and smelled of damp earth. There wasn't a lot of energy coming from the box and she wondered why.

"You opened it without me," Darci said petulantly.

"Just once and quickly," Jack said. "I reached in, grabbed the egg, and closed the lid." He was standing behind her and looking down over her shoulder. "I turned the key just to make sure that it was safe. I was a little worried that maybe something awful would happen, since turning keys around you is a bit dangerous."

"*You* caused the trouble with the key, not me. I would have waited before opening that box. Anything bad that happened, was *your* fault."

"We can discuss that later. Open the damned thing!"

"There's no need for cursing," she said, her hand on the lid. "And you know, don't you, that I can tell whether you've lied or not?"

"So help me —" he began, then cut off when Darci opened the lid of the old box.

"Oh!" she said. "Look at that!"

"What?" Jack asked, looking inside the box.

"The light," Darci said in awe. "The light. See it? It's blue. No, it's more than blue. It's . . . it's the exact shade of Henry's aura." There was suspicion in her voice as she said the last. "Devlin! Is that you?"

"Home sweet home," Jack muttered, reaching into the box. "Dead people everywhere. Tell him not to slime around on the antiques. They're valuable."

Darci was watching the light float around the room. "You blocked the energy, didn't you? So help me, Devlin, show yourself so I can kill you! Why wouldn't you help me when I was back in time? Was it Henry who took away my power? Stop it, I say!" The light was going 'round and 'round in a spiral, then started bouncing on the bed like a giddy three-year-old.

"Look at this," Jack said, removing a leather pouch from the box and dumping garnets into his palm. In the next moment he had to sit down, for they were the garnets that had been given to him when Lavender had danced on top of the buckboard. "Will I ever see her again?" he whispered.

Darci didn't tell him, but behind him Devlin had formed himself into Lavender. She was smiling and reaching out to touch Jack's hair. "That's not funny," Darci hissed at the Shape Changer. "Get out of here! Leave us alone!"

The ghostly vision of Lavender looked over Jack's bent head at Darci, the eyes defiant. They weren't Lavender's beautiful, kind eyes, but the eyes of a mischievous spirit.

Darci still had the egg in her hand. She held it tighter, feeling the energy from it flow up her arm, then gradually into the rest of her body. "Go!" she said to Devlin.

Lavender's face looked smug, then it changed to confusion, and in the next second the vision was gone.

For a moment Darci stared at the blank wall.

"What's wrong?" Jack asked.

"I'm not sure." She looked at the egg. "I think maybe I just made Devlin leave the room."

"So?"

"He once told me that when I could keep him from leaving the room I'd be ready. I wonder if the opposite holds true?"

"Ready for what?"

"I don't know what. It's another one of those great mysteries that's been dumped on me. My guess is that it's some kind of test. What else is in that box and who put all this together? Is the crucifix in there?"

Jack dug around in the box and withdrew a little pouch. "Is this it?"

Taking the pouch from him, Darci dropped the crucifix into her right hand. "Oh my," she said. "Oh my goodness. My, oh, my."

Jack watched her standing in the middle of the room, an old iron egg in one hand and the little crucifix in the other. She closed her eyes, bent her head back, then seemed to go into such ecstasy that he was envious. He couldn't take his eyes off her, as her face took on a look of such sublime pleasure that he feared for her life.

He couldn't take it. He grabbed both objects from her hands and put them on the table. "I don't think that's what those things are to be used for," he said primly.

Darci looked like she might cry, but she recovered herself and straightened her shoulders. "Whatever you're thinking, it's not right. They hum and when I put one in one hand and the other in the other hand —"

"Yeah, you start humming, too." He removed the breakfast tray off the bed and started to put the box on the bedspread, but Darci ran to the bathroom and got a towel to set the dirty box on.

"Now," Jack said sternly, "I want you to stop playing around and doin' the dirty with a bunch of magic things and tell me what you feel about this box."

Darci gave a longing look at the egg and crucifix on the table and thought about putting Jack to sleep so she could take some time to figure out what the things did. What power did they have? How did they work with the other objects she had? Or did they? Had Devlin been trying to steal them or protect them?

Sighing, Darci put her hand on the metal box. "Simone," she said. "And

338

Adam. But, no, not Adam. Not much, anyway. Mostly Simone. But Tom did the actual digging. And Tula. Yes, Tula took over after Simone died. Oh!"

"What now?"

"I just felt Simone's spirit. I think she's trying to contact me." Darci looked at Jack in wonder. "I've never dealt with other psychics before. Except for Linc's son. And a few people without bodies. And Henry, of course."

Shaking his head at her, Jack turned his attention to the box. On top was a small leather portfolio tied with silk. As Jack opened it, Darci said, "It's from Adam. He wants me to try to go back to him."

Inside was a small portrait of Adam's wife, Diana, and a lock of her hair.

"She could be you," Jack said, looking at the picture. "She's a dead ringer for you."

Darci took the two items and held them. She knew that Adam hadn't written her a note because he was trusting her to re-member and — if possible — bring his wife back to him.

Darci set the items on the bedspread and looked at the big package that Jack was re-moving. It was a large piece of embroi-dered cloth, folded around what looked to be newspaper clippings. The cuttings were old and fragile, yellowed, dried-out, and damp at the same time. Jack touched them gingerly, knowing they could fall apart at any moment.

He held up a finger to mean, *Wait a minute,* then left the room. "And don't touch those things on the table," he called from down the hall.

Darci picked up the little portrait of Diana and held it. The woman had been very ill when the picture was painted. She'd known it but she'd told no one. Her love for her family came through the picture, and Darci could almost feel Diana's spirit close by. I can find her, she thought, and put the picture down.

Lying back on the pillows, she stared at the items on the table across the room. The egg especially intrigued her. She glanced at the doorway. Maybe if she was quick, she could . . .

When she looked back at the egg, it seemed to be moving. Just a bit, but it seemed to be rocking. "Come to me," she whispered, concentrating on the egg, and holding out her hands. When the egg began rolling slowly toward her, Darci smiled, even though she didn't know what would happen when the egg reached the edge of the table. Would it fall or could she make it sail through the air?

She didn't find out because Jack appeared in the doorway with a pile of photocopies in his hands. "Now we can read them without worrying about the old paper flaking."

He glanced at Darci, saw that she was looking guilty, then turned and saw the egg balanced on the edge of the table. "I don't even want to know what you were doing," he said as he pushed the egg farther back.

"Here, let's read these," he said, moving the chair next to the bed and sitting down. "We'll start with the letter from Simone."

Simone had written that she was going to entrust her son and daughter to put anything pertinent into the box, and she hoped Jack and Darci would someday find it. She went on to say that she couldn't guarantee that anyone past Tula would put items into the box, but at least there would be a few years' worth of information.

The first clippings were about the deaths of Lavender Shay and John Marshall. The town had mourned the loss of the young people for many months.

"Look at this!" Darci said, sitting up straighter. "It says that Mr. and Mrs. Ulysses Shay, in memory of their only child, adopted Miss Millicent Brown, who would now be known at Millicent Shay." Darci looked at Jack in wonder.

"Here's another one!" he said. "It's dated 1848. 'Miss Millicent Shay has been . . . ' " He looked at Darci. " '. . . accepted as one of only twelve women students in the Boston Female Medical School. Miss Shay has been quoted as saying that she's entering medical school in memory of her dear friend and adopted sister, the late Miss Lavender Shay.' "

Jack looked away for a moment. "Lavey wanted to study medicine, but her father said no. He said ladies didn't touch sick people. I guess he learned what was important in life."

"Here's another one," Darci said. "It says that Dr. Millicent Shay opened a free medical clinic for women and children in the Appalachian Mountains in 1854." Darci put down the paper and looked at Jack.

"I wonder what happened to her brother?" he asked.

"He stayed with Millie through everything. He only trusted her. He drove an ambulance wagon during the Civil War."

"Does it say that in there?"

"No, I just know it." She grinned. "I *know* it. Isn't that wonderful? I don't have to read about it or strain my mind trying to figure it out, I just *know* it."

"How nice for you," Jack said, sarcastic. "Okay, what's next? Let's see. Here's one on Adam Drayton, of Drayton Falls." Silently, he scanned the article, then put it down on the bed. "What else is in there? What happened to Tom and Tula?"

"Give it to me," Darci said softly. "I want to see what happened to Adam."

"I don't think —" Jack began, then, as Darci stared at him, he had an overwhelming compulsion to give her the paper. He had to, couldn't stop himself from handing her the paper.

"Oh no," she said. "Not Adam." As her eyes teared up, she handed the copy of the article to Jack so he could read it aloud.

About three weeks after Lavender's and Jack's deaths, Adam Drayton had been discovered by Fontinbloom Nokes inside the tunnels with a keg of gunpowder and fuses. Adam was planning to blow the tunnels up. Nokes shot Adam Drayton, killing him with one shot. At his trial, Nokes said that before he died, Adam had said that he was going to blow up the tunnels so they couldn't be used for evil later.

Darci fell back against the bed, tears in her eyes. "Adam did it for us. Because of us. If we hadn't gone to him, he'd never have known about those tunnels and would never have tried to destroy them."

"Wait," Jack said. "Look at this one. It's dated 1850, and it says that the old garnet tunnels are said to be haunted. 'There have been two serious attempts by Fontin-bloom Nokes's heir to see if there are still garnets to be mined, but the sounds of two men arguing and of a single gunshot that echoes through the tunnels scares all workers away. Frustrated, Mr. Nokes's nephew boarded up the entrances to the tunnels and went back to his country of origin, Australia. He left warnings that all trespassers would be prosecuted.' "

"I wonder if the tunnels stayed empty until the witch began to use them?" Darci asked. "All those years of sitting there empty when they could have been destroyed."

"But wouldn't she have just gone somewhere else?" Jack asked. "There are lots of tunnels around the world, and it was my understanding from the file I read that she had special reasons for wanting your sister-in-law. And you," he added softly.

She held up her left hand. "Nine moles. She'd foreseen that the person who would kill her had nine moles on her left hand."

"Too bad she could foresee anything," Jack said.

Darci's eyes widened. "Take away her ability to foresee the future and she wouldn't know what was going to happen to her or who was going to do it."

"If you take away her ability to foresee the future, do you still have a witch?"

Darci thought of several replies to that, but before she could say anything, the phone rang and Jack answered it.

"Greg, old man, how are you?" Jack said cheerfully. "No, nothing's wrong with me, I'm just in a good mood, that's all. Now, now, Greg, that's not true. I've been in a good mood before."

Pausing, he smiled at Darci. "Uh, no," he said, "we haven't made any progress in finding my father. Yeah, I know where my relatives are. No, Darci didn't do it. She was asleep. *I* sent my relatives to work in the homeless shelter. Yeah? That clean, huh? Send them to another one. Yeah, we'll report to you if anything happens." He hung up the phone.

"Let me guess," Darci said. "Greg wants us to do what we're supposed to be doing."

"More or less," Jack said, sitting back down and looking at her. "Can you still feel my dad?"

"Yes. He's safe. In fact, he's more comfortable today than he was yesterday. He's waiting for something. I'm not sure he's a prisoner at all."

"Ah."

"What does that mean?" Darci asked.

Jack looked at the two objects on the table. "You have that healing ball with you?"

"Always. What do you have in mind?"

"I wonder what would happen if we went into that room in my father's bedroom and took all these things in with us."

"You mean the box and key, the crucifix, the egg, and the Touch of God?"

"Yeah. If two of them together hum, what do you think all of them together would do?"

"Find spirits?"

Jack jumped up. "I'll get these two, you get the other two. Meet you in the secret room."

"I'll get there before you do," Darci said and took off running.

Chapter Eighteen

"I don't know what they are or what they do," Darci said, looking at the eight objects before them.

"You're the soothsayer," Jack said, "so why don't you know?"

"You're the FBI agent, so why don't *you* know what these things are and where your father got them? Was he involved in some nasty occult thing? Maybe he's a warlock."

"If you knew my father, you'd know how absurd that was. And how do we know these things have anything to do with the occult? Maybe he just liked them. Or maybe they were here when he bought the house and he doesn't know about them. The previous owner died and my father bought the house from his heirs, so maybe the last owner put them in here."

"Is the man you're now defending the same man you used to despise?"

Jack grinned. "Yeah, but back then I . . ."

"Had a very angry spirit around you."

He cocked his head at her. "You don't think that schizophrenics have other spirits around them, do you? And what about those people who hear voices?"

Darci decided it was better not to answer that question. They'd spent over an hour in the hidden room and had been unable to figure out anything. She had four objects that hummed in a way that even Jack could feel, but their vibrations didn't increase when she put them next to the four objects that had been in the room. They had all eight of them lined up on the shelf beneath the gory painting and had looked at them in every way possible. They'd even tried to fit them together.

"What interests me is that there are like items," Darci said. "It's like in the coloring books of my daughter and my niece. Match the objects."

Jack put the Touch of God next to the blue glass ball, the iron egg next to the stone egg. The ivory statue of a Biblical-looking figure went next to the crucifix. The key went next to the silver box. "We know that those two go together."

She looked at him suspiciously. "You're not thinking of putting the key and that box together again and going back to Lavey, are you?"

"No. I had a night to sleep on it and the lack of dentists began to scare me. I think I'll bide my time and let you find her here."

"Hope she's what you want," Darci muttered, but Jack wasn't listening. He was looking up at the painting of the man with the branding irons.

"We haven't paid any attention to this thing. Other than probably being worth millions, I wonder if it has any significance."

"Except to scare away evil spirits?"

"Or to attract them," Jack said, his face pressed to the wall as he looked at the back of the frame of the painting. "Get that side and help me get it down."

It took them several minutes, as the painting was large and heavy, but they eventually managed to get it down and set it against the far wall. When they turned they saw a little door set into the wall.

"We're good," Darci said.

"The best."

"My abilities and your devious mind."

"Glad to be of service," Jack answered.

They both expected a lock to be on the little door, but there was none. But before he opened the door, Jack made Darci stand as far away as possible. "Last time we used anything from this room we ended up a couple of centuries from here. I don't want to take any chances with this."

"All caused by you," Darci said, but she smiled at him.

Slowly, he opened the door and looked inside.

"What's in there?" Darci asked from close behind him. "I don't feel any energy, so it can't be too bad or too powerful." Disappointment was in her voice.

Jack put both his hands into the compartment and withdrew an object that he set on the shelf. Both he and Darci peered at it.

"What is it?" he asked. It seemed to be a blob of fired clay, rather like a kid's science project of a volcano, except that it looked as though it had been knocked around a bit. There were some holes and dents in the surface.

"I have no idea." Darci ran her fingers over the thing. "It seems to be ceramic, but then again it's almost like it's metal. It's certainly cold enough to be metal. I feel absolutely nothing from it. Which means that it's probably the most powerful thing I've ever touched."

"How do you figure that?"

"Even pencils give off energy. Trees do. Someday I'll tell you a story about a tree in Alabama that was angry because a car had hit it. I — What are you doing?"

He'd picked up the stone egg and was holding it near the thing they'd found in the cupboard. "This has to work with these things. Somehow, they must be related."

Idly, Darci picked up the iron egg and did what Jack was doing, moving the egg around the sides of the object. It was fairly large, about a foot square and eighteen inches high. Since it exactly fit into the cubbyhole behind the painting, she was sure the cabinet had been made for the object. But who had done it? And more importantly, why?

"Oh!" Darci said as the iron egg suddenly stuck to the blob. "Oh!"

Jack looked at her, then at the thing, then at the egg he was holding — and they had the same thoughts at once.

"They fit," Darci said. "The objects they had are the right shape and size, it's just that —"

"They aren't magic. They're not the correct items."

"Exactly," Darci said. She glanced at the blue glass ball as she picked up the clear

Touch of God. "Whoever collected these wanted this, but settled for that." When the Touch of God was grabbed by the base, she grinned at Jack.

He picked up the silver box and waved it around the base. In a second it, too, found its place.

When he picked up the key, Darci grabbed it out of his hand. "Oh, no you don't. I have a feeling that sticking that key back into that box activates the whole thing, and we're not doing anything until I figure out what all this means."

"I guess I should be grateful you're saying 'we.'" He picked up the last item, the crucifix, and looked at it. "What do you think will happen when I put this into place?"

"I don't know," Darci said, shaking her head. "It would be too much to hope that it would give me a way to find my husband."

"Or my dear ol' dad." Reaching out, he touched the ceramic base to turn it, then drew back his hand. "Ow! That thing is hot."

Darci held out her hand over the base, but didn't touch it. She could feel the heat of what had, minutes before, been ice cold. "Oh yes," she said. "We are doing something now."

"I just wish I knew what," Jack muttered as he moved the crucifix around the base. When it was sucked into place, he put his burned fingertips into his mouth, then took Darci's arm and pulled her to the far side of the room. "Stand back," he said, one arm raised as though he meant to put it over his face in protection. The other arm he put around Darci, ready to throw her to the floor and fling his body over her.

Nothing happened. The base just sat there on the shelf, the four items attached to it, but it did nothing.

"Look outside and see what year it is," Jack said.

"You look outside." Darci moved toward the base and the objects, which were so hot she couldn't touch them. "There's energy here," she said softly, "but I don't know what kind. I think — Oh! Here's the problem. There's something missing."

Jack looked at the side of the base and there was indeed a small, oval indentation that would fit another object. He looked at the three objects left on the shelf. None of them would fit the space. "The key?" he asked.

Darci had the key in her hand, held tightly as though she thought Jack was going to wrestle her down and take it from her. Cautiously, while trying to keep the key away from the box, she held it near the depression. "Nothing," she said. "I feel nothing at all, not even any energy."

"May I?" Jack asked. "And don't give me that look. I'm not going to use it on the box." As he held the key near the base, he said, "It's cooled off." The base was yet again cold to the touch. When he tried to remove the iron egg, it came off easily and went back on easily, but the base didn't heat up again.

"We're missing something," Darci said again. "I can feel it, but I just wish I knew what it was — and what happens when we put all the objects together."

"Isn't there somebody — alive or dead — that you could call and ask?"

"I think that right now we're on a higher plane than what anyone I've ever met knows about. Although Henry probably knows —" Her head came up. "Devlin!" In the next second, she said loudly, "Devlin, come here!"

Jack, his eyes on Darci, thought he saw a movement behind her so he looked up. "I'm not sure, but I think I just saw the paneling blink." He was swallowing hard, working to keep himself from running from the room.

Turning quickly, Darci narrowed her eyes at the wall. "Come here this minute and stop that!"

Gradually the room filled with a blue smoke that neither Jack nor Darci could smell, and from the smoke formed the upper half of a body — a large body with black hair and a huge black mustache. The figure loomed over them, its massive arms crossed over its huge chest.

"What do you want of me?" came a voice that filled the room, making it vibrate. Neither of them flinched.

"I really am going to tell Henry on you," she said, glaring up at Devlin.

Jack glanced up at the figure with one eye. "Too bad you can't make him get into a bottle and we could put a cork on it."

When he said these words, Darci saw the light that was Devlin flicker. It was only for a split second, then he was back to being a looming giant, trying to intimidate both of them. "Say it again," Darci said to Jack.

"Say what? You mean about putting an evil genie in a bottle?" When he looked up at Devlin, he, too, saw the tiny flicker. Jack stood up straighter. "I said," he said loudly, "that if you can control him, as you now seem able to do, maybe you can command him to put himself inside something, like, say, a bottle. Then we could put a cork in the bottle and leave him there. That would be great, wouldn't it? You'd have your own personal genie whenever you wanted him."

While Jack had been talking, Devlin had been growing smaller, looking like a balloon that was deflating. He still looked like a child's image of a pirate, but he was smaller. By the time Jack finished, Devlin was the size of Darci, much smaller than Jack.

Darci stood there blinking at Devlin for a moment, then said over her shoulder to Jack. "Now what do I do with him?"

"Beats me. You're the psychic, not me."

"Technically, I'm not a psychic since I can't read minds. And I really can't tell the future, so I'm not a soothsayer, as you called me. I think maybe I'm —"

"A procrastinator," Jack said. Both of them were staring at Devlin, who was defiantly staring back, but saying nothing. "Ask him something."

"What will happen if we get all the pieces put into the base?" Darci asked.

"You'll have to find that out for yourself," Devlin answered.

"He really is an evil genie, isn't he?" Jack said. "Where do you think we can find one of those jeweled bottles like they have on TV? Or should we just use an old beer bottle?"

When Devlin shrank a bit, as though he were frightened, Jack smiled maliciously. "How much does he have to obey you?"

"I don't know," Darci said. "This is new to me. I don't even know why he now has to obey me. Have I gained some new power, or have these objects given me more power? And if so, which one or what combinations?" She looked at Devlin. "Either you start talking or I will let him go get that bottle and a cork."

At that, Devlin seemed to recover himself somewhat. In a flurry, he changed into coveralls with prison stripes, with a ball and chain around his ankle. He was a mousy-looking little man who portrayed innocence and persecution.

"Really!" Darci said. "You are too dramatic."

Devlin, with chained wrists, gave her a slight bow. "If you put all the pieces together, the egg will open."

"What's inside it?" Darci asked quickly.

"Something that you can use."

"Wasn't there an empty wine bottle from last night?" Jack asked.

Devlin, now seeming over his fear,

turned himself into an Elizabethan courtier, all velvet clothes, with jewels winking. "If you have everything, you will be able to find all that you want to find." He gave a sly look. "Even to finding the two people you seek."

Darci drew in her breath. "How?" she whispered.

"As you so clumsily found out, the box opens to allow you into the past, but with the box alone you have no control as to where you go in history. This time you were guided by another, but soon you will be on your own."

"You mean when Henry dies, don't you?"

Devlin shrugged. "Your earth bodies die easily and quickly."

"So how do I choose the time periods and what do I do when I get there?"

Devlin gave a little smile. "You will discover what you need to know when you need it."

"I've about had enough of this psychic mumbo jumbo," Jack said, stepping toward Devlin. "Darci doesn't seem to know the power she has, but I could help her find out. I'm not nice like she is, so either you tell us all of it, or I'll have her stick you in an aspirin bottle."

Darci narrowed her eyes at Devlin. "Or maybe I'll put you in a string cage with a rock inside it."

At that, Devlin almost disappeared. All they could see of him was a shape in the paneling and two eyes — eyes that were full of fear. "If you put all the objects into the vessel, you will be able to see what can be changed, and what will happen if the world is changed."

"You mean I'll be able to see that if I go back in history and say, stop Pearl Harbor from being bombed, I'll see the repercussions to today?" Darci asked.

"Yes," Devlin said simply.

"Can she see what would happen if Lavender lived?" Jack asked.

"Yes."

"What else does it do?" Jack asked.

Devlin stuck his head and shoulders out of the wall. Now he was wearing a soldier's uniform of about 1870, and he had a big metal horn to his ear, as though he were deaf. "What? I can hear no more. I have been given my orders and I can tell no more. You must find the missing piece on your own." He looked at Jack. "You know what and where it is."

"I do not —" Jack began.

"How can I find the spirit of someone

from the past who is living today?" Darci asked quickly.

"You can do that now," Devlin answered, then grinned. "My other master calls. He, too, has a bottle." With that, he disappeared.

"I can't say that I really *like* that . . . whatever he is," Jack said as he looked at Darci, who was thinking hard. "*Can* you find spirits now?"

"Maybe. I never tried to find one."

"What have you done with your abilities all your life?"

Darci sighed. "Truthfully? I've spent most of my time trying to keep people from finding out what I can do."

"Interesting."

"What does that mean?"

"You use your powers as little as possible, then your husband is taken from you and you're thrown into situations that require that you learn a lot about your powers. And you find a whole lot more power. That's interesting."

"I just wish I could find out who's guiding all this. I think it's Henry, but it could be someone I've never met."

"What you want to know is, who's turning power over to you."

"What makes you say that?"

Jack smiled. "That Devlin. You told me that you had no power over him, but now you seem to be able to command him — to an extent."

"Except when his 'other master' calls and he has to go."

"Exactly," Jack answered. "Are you hungry? No, sorry I asked. How about some lunch?"

"Great. And you can tell me what and where the missing object is that we need to put into that base."

"Haven't a clue," Jack said, holding the door open for her. Ten minutes later they were in the kitchen with a plate full of sandwiches and steaming cups full of homemade soup. "Who would have thought my aunt was such a great cook?" Jack asked, mouth full.

"Chrissy," Darci said. "She made all this."

"That so? Maybe she's found her calling."

"No, she'll end up old, alone, and unhappy."

"I thought you couldn't tell people's futures," Jack said.

"I can't. Except for sometimes. Sometimes I have visions about people and —"

Jack used his napkin to wipe his hands,

then held out his palm to Darci. "Tell me what you see."

"My goodness!" she said. "Your hand has turned purple."

It was a second before Jack got the joke and in that second he turned pale. His expression showed how much he'd come to trust Darci in the last days. "For that one, you're dead meat," he said, then lunged for her neck.

Laughing, Darci tried to paralyze him, but she couldn't concentrate, so she managed to only paralyze three fingers on his right hand — which made Jack laugh too.

And that's how Greg Ryerson found them. Darci had been so involved with the objects they'd found and laughing with Jack that Greg had been able to enter the house without her feeling it.

When Jack and Darci looked up and saw Greg, they were both startled into speechlessness.

"Jack, may I see you alone?" Greg asked stiffly, his body language revealing what he thought of the two of them laughing together.

"I'm sorry," Darci whispered to Jack, meaning that she was sorry for having neglected what she'd been sent there to do, and sorry that Jack had been caught playing on the job.

Jack winked at her, then followed Greg into the library.

Greg waited until the doors were firmly closed. "You want to tell me what the hell is going on here?"

"You wouldn't believe me if I did tell you," Jack said.

"Try me."

Jack opened his mouth to tell Greg that he'd been time traveling, but he changed his mind. "Did you come here because you were worried about me?" He was flexing his hand, getting the blood to flow after Darci's paralyzing of his fingers.

"I came here because we received a ransom note."

"For Dad?" Jack asked, taking a seat in one of his father's leather chairs.

Greg stared at his friend. "What's happened to you? You've never called him 'Dad.' It's always been 'the old man.' So why this title now?"

"Who knows? Maybe I'm getting mellow as I get older."

Greg narrowed his eyes at Jack, willing him to talk — and confide, but Jack was silent.

"Tell me what you've heard."

"I'm being told as little on this case as

possible so I don't know what's up. I was told that a ransom note had been sent."

"To whom?"

"That's just it," Greg said. "I don't know who got it. The president of the United States, for all I know. All I was told is that fifty million is to be delivered somewhere tomorrow at six p.m."

"Why so low?"

"I was told that it's the cash on hand your father has."

At that, Jack and Greg looked at each other and laughed. And with their laughter their coolness toward each other vanished.

Greg took a seat across from Jack. "You want to tell me about . . ." He nodded toward the kitchen. "Two days ago you two hated each other and now you're playing footsie. You two spend the night together?"

"Yeah, but not like you mean. She eliminated someone for me."

"Killed them? Look, I don't think the bureau's going to —"

"It wasn't like that. Could we drop this? There's nothing between Darci and me — at least not like you think. If I'd had a sister she would have been it."

"Your sister? I thought you thought she was a freak."

Jack turned angry eyes on Greg. "Don't

ever let me hear you say that again. She can do certain things, but she's not a freak."

"Jack, you've got to keep this in perspective. I like the woman, personally *like* her, but she can kill people with her mind. She can paralyze people. She can —"

In an instant, Jack grabbed Greg's collar and lifted him up. "Keep your mouth shut about things you know nothing about."

"You planning to kill me, Jack?" Greg asked softly. "Because if you are, let me call my wife and see if my insurance is paid up."

Blinking, Jack dropped his friend, went to the bar against the far wall, poured two glasses full of cold ginger ale, and gave one to Greg. "Let's stop this, all right? Some things have happened that I can't tell you about, and as for Darci, she's been through a lot, can do a lot, and —" He downed half his drink, then looked back at Greg. "Tell me what you came here to say."

Greg was looking at his friend in speculation. "I've been told that the bureau wants you off the case."

"Why?"

"I don't know. I'm considered too lowly to be told much of anything. You and I and your little sister out there . . ." Greg was making a joke but Jack didn't smile. "Darci

Montgomery is also to be removed from the case and she can go home. Tomorrow evening at six a specially delegated agent will deliver fifty million dollars in cash to a drop spot that I don't know about. It's hoped that the kidnappers will release your father after they get the money."

"And how likely do you think that is?"

"About as likely as your thinking that a psychic is the sister you never had."

Jack ignored the comment. "The way I see it, my father has until six tomorrow to live — if he isn't dead already."

"That's what the psychic is supposed to know, isn't it?"

"You call her that one more time and I'll make you sorry," Jack said.

"I'm shaking in my boots."

Jack gave Greg a hard look, but Greg just smiled in return. "So what have you two been doing these last days that's made you so chummy?" Greg asked.

"Popping in and out of time," Jack answered quickly. "This whole thing about Dad is fishy, but I can't figure out what's wrong with it. Darci says that Dad is comfortable. Does that mean he has clean underwear every day, or does it mean he's up to something in the murky world of crime so he's with friends?"

"*Your* dad? Do you forget that I sit behind a desk all day? I do little but read files, and with my clearance I have access to all sorts of documents. There's nothing in your father's life that isn't squeaky clean."

"Oh yeah? Then how come he has a hidden room off his bedroom that's full of magic objects?"

"Does he?" Greg asked. "How interesting. Let's go see it."

Jack looked as though he might be about to get up, but he stopped himself. "There's an object I need to find. It's about this big and this wide." He held up his fingers to indicate something small, no more than an inch in either direction.

"That covers pretty much all the rocks in the driveway."

"It's asphalt, not gravel," Jack said, not smiling.

"What about in the bottom of the fish pond?"

"Could be. Nothing stand out in your mind?"

"Jack, what the hell are you up to with that woman? Is it sex? Is she so great in bed that you can't think straight? Or has she hypnotized you with her powers? That's it, isn't it?"

"It's not anything like that," Jack said. "She and I . . . Darci and I . . ." He waved his hand. "I can't go into that. I need to find something. I need this small thing."

"Couldn't you give me a better description than just the size? What's it made of? What's it used for? Where and when was it made? Is it natural or manufactured?"

"I don't know," Jack said. "But I'd guess that it's an important thing, not just a rock lying at the bottom of a pond." Pausing, he smiled. "Besides, Darci has the rock locked up." When Greg started to say something, Jack waved his hand. "That's not important now. I need to find this thing so I can find Lavender."

"Lavender? Like the color? Someone named their kid Lavender?"

Jack put his fingertips to his temples for a moment. "Does Dad have a safe deposit box and can I get into it?"

"I have no idea and the only way you'd be allowed to get into the box is if you declare who you really are. You ready to do that?"

"No, of course not. Although I don't feel the . . ." Jack smiled. "I no longer feel the anger at that idea that I once did. Where's the money to be dropped?"

"No idea." He was staring at Jack, trying

to figure out what was wrong with him. "I'll give Mrs. Montgomery a ride home, and you can go back to what you were doing when we picked you up. You remember? Before the jewelry store?"

"That seems like a thousand years ago. Six tomorrow, huh?"

"You can't interfere in this, Jack. No one knows that you're Hallbrooke's son and if you want to keep it that way, you have to stay out of it." He looked at his watch. "I have to go. I have a meeting with the big shots. Look, Jack, take my advice and let this go. Nothing's been said, but I agree with you: There's something not right about this kidnapping — if that's what it is. None of it sits well with me. First I'm told to use the psychic, then I'm told to find you, then —"

"Then what?"

Greg ran his hand over his eyes. "All I know is that something's not right. What's in this hidden room?"

"Nothing that would interest you, just some old stuff. An iron egg, for one thing."

"Right. An iron egg. Your father found an iron egg and hid it in a secret room off his bedroom."

Jack raised an eyebrow. "Actually, an old woman gave Darci the egg back in the nineteenth century, but Darci couldn't take it with her, so she had Tom the driver hide it by a church in Camwell, Connecticut. Remember the box you had the agents dig up? The tunnels are in Camwell, you know. They were haunted by Adam Drayton and Fontinbloom Nokes because Adam gave up his life to try to save a lot of people in the twentieth century."

"All right," Greg said, getting up. "I can take a hint. You don't want to tell me anything. Should I take Mrs. Montgomery home or do you want to?"

"I will," Jack said, opening the library door. "She'll stay here tonight. Don't give me that look. Do you guys at the bureau think of nothing except sex? She's my guest and — What's that look for?"

They were at the front door and Greg had stopped to look back at Jack. "What about that ruby that was on your father's watch?"

Jack had no idea what Greg was talking about. "Ruby?"

"Or whatever it was. Remember the red stone he had hanging from that old pocket watch he used to carry?"

Jack's face lit up. "Yes! I remember. You and I used to say it was the key to all his wealth."

"You said that if he lost it he'd lose all his money."

Jack clapped Greg's shoulder. "If that stone is what we need, the irony may be that I might have been right. Maybe his wealth *is* connected to it."

"Someday I want you to tell me every word about what you and Mrs. Montgomery have been up to these past days. And I want to know why you've had such a change in personality. She hasn't exchanged your spirit with somebody else's, has she?"

Greg meant the last as a joke, but Jack didn't seem to think it was. "Yes, in a way, maybe she has," he said so seriously that Greg took a step back.

"Are you all right?"

"Fine," Jack answered, then put his hand on Greg's shoulder and half pushed him out the front door. "There's something I have to do now, so I'll see you later."

"What about your relatives?"

"Relatives?" Jack asked, his mind elsewhere.

"You know, Chrissy, Holcombe, your aunt and uncle? Your aunt's dreadful husband? You remember them, don't you? I'm not convinced that they aren't involved in your father's disappearance."

"Darci would know that, so they aren't. Where are they now?"

"Cleaning their fifth homeless shelter," Greg said, smiling.

"Great. Any orphanages around? Send them there. Just keep them out of here. Oh, wait, you might send Chrissy back here to make us dinner."

"Chrissy?" Greg asked. "Cook? Dinner?"

"Yeah. Look, Greg ol' friend, it's been great fun, but I have to go. Darci and I . . . I mean, I have some things to do."

"You wouldn't go after your father, would you? I was told to tell you that you are *not* to become involved in this ransom for your father. You're to stay out of it. Completely out of it."

"I wouldn't think of disobeying an order," Jack said, smiling at Greg, then shutting the door before he could say another word.

Three minutes later, he was back in his father's bedroom, where he knew Darci would be. "I think I've found it," he said, not bothering to explain what "it" was. Turning, he went into the room where the objects were. In the middle of the shelf was the base and on it were four objects. Picking it up, Jack examined the small, empty depression in the side. "My father has always carried an old-fashioned pocket watch and on the chain of it is a little red jewel. It's cut round, not brilliant."

"Cabochon," Darci said.

"Right. The ancient way of cutting a stone. I think it would just about fit in this space."

"So," Darci said, as she left the room, "it's all coming into place. I knew I was directed to you and to your father, and now I'm beginning to understand why."

"Yeah," Jack said seriously. "You're to find the woman I love."

"And the man I love," Darci said, smiling back at him, then she grinned. "So where do you think your father and this jewel are?"

Taking her arm in his, he led her down the hall. "That, my dear little sister, you and I are going to have to find out. You said you have visions and go into trances. I want you to do that now and tell me everything you see. Between your power and my —"

"Knowledge of low-life, underworld characters —"

"Exactly. Between the two of us, we should be able to find out where Dad is."

"And if we can't find him, we'll call my cousin Virgil."

"A cousin from Kentucky? Some redneck with a pickup and a rifle?"

"He's in Hollywood and he lives in my mother's mansion."

"Mansion? Your mother?"

"Jerlene Monroe."

Jack stopped walking. "Your mother is Jerlene Monroe? The movie star? The one who won the Best Supporting Actress Oscar this year? The woman the American people voted as the most beautiful person in the world?"

"Did you think my mother had three teeth and smoked a corncob pipe? And why didn't you know about her? I thought you read my file."

"I guess they forgot to tell me that little detail." He was being sarcastic. "And your cousin lives with her?"

"Don't start turning Yankee on me. My mother isn't having an affair with her cousin. Just because we're from the South doesn't mean — Anyway, Virgil has a natural ability to deal with the lowest of the low."

"He should work for the FBI."

"He'd have a heart attack if anyone asked him to do that. He works for my mother and keeps people away from her."

Jack smiled. "Think I could meet her someday?"

"As long as I don't have to go with you."

"Ah."

"What's that supposed to mean?"

"You and I, little sister, are a therapist's dream." At the library door he stopped. "Let's do it in here. Ready?"

"I hope so."

Chapter Nineteen

"If you start crying again, I'll . . ." Jack said under his breath to Darci.

"I am not crying. I just got a little misty, that's all. And besides, *what* would you do to me?" She glared at him.

"Nothing," he said, checking his rifle yet again. Concealed in his black clothing were three handguns, two knives, four round throwing disks that Darci called "ninja things," and a vial of poison. "I don't know what you're so upset about, just because you're wearing a black leotard. You don't look bad. If you weren't like a sister to me, that is." Grinning, he slipped another knife into a concealed pocket of his loose trousers.

"I'm not upset about that, it's just the memories that wearing a catsuit bring back to me. I bought mine when I was with Adam the first time. I wore it into the tunnels that first night. That all seems so very long ago now."

"Come on, buck up," Jack said. "You looked into this and you said it would be all right."

"I can't see the future. If I could, I'd look ahead and see how I find Adam, then I'd go get him."

"That's my girl! Not if, but how. So, now, dry your eyes and let's get out of here."

"I'm not sure we should do this," Darci said. "Maybe Greg and the FBI should handle it."

"We've been through this enough," Jack said. They'd spent yesterday afternoon and into the night with Darci putting herself into trances to see what she could concerning the whereabouts of John Barrett Hallbrooke. Jack had given her everything he could find that his father had touched so she could feel the items and see what she could.

"Safe," was the main word that she came up with. His father was safe. Finally, they'd begun looking at what was around Hallbrooke in her visions. It was confusing because Darci's visions often showed where he'd been in the past. She'd touch an item on his desk and know that he'd liked or not liked the person who had given him the gift.

"He's rich but people outdo themselves in trying to give him expensive gifts," Jack said as he picked up an eighteen-carat-gold paperweight. By 10:00 p.m. they gave up on the office and went into his bedroom to try to find something personal, but they found nothing. At midnight they went up to the attic and found a trunk full of old photos.

Darci held some pictures of Jack as a young man up against his face and compared them. "Big change," she said. "Did they have to use a jackhammer to get rid of that nose?"

"By the time the steering wheel smashed it flat it was easy to remove the pieces."

She held the photo tightly. "I can feel the anger in you back then, and I can almost see Millie's angry spirit hovering over you."

Jack didn't say anything, but she knew how glad he was to be rid of that spirit.

Darci held up another photo. "This is your mother, isn't it? She was very pretty."

Jack had seen few photos of his mother and knew little about her. Although he'd asked his father many times, he'd never received any answers. "So this is where you tell me that he loved her and my father's coldness is from his misery at her death."

"No," Darci said. "As far as I can tell, your father was born cold. Displays of emotions disgust him. I think he feels emotions, but he didn't feel any love for your mother."

"So why'd he marry her?"

"To procreate himself, of course. Continue the species."

Jack laughed. "Failed there, didn't he? He got me instead."

"I don't think he feels that he failed," Darci said softly.

"What about my mother?"

"Money. All she wanted was money. She was much colder than your father. Truly cold. She resented every penny your father gave to anyone besides her." She looked at Jack. "I think you were lucky that the mother you knew was Greg's mother."

Jack took a photo and looked at it. His beautiful socialite mother. She'd died in a swimming accident when he was only three. "How did she die? I was never told the details."

"Drunk," Darci said. "With two lovers. She jumped into the swimming pool, but it had been emptied for the spring cleaning. She broke her neck."

"Ah," Jack said and put the photos down. It was probably much better that he didn't remember her, and hadn't grown up near her.

At 3:00 a.m. they at last got a break. They'd been going through Jack's father's filing cabinets. Everything was meticulously organized, all of it boring and predictable.

"No receipts for objects believed to be magic," Jack said as he tossed aside a folder with a single piece of paper in it.

When a little charge went up Darci's arm, she reached for the folder, but she didn't open it. "This is where your father is."

"Yeah?" he said, opening the folder. Inside was a deed of ownership to a house about a hundred miles from where they were. "I know this place! I've been there. I went with Greg and his parents when we were eight." He looked at her. "You're sure he's here? He owns this, so I doubt if the kidnappers would have taken him there."

Darci put her hand on Jack's arm. "I think we should tell the FBI where your father is and let them go get him."

"This isn't the place the FBI knows about? Where the ransom drop is?"

"No. I can't feel that it is. I think they believe he's in another state. I'm not sure about that, though. I got all I could from

Greg's glass, but he didn't know much."

"If I tell the FBI, they'll go in with a dozen men and helicopters and my father will end up dead. I'm going in to get him myself. Alone."

"Without me?" Darci asked innocently.

"That's right. Without you."

"And how do you plan to leave me behind?" She stared at him for a moment, then Jack sneezed.

When he was on his twelfth sneeze, he said, "You don't play fair."

"Never have, never will. Let's get some sleep and tomorrow —"

"By tomorrow night my father will be dead," Jack said, blowing his nose. "Whoever has him is going to get the money today and kill him tonight. And, no, don't try to find that out psychically. I've worked on cases like this for years and I know what happens."

Darci sat back on the floor and looked up at Jack. She'd felt a lot of things that she hadn't told him about. The main thing was that Jack *needed* to do this. He needed to find his father if he was to heal old wounds. And he also needed Darci. She wasn't sure what was going to happen, but she could tell that he needed her to make it all happen.

In the end, Jack had his way and they started getting dressed. It would be the foggy light of dawn by the time they got there, so Jack had them both dress in black. They'd rummaged in Chrissy's room and found a black one-piece leotard that Darci could wear.

Jack had been unprepared when Darci looked at herself in the mirror and started crying. While he was dressing and loading himself with weapons, she sniffled and talked about Adam and their life together.

He got her into the car, with a cooler full of food in the back, and he drove while Darci talked. After the first few minutes he managed to direct her away from her wondrous life with Adam Montgomery and onto what happened when she'd helped the actor Lincoln Aimes find his son.

What interested Jack was that she could read Aimes's mind when she touched him. Since he'd met Darci they'd had no time to explore what could be done between the two of them. Irrationally, Jack felt a wave of jealousy over Aimes and Darci.

"Aimes's son can heal?" Jack asked in wonder.

"Yes. I think he has more ability than he knows about, but he's learning. He lives in East Mesopotamia, Georgia, with his grandfather, and Linc visits him often. I think there's a young lady there who Linc likes. She's not impressed with his beauty or his success."

"What else does he have?" Jack asked snidely.

"Kindness. And he wants to make the world a better place to live."

Jack didn't say anything for a while, but a small idea entered his head. Maybe if he and Darci found the missing piece and put it in that base, maybe if what Devlin had said was true and Darci could change history, maybe she'd want some help. Maybe he and Darci, and maybe this Aimes character, could work something out. Helping people, something like that.

"What are you thinking about so hard?" Darci asked.

"What will you do with your life if you don't find your husband?"

"I refuse to think of that," Darci said, looking out the car window for a moment, then she looked back at Jack. "I think I need to stay home with the girls. I need to quit running all over the world."

"Not to mention throughout history."

"Right," Darci said softly, turning away.

Jack slammed on the brakes, then backed up. "This is the road I want. I don't want to use the paved road or they'll hear us."

It was still night and Darci dreaded trying to walk through the woods in the dark. Jack pulled the car off the overgrown dirt road, parked it, then piled long branches on top of it. If you weren't looking for it, you'd never see the car.

Getting out, Darci immediately knew that there were people near them. Not too near and she couldn't tell how many, but there were people, hiding and waiting for something. For them? Or for the FBI?

She put her finger to her lips for Jack not to speak, then she pantomimed that there were people near and pointed in their direction. Jack shaped a house with his hands and pointed the same way as the people. She nodded in understanding.

Crouching, Jack started down the old roadway, Darci close behind him. Over the leotard, she had on one of Chrissy's jackets, the sleeves rolled up. It was big, bulky, and cumbersome.

It seemed to take them forever to go the mile or so before they could see the roof of the cabin. The sun seemed to be trying to make up its mind whether or not it wanted to show itself. When the first drops of rain hit Darci's face, she knew that the sun was going to retreat to somewhere warm.

Jack, gun drawn, motioned her to move beside him. Seeming to be oblivious to the rain that was starting to come down harder, he flattened himself against a muddy bank. When Darci hesitated, he threw his arm around her shoulders and pulled her down beside him. She managed to keep her face out of the mud, but her chin sank into the oozy mass.

Jack motioned for her to tell him where the men were. She knew they were men by the feel of them. There were at least four of them and they weren't evil, but they were out to do harm. She felt that the men were very excited and were looking forward to whatever was coming.

Putting her mouth close to Jack's ear, she whispered, "It's *you* they want."

Nodding, Jack motioned for her to stay down while he went up the bank alone. He meant for her to stay safely behind the hill.

She shook her head vigorously and clutched onto his jacket, forcing him to get back down. She pointed to a tree at the top of the bank. She would sit there and use her mind to help him. She motioned that she'd paralyze them. She watched Jack as he seemed to try to decide if paralyzing men was considered fair play or not.

She glared at him, letting him know that she could always keep *him* from going after the men.

Jack gave her a little smile, then crawled up the hill on his belly. After he made sure that he saw no one, he motioned for Darci to come up. He helped settle her under the tree, even to dumping wet leaves over the lower half of her body. When he felt that she was camouflaged enough, he started to leave, then turned back and looked at her.

On impulse, he kissed her forehead, then he turned and disappeared into the rain.

Darci drew up her knees to her chest and concentrated, using her mind to find the other men who were out there. One of them knew that Jack was near and was beginning to move toward him. How she wished she could warn him!

Concentrating, she tried to stop the man who was going after Jack. At the same time, she tried to paralyze the men who were much farther away, but the distance was hindering her.

And this time, she had no help.

In spite of herself, the vision of years ago, when she'd killed the witch and her cohorts, came back to her. The more Darci concentrated, the more she seemed to be transported back to that night. She'd never told anyone, but what she'd done that night was to use the energy of the captive children. Later, everyone had told her what a saint she'd been to put the children to sleep so they saw nothing of what happened, but that hadn't been what Darci had done. She'd taken the energy of the children, their fear, their loneliness, their yearning for the comfort of people who loved them, and she'd added it to her own powers.

In Darci's mind it had been those children who'd killed the witch and the others. The children had so wanted their freedom, had so wanted to *live* that they'd allowed Darci to take their auras from them. They had allowed Darci to take their anger and hatred and fear, and blend it with her own powers, until Darci was in possession of a ball of rage and fear that could have killed a thousand people.

That night when she'd started, when she realized that she could take the energy she saw around the children and use it, it was as though spirits that were trapped in the tunnels began to wake up. Darci had been blinded by what was going on. Her eyes couldn't see, but her mind had seen and felt a thousand spirits running toward her. They flew through the air, gathering, crawling, floating. They'd filled that room until there was nothing but the energy of spirits.

The witch had known. The three others, merely peons to do her bidding, felt nothing, but the witch had felt it all. "You think you can defeat me," she'd cried. "I have beaten you before and I will do so again."

Her words, meant to intimidate, had the opposite effect. The energy — black, angry energy — increased. Darci had been weakened physically by what was being done to her. And her mind wasn't at its peak, either, for she'd been told that Adam was dead. Somehow, with some magic object, no doubt, the witch had been able to cut Adam off from Darci so she couldn't feel him. When she'd been led into the chamber, she hadn't cared whether she came out alive or not. It had seemed that her whole life had been such a struggle that she was no longer willing to continue. With Adam, she'd seen what life could be, but if he were taken from her, she'd return to being alone.

It had been the children who'd revived her. A cage full of them. Like little animals, all heaped up together, most of them too young to speak. They couldn't speak, but they could feel, and the cloud of black and red auras above them told of their rage and their tears.

Darci was pulled past the cage and she saw the colors around the children and thought, If they don't give up, I won't, either.

She'd told Jack that she didn't know what she could do, but when the chips were down, she'd found out what she could accomplish. When Linc had been killed, she'd used a holy object and the love of two people long dead to bring him back to life.

And in the tunnels she'd found that she could take other people's energy — their very souls — and, with their permission, use it.

That night she'd been able to speak to the children with her mind. Maybe it was because they were so young and so newly arrived from being with God, but they heard her and, one by one, they'd sent her their anger. And as each child parted with the energy that kept him alive, he fell down into a coma, and Darci knew that if she died, so would they. People cannot live long without their life forces.

But Darci didn't die. She gathered the energy from the children who still had bodies, and she accepted the energy from those people the witch had killed before, and she turned it all against the witch.

Her three henchmen had been easy to defeat, but the witch had never so much as blinked as they fell at her feet, their brains gone. It had taken more, it had taken all Darci had and more to bring that woman down — and after a while Darci knew she was losing. She could feel the life being drained from her as the hatred of hundreds used her body to send their rage to the witch.

It was at the end, when Darci knew that she could hold out no longer that, suddenly, everything stopped. In an instant, she found herself outside her body. She could see herself standing there, glaring at the witch and the witch glaring back — and she could see that evil was winning. The absolutely pure evil in the woman was feeding on the good in Darci — and the woman was winning.

But as Darci stood there, bewildered, looking at herself, she felt a warmth to her right and turned to see a bright light. She put her arm up to shield her eyes, but when the warmth increased, she lowered her arm and smiled. There in that light was such a lovely-feeling life. It was what she was sure heaven felt like.

Opening her eyes, blinking, she looked into the handsome face of a man with dark, curly hair. She didn't know how, but she knew who he was: Saint Michael, the archangel who ruled the earth. He was dressed like a Roman soldier, with chest armor and a leather skirt that showed his strong legs.

"We are pleased with you," he said. "And you will be rewarded."

Darci just stood there staring at him and smiling. He had a wonderful feeling about him and she hoped he would welcome her into heaven when she got there.

"Not now," he said softly. "I will see you here later. For now we have something for you to do."

He smiled at her again, then he was gone, and Darci was back in her own body. Her head hurt and her body was giving out, but she knew then that she was going to win. The sure knowledge that she could not fail gave her new energy. She doubled her concentration. There was no more holding back, no more thinking that she had no right to take a human life.

She smiled at the witch, then she took a step back, and she let the others come into her fully. She let their hate and fear take over her body completely, and that anger went from her into the witch.

Darci would never forget the look on the woman's face when she realized that she was going to die. It was surprise more than anything else. She had begun to think that she couldn't be defeated; she'd begun to think she was immortal.

In the last second, the witch opened her arms as though to embrace all the hate that she had caused, and the spirits around her clasped her to them, covering her, making her human body part of their bodiless spirits.

Darci thought she was used to spirits and what other people thought was strange, but even Darci's eyes widened when she saw the spirits pull the witch's soul from her body and lift it out. They took it away to a place that Darci didn't want to see, and when the spirit was gone, the witch's old body collapsed to the floor, dead.

For a moment, Darci opened her eyes and looked around her. It was quiet in the tunnels. To her right was the cage full of children, sleeping now, their auras once again with them, auras that were now blue and green, one creative little fellow's yellow, one daredevil's aura pink and red.

Smiling, Darci thought how good it was to see them well and healthy once again. She also thought how good she felt, a bit tired but not much. Turning slowly, she looked at the black end of the tunnel where she'd seen the angel. Or had she? Had she really and truly seen an angel? *The* angel? And what was it he'd said? At the moment she couldn't remember.

I must find Adam, she thought, then turned as though she meant to walk away. But she didn't take a step before she collapsed on the floor, and that's where Adam found her hours later.

When she awoke, she was in a hospital and Adam and many of his family were there. Even her mother was there, which surprised her more than everything else that had happened. Seeing an angel was more normal than seeing her beautiful mother at her bedside. And Darci was told that her mother had risked her life to save her.

Now, smiling, Darci came out of her trance of memory and was horrified to realize that she hadn't been protecting Jack. The man stalking him was very close to him. Jack! she said in her mind, wanting to warn him, but now that Millie's spirit was no longer around him she couldn't talk to him with her mind. Not directly anyway, not with words, and not quickly. She knew that if she took her time she could send him thoughts, but the ability to actually talk between minds was something she shared only with her husband. And she couldn't paralyze the man, for he was too far away.

She knew that there was only one way to help Jack and that was the human way. Standing up, she put her head back and gave a scream that she knew would carry through the forest.

She felt Jack turn, felt that he had stopped his assailant, but in the next minute a shot rang out. Darci felt a burning pain in her shoulder and thought, My goodness, I've been shot.

In the next second she couldn't see or hear anything.

"Don't die on me now, baby sister," Jack said as he bent over her, gently smacking her cheeks. "Wake up, honey."

"I'm all right. I'm sorry. I didn't do what I was supposed to do."

"As far as I know, you haven't done what you were supposed to do since the day I met you. Tell me, in your whole life, have you ever done what you were *supposed* to do?"

She tried to sit up, but Jack pushed her back down to the damp ground. "Where are they?" she asked.

"Don't you know? I was hoping you'd be able to tell me. I took two of them out, but there's another one around. Tell me where they are."

"I don't know," Darci said, holding onto the front of Jack's leather jacket. "I can't feel anything. This can't be happening to me again. What year is it?"

"Ssssh," Jack said, ducking down to lie flat beside her. "I heard something."

For a moment they lay in silence, listening, but there was nothing they could hear over the gentle rain.

"Listen to me and don't argue. I've got to get both of us out of this. There's something really wrong about all of this and I mean to find out what it is."

"Jack," Darci said softly, "are you hurt?"

"Just a little. Probably less than you are, but it's enough that I'd like to get out of here."

"Help me up and we'll go to the car."

"Can't. They took it. I saw them drive off in it about thirty minutes ago."

"How long was I out?"

"About an hour. I didn't want to wake you as long as you were dry, but the rain has seeped in under even this monster tree, so we've got to move."

"Jack, contact the FBI. Greg would be here in minutes."

He acted as though she hadn't spoken. "I haven't heard anything since they took off in my car. Listen to me and this time I want you to obey me. I'm going to carry you to a shed that's behind the cabin and leave you there."

"Leave me! Then what do you do?"

"What I came here to do: Find my father."

When Darci moved, she felt the pain in her shoulder, but she didn't want to look at the wound. If it was bad she feared she wouldn't have the courage to go on. "I'm going with you. There's someone else here. I can feel him."

"Sure it's a 'him'?"

"Yes. Very male and powerful energy."

"That's got to be dear ol' dad," Jack said with a smile that held a trace of pride in it. "Can you stand up? I'm going to put you over my shoulder and carry you that way. I'm afraid that my left arm is out of commission for the moment."

"Jack, please . . ." Darci began as he helped her stand. "I can walk. I can —"

She broke off when Jack knelt and put

his shoulder into her stomach. The next second she was being carried through the forest. Since she was touching him, she could feel some of what he'd just been through when fighting off the three men. Without any help from me, Darci thought in disgust.

"Jack, I really am sorry," she said against his back.

"Save it for later." Moments later he stopped at a little toolshed in the back of the cabin she'd only seen from a distance.

"There's only one man in there," she said as he set her down. "And he's in no danger. And I no longer feel any danger around here. Not to you and certainly not to the man inside."

"Nice try, Mrs. Montgomery," Jack said, "but I think I'll do it my way."

"Okay," Darci said, looking at him hard and willing him to not be aware that she was going to be right behind him. "I'll just wait for you to come back and get me," she said demurely, again willing him to believe her. She'd let him down once, so she wasn't going to let him down again.

Jack set off toward the back of the cabin, through tall weeds and piles of winter logs. Not far behind him, Darci walked slowly, being careful not to move her arm. It hurt, but she willed herself to ignore the pain.

When Jack reached the back door to the cabin, he plastered himself against the wall, gun drawn, then grimaced when he saw Darci across from him. He pointed at her, meaning for her to stay where she was.

Jack silently tried the latch of the door; it was unlocked. Raising his fingers to Darci, he counted to three, then grabbed the latch and flung the door open. A yard behind him was Darci.

Inside, it was an ordinary-looking cabin, with the requisite pine furniture and a stone fireplace on the far wall. Sitting in the middle of the room was a man with a newspaper before him. They could see his profile and he didn't look up when Jack burst in with his gun drawn.

"There's hot coffee in the kitchen," the man said in a deep voice. "And hot chocolate. Help yourself."

"Mr. Hallbrooke," Jack said in a very official voice. "I'm FBI agent Jack Ainsley, and I have come here to rescue you."

The man turned a page of his newspaper, but he didn't look at Jack. "Don't be ridiculous, John. You're my son and I brought you here."

Before Jack could reply, Darci said, "There's a car coming."

The man turned another page of the newspaper. "I can assure you that it's safe. They're my men."

In the next moment they heard a car skid to a stop just outside, and seconds later the front door of the cabin burst open. Two men rushed in, one of them with his arm in a sling that looked to have been made from a T-shirt, the other one with a gun drawn — and aimed at Jack's head.

"We have him, sir," the man with the gun said.

At that, the man in the chair gave a bit of a laugh, slowly and neatly folded his newspaper, put it on the table beside the chair, then turned and looked at Jack and Darci.

While this was going on, Darci took the opportunity to freeze the two men across the room into place. She even froze their lips so they couldn't speak. Maybe she'd be able to make up to Jack for her earlier failure.

"Is this one of your games?" Jack asked his father, hostility in his voice.

"Is it a game to want to see my only child every now and then?" the man asked.

Darci was concentrating on holding the two men in place, but she managed to sneak a look at Mr. Hallbrooke and saw that he looked very much like Jack had before his surgery. He wasn't a handsome man, but he was a powerful one. He had an aura that was so solid it could have been made out of bricks. And it was green, the color of money.

"Your only child?" Jack said, his voice rising in anger. "Did you care when your only child was killed?"

"I would have, yes," Mr. Hallbrooke said calmly, "if my child had been killed. You don't think that *I* was told the same lie as the public was, do you, John? Surely you must have guessed who paid for your expensive plastic surgery. You don't think that the U.S. government brought in the finest surgical team ever assembled, do you?"

Darci could feel Jack's temper rising. She couldn't turn enough to see his aura, but she was sure it was now shooting little flames of red and yellow. "Could those men leave now?" she asked tiredly. "Holding them is beginning to give me a headache."

She had the satisfaction of feeling John Barrett Hallbrooke the second turn his full attention onto her.

"Get those bozos out of here!" Jack yelled at his father.

"You may go," Mr. Hallbrooke said over his shoulder, then turned in surprise when the men didn't obey him immediately. For several moments he stood there looking at them. Their eyes were the only things they could move and they were nearly shouting with them.

"Darci," Jack said at last. "Please let the men go."

With a sigh of relief, Darci released the two men. They gave her a look she'd seen too many times, then ran out the door.

Jack was glaring at his father, and Mr. Hallbrooke was staring at Darci as though he wanted to put her in a jar and study her.

"Mind if I have some of that chocolate?" she asked. When neither man answered, she went across the room to the little kitchen and helped herself. When she looked back, neither man had moved. So much for having removed Jack's anger, she thought. On the counter was a box of pastries and she helped herself.

While she ate and drank, she did her best to calm both men down. For all that Mr. Hallbrooke seemed disconnected and calm, she could feel that he was very excited. Why? she wondered, then smiled. He was excited at seeing his son again.

Her pastry finished, Darci refilled her

cup and went back into the living room. "Could one of you help me get this jacket off?"

Angrily, Jack started to snatch the jacket from her, but when she yelped in pain, he stopped.

"If you've hurt her mind," Jack said to his father, anger shooting out of him, "I'll see that you answer for it."

Puzzled, Mr. Hallbrooke looked from one to the other. "Her mind?" He looked at Darci, now sitting on the couch. "What are you?"

"The usual," she said, waving her cup as though to say she wasn't any different than anyone else.

"I must say, John, that I wasn't told you were working with . . . with . . ." He didn't seem to have a label for Darci.

Jack turned to his father. "You want to tell me what this is all about? Why have you wasted my time, and the time and money of the bureau?"

"Since when did you become conscientious? Coffee?"

Darci concentrated on Jack, telling him to sit down and talk, and to stop acting like a rebellious schoolboy, but his aura had begun to weaken and his face was turning pale. "Jack?" she asked. "Are you all right?"

She saw that there was a small pool of blood on the floor under Jack's left hand. When she looked up at Mr. Hallbrooke he was also looking at the blood. Externally, he didn't move, but his aura shot out around him in alarm. Well, she thought, you big fat liar. You act like you don't care, but you're mad about your son, aren't you? You probably loved it every time he told you off.

Darci went to Jack and helped him sit down. She sent the thought to his father to get help, but he was already on his cell phone.

"I'm fine," Jack said, "just a little weak. Give me a minute and I'll be all right."

Darci glared up at Mr. Hallbrooke. "You meant to play a joke but those bullets were real," she said.

"They weren't meant to be," Mr. Hallbrooke said softly, and Darci could see the anger under his cool exterior. Had he meant for the men to use rubber bullets? Tranquilizers? Why had they disobeyed?

As Darci thought these questions, she was sure that everything in her life now had a reason. If she and Jack had been shot with real bullets, then that was what was meant to happen. The words "blood sacrifice" came into her head, making her shiver. She put her mind back onto the matter at hand.

Mr. Hallbrooke calmed down and looked from one to the other, seeming to wonder what they were to each other. "Help is coming."

Suddenly, his face lit up as he looked at Darci. "I know who you are. You're the —"

"Say it and you'll never see me again," Jack said.

"I wouldn't demean myself by repeating something from a tabloid, if that's what you mean." He looked back at Darci. "You're the one who helps the FBI, aren't you? Have you found your husband yet?"

"No," she said, "but I have some leads. Mr. Hallbrooke, you don't happen to have your pocket watch with you, do you?"

"Yes, of course I do." He reached into his pocket and pulled out the watch. He wasn't wearing sweats or corduroy like most city people who spend time in the country, but had on a well-tailored tweed suit, complete with necktie.

Taking the watch, Darci held up the red cabochon jewel for Jack to see. "Think it'll fit?"

"Perfectly."

"Might I ask what that will fit?" Mr. Hallbrooke asked.

Jack was trying to hide his pain, but Darci could tell he was feeling faint from it. Maybe she shouldn't try to calm him down. "Where the hell did you get all those things in that hidden room?" he half yelled at his father.

"Hidden room?" Mr. Hallbrooke asked, sitting down on the couch across from Jack. For the first time he looked bewildered, not in control of the situation. "I have no idea what you're talking about."

"The room off your bedroom," Darci said, removing the jewel, then handing the watch back to him.

"Ah," Mr. Hallbrooke said, sounding just like Jack. His lips curved into what might possibly be called a smile. "That was there when I bought the house. The electricians doing the rewiring found the room. I have no idea what it was for or what the things inside it are. I bought the house and contents from the previous owner's heirs."

"And that?" Jack asked, nodding toward the jewel.

"I liked it, so I put it on my watch. Would you mind telling me what this is all about?"

Darci started to answer but the sound of a helicopter stopped her. Mr. Hallbrooke

hadn't bothered with an ambulance finding its way to the cabin; he'd called for a
chopper.

"I think we should discuss all this later,"
Mr. Hallbrooke said, standing up.

Jack made a lunge to take the jewel from
Darci, but she pulled it away. "After you
get patched up," she whispered.

Mr. Hallbrooke went out the front door
to the helicopter.

"You're awfully calm about this," Jack
said, putting his arm around her shoulders
as she helped him to stand up.

"One of us has to stay sane and since
you're making a fool of yourself —"

"Excuse me?" Jack said. "A fool, did you
say? Let's see, I just got shot trying to
rescue a man who didn't need rescuing in
the first place. And what about those men
I shot? Did they deserve that, no matter
how much my father pays them? And what
about you? How's your shoulder?"

"Fine," she said, then reached inside her
jacket and pulled out the Touch of God. "I
brought it just in case we needed it. I stuck
it in my upper pocket and I'm pretty much
well."

"Give it to me," Jack demanded, but
Darci pulled it back. Jack looked hurt that
she wouldn't give him the healing stone.

They were at the door now and the helicopter was making so much noise that they could barely hear each other. Mr. Hallbrooke was talking to the pilot, who was nodding in agreement.

"Jack!" Darci yelled up at him. "Everything that's happened has led us to something else, right?"

"Yeah."

"So I think you *need* to go to the hospital. If you're healed, you won't need to go. And, besides, your father has some things he wants to say to you."

"Such as?" Jack asked, practically sneering.

"He's tired and he wants you to work with him."

"You're crazy."

"He loves you."

"You're insane."

Darci saw that Mr. Hallbrooke was coming toward them, so she spoke rapidly. "Trust me. I know that your going to the hospital with him is important. Stay with him. He's dying to tell you something, or offer you something. He did all this kidnapping because he knew you wouldn't come to him unless you were forced to do so. Listen to him."

Jack was looking skeptical, but Darci

stood on tiptoe and kissed his cheek. "Do it for me, big brother? Can you trust me on this? I'll go to the hospital in a couple of days and you'll have a miraculous healing, but for right now you need to be the wounded hero."

That made Jack smile. "Yeah, well, okay, but you're going with us, right?"

"I . . ."

"And you'll wait until I get out of the hospital before you put that jewel on the base, right?"

"Oh . . . uh . . ."

"Darci!" Jack said in warning as his father approached. "So help me, if you do anything when I'm not there I'll — Oh, no you don't," he said as her eyes became pinpoints of concentration.

"Help!" Darci yelled and Mr. Hallbrooke hurried forward. "I think he's fainted."

Mr. Hallbrooke caught his son and held him upright as the pilot came running. "Paralyzing him would have hurt his wound, wouldn't it?" he asked her.

Darci's face turned red. The man caught on quickly. She couldn't help a small smile and a nod.

The pilot and Mr. Hallbrooke half carried Jack's inert body to the helicopter, then got him inside and strapped him in. Darci stepped away.

"Go with us," Mr. Hallbrooke yelled over the noise of the chopper.

She shook her head. "I have something I must do. Do you have a car?"

Without a question, he tossed her a set of keys, then climbed in beside his son. "What about you?" he yelled, motioning to her shoulder.

"Healed," she said, and couldn't resist pulling her shirt to one side to show him the wound that had closed now.

Mr. Hallbrooke drew in his breath, and his eyes opened wide.

His astonishment made Darci laugh as she stepped back and let the helicopter rise into the air. She waited for a long while, until all was quiet again, then she went in search of the car that fit the keys.

"Where is she?" Jack asked when he was being wheeled down the hospital corridor on a bed.

"Mrs. Montgomery?" his father, walking close beside him, asked.

"You know exactly who I mean. Where is she?"

"She said she had something she had to do, so I gave her the keys to my car."

Jack closed his eyes for a moment. "I'm going to kill her."

"I think perhaps she might be able to prevent your doing that."

Jack looked at his father. "How much do you know?"

"Not nearly enough, and I can tell you that I plan to find out a great deal more."

"You won't be able to," Jack said, smiling at the thought that there would be something his father couldn't find out. "No one knows about the things that happen in her life."

"Except you."

"Not even me. I know what she and I have done, but —"

"Such as?"

Jack chuckled. "You wouldn't believe me if I told you." Looking up, he saw the face of the male orderly pushing the bed. It was a uniform he didn't recognize. "Where is this place?"

"You don't think I'd take my son to the local emergency room, do you? You're in a private clinic and you'll be meeting with my private physician."

"I should have guessed. You know that there are people out there dying because they have no health care?"

"Perhaps you should set up a free health

410

care service in this country."

Jack looked at his father suspiciously. "Now we're getting to the heart of the matter, aren't we? I give up my job to work for you."

"It's a possibility."

"And that's what this is all about, isn't it? The truth at last."

"Mrs. Montgomery tell you?"

"Yeah," Jack said, unable to suppress his smile, but the movement sent pain up through his shoulder. He really was going to kill Darci. She could have healed him with her little glass ball, then the two of them could have fit the jewel into the base.

And then what? he wondered. What would happen then? Would the world go up in smoke? Or had Devlin been telling the truth and Darci would be able to look at history?

"Here's where I have to leave you," Mr. Hallbrooke said as they came to closed double doors. Throughout all of it, the man had never lost his stiff formality, had never bent from his rigid posture. "When this is over, you and I will talk. I have something to discuss with you."

"Yeah, sure," Jack said. "And we'll toss a ball around in the backyard."

"I hardly think —" Mr. Hallbrooke

began, then gave that tiny smile. "Yes, I see. Perhaps we'll talk about that hidden room and what's in it. I didn't quite tell the whole truth. I removed some of the items from the room. Perhaps you can use them to blackmail Mrs. Montgomery into doing what you want her to do."

For a moment Jack looked at his father with his mouth agape, then he let out a laugh that could be heard all the way down the corridor. "Now I know where I got everything," Jack said. "Sure, Dad, we'll talk as soon as we can." The orderly pushed the bed through the doors.

"Dr. Shepard will be here in a minute," the orderly said.

"Glad to hear it," Jack said, closing his eyes, trying to think about all that had happened in the last few hours. His father had faked a kidnapping to get his son to come after him. "What made him think I'd do it?" Jack muttered.

"You say something?" the orderly asked.

"No, just mumbling." Jack tried not to think of Darci and how she'd betrayed him. If she'd used that ball on him, he could be with her now. They could be trying to find Lavender. Instead he was on a bed, weak, light-headed, frustrated that he couldn't do anything, and angry that his father had played him for a fool.

"I'll go see if I can find the doctor," the orderly said and left the room.

When he was alone, Jack suddenly missed Lavender so very much. In the few days since he'd seen her, he'd tried to keep so busy that he couldn't think about her — or remember her. But now that he was incapacitated, all he seemed able to do was think about her. He remembered her eyes, her sweet ways, the night she belly danced atop the wagon. He remembered holding her hand while they both died. He hadn't told Darci, but after they'd returned to the twenty-first century, he'd remembered the time after he and Lavey had fallen. He remembered the long, long fall down, remembered the crash onto the hard ground. He remembered touching her. He knew exactly when her spirit left her body, and he'd willed his to go with her. They'd held hands and looked down at their bodies on the ground, then they'd drifted into the light, happy at last.

"Here, now, none of that," said a gentle voice, and a soft tissue wiped at the tear that had trickled from Jack's eye. "We'll have you up and about in no time."

Embarrassed, Jack opened his eyes to look into . . . into Lavender's eyes. He stared, unable to blink. Her head was turned slightly away from him, but he could still see her eyes. He gasped loudly.

"I know," she said as she cut away his jacket to get to the wound, "purple eyes are strange."

"Lavender," he said hoarsely.

"That's what I say they are, too." Her attention was on his arm, not his face. "But the kids all say they're purple. Now hold still, this might hurt a bit."

Jack could only look at her; he couldn't speak. There were physical differences between her and the Lavender he'd known in the nineteenth century, but he knew who she was.

"You're a good patient," she said, then turned and, for the first time, looked into his eyes.

For a moment, they stared at each other, unable to speak, just looking at each other in silence.

The swinging doors opened with a crash. "Mr. Hallbrooke is outside and he's antsy. Wants to know what's going on," a man said. When the doctor didn't answer, he said, "Doc! Earth to Dr. Shepard. Come in, please. The man who owns the hospital has asked a question so it must be answered."

"Uh . . . yeah," she said after a while and finally broke contact with Jack's eyes. "Mr. Hallbrooke."

"Yeah, the head honcho. The big daddy." He glanced at Jack on the bed. "What do you have to do with Hallbrooke?"

"He's —" Jack hesitated. Whatever decision he made at this moment would be forever. He wouldn't be able to take it back. "He's my father," Jack said at last.

"Yeah? I thought he was childless. I heard —"

"You heard too much," Dr. Shepard snapped. "Now go tell Mr. Hallbrooke that his son is doing fine and he'll be —"

Reaching up to the side of the bed, Jack put his fingers over hers. She didn't look down, but her neck became very pink. She straightened her shoulders. "Tell Mr. Hallbrooke that his son needs a great deal of rest — and many tests. I think he's going to have to be in this hospital for a great many days."

The orderly looked from Jack to Dr. Shepard, back again, then he smiled. "Sure thing, doc. You're callin' the shots. I'll tell him that his son will be well looked after. Very, very, very well looked after." Chuckling, he left the room.

When they were alone, Dr. Shepard

looked at Jack in embarrassment. "I didn't mean to hit on the boss's son," she said. "I mean, I don't usually —"

"You don't by chance know how to belly dance, do you?"

Her eyes widened. "I started taking lessons for Middle Eastern dance when I was only six."

Closing his eyes, Jack smiled. "Ever hear of a stone called Nokes garnet?"

She reached into her blouse and pulled out a chain that held a pendant of what looked to be a five- or six-carat stone. "My favorite, but most people have never heard of them. How did you —"

He still didn't open his eyes, but his smile grew broader. "Where did you grow up?"

"Camwell, Connecticut, and if you say one word about witches I'll let another doctor work on you."

Jack had no intention of saying anything about witches. Opening his eyes, he looked at her. "Do you have a first name?"

"Lillian," she said. "And you?"

"Jack, short for John Hallbrooke the fourth. Do you mind?" They both knew he was asking her if she minded that he had a father who had too much power and far too much money.

"I don't mind," she said softly. "Now, let's look at that wound. I wouldn't want you to die now that I've found you again."

Jack smiled, knowing that she had no idea she'd said "again." She'd found him "again." As he watched her, he forgot all about Darci and the jewel and the magic objects. Jack knew that he was where he should be, doing what he was supposed to be doing, and, most of all, he was with who he was supposed to be with.

Smiling, he closed his eyes again. At last, all the anger he'd held inside of him all his life was gone.

Chapter Twenty

Darci took her time when she got back to the Hallbrooke house. She knew she needed to sleep, but her adrenaline was pumping too hard for her to be still.

The first thing she did was sit down in Mr. Hallbrooke's bedroom and visualize that no one would disturb her. She made sure that if anyone showed up, he wouldn't come into the house.

Holding the jewel in her hand tightly, and the papers Simone had left her under her arm, and a tray with a big bottle of fruit juice and a glass in the other hand, she went into the hidden room. For a while she stood looking at the base with the artifacts stuck to it. After setting down the things she carried, she put the Touch of God back into place, then smiled when the base grew warm. She felt it grow warmer by the second, and when she held out the jewel, it was almost greedy in the way it drew it into place.

Once all the objects were on the base, Darci stepped back, smiling with deep satisfaction. In her heart, in her soul, she knew that she had finally come to the right place. If she was ever going to see her husband again, now was the time.

The base began to hum in a pleasant, happy way, and it grew so hot that she could feel the warmth all through the room.

When she picked up the key to the silver box, she was almost afraid, but she let out her breath and told herself to calm down.

Slowly, she put the key into the hole in the box, then waited. What will happen now? she wondered.

In the next instant, to her right, against a wall of plain paneling, a tiny drop of what looked to be water appeared. As Darci watched, the drop grew and enlarged until it was a huge round surface, wavy at the edges, but clear in the middle.

Cautiously, she reached out to touch it and saw her hand disappear. Quickly, she drew back, almost afraid that her hand had been taken from her. When she saw that her hand was all right, she put it back in to the elbow, and when that was safe, she put her face into the circle to see what was in there.

What she saw was history — if that were

possible. Scenes of time seemed to be whirling about her. Here a horse-drawn carriage, here an automobile that drove even though it had no wheels, there a castle, there a cave dwelling. When a toothless man leered at her, she drew back to the safety of the room.

She poured herself a large glass full of cran-raspberry juice and thought about what she'd just seen. For a moment she thought of commanding Devlin to appear so she could question him, but she didn't want to have to deal with his arrogance and his eternal body changing.

Putting down her glass, she went to the circle and looked at it. "I want to see Adam Drayton with his wife," she said, then stuck her face into the circle.

Before her was an idyllic setting of apple trees in bloom and Adam Drayton teasing a young woman who looked very much like Darci. With her powers intact, Darci knew that her guess had been correct: Diana was ill and it was her heart. There was something wrong with one of the valves, a hole in it perhaps.

Drawing back, Darci smiled. Yes, she could see the past. But what she needed was to be able to see what would happen if the past changed.

She put her face back into the circle. "I want to see what the world would be like if Lavender Shay had lived."

To her disappointment, all she saw was the world as it currently was. She could see nothing different. But that was good, wasn't it? she thought. If Lavey lived, it would change nothing.

She looked back into the circle. "Let me see Camwell, Connecticut, three years after Lavender does not die." It was an awkward way of stating it, but that's what she wanted.

To Darci's horror, Camwell seemed to be mostly charred buildings — and she knew that Millie had been the cause of the fires. Curious, Darci looked back at the shelf in the hidden room and saw that all the papers that Simone had left her were gone. Millie had burned down the church. "Where is Tom?" she asked, and was shown a gravestone.

Stepping out, Darci had to think about what she'd seen. She'd wanted Lavender and John Marshall to live and have a happy life together, but if they did, the anger of Millie would hurt a lot of people. She felt bad about this, but at the same time she felt good. She and Jack had changed history for the better. They'd changed history in a small way, for what did one town burning down matter? But what they'd done had made a big difference to some very deserving people.

She looked back at the circle. "Show me the witch in 1992," she said. If Millie burned Camwell down in the 1800s, perhaps the witch . . . no, it seemed to have no effect on the witch. She was still in the tunnels and still had Adam's sister as her captive.

Darci drank more juice and realized that she was going to have to leave it that Lavender and John Marshall had been killed. Millie's going to medical school seemed to have been the right thing in the long run.

"I want to see what happens if Diana Drayton lives," she said as she put her face back into the circle. She was shown a happy Adam and Diana, both gray-haired and walking arm in arm. "More," Darci said. "Farther ahead." She was rewarded with seeing a great-great-grandson of theirs, the descendant of a third child. He had invented something that would help cars in the twenty-first century operate on very little gasoline.

"Nice," Darci said, smiling. Originally, Diana had died before having a third child. Now all Darci had to do was figure out how to make it happen.

As she sipped her juice and contemplated, she knew she was a bit afraid to step fully into the circle. What if she couldn't get back? When she'd gone back in time before, her powers had been taken from her. What if she stepped through and the circle closed behind her and she was trapped somewhere with no powers?

"Then I won't step all the way through," she said. But how did she change things without being there? And when did she want to arrive? Smiling, she set down her glass, went to the base, and put her hand on the Touch of God. "May I borrow this?" she asked, and wondered, if she did, would the circle disappear?

To her pleasure, it seemed that the funny-looking little sculpture changed its tune and was now humming something that seemed to be assent. Like the tree, Darci thought, smiling, and vowed to someday explore this concept of inanimate objects having feelings.

She took the Touch of God, said "thank you," and the sculpture seemed to hum a "you're welcome."

Darci went back to the circle. "I want to see Diana when she was a child, and I want her to be alone. I want her close to the edge of the circle."

When Darci put her face through, there was a little girl, about six, sitting under a shade tree playing with her doll and singing to herself. Darci stepped halfway through the circle, keeping her left arm and leg in the room.

"Who are you?" the girl asked, looking up at Darci with curious eyes.

"I'm your fairy godmother and I want to show you something. Let me hold this onto your heart."

It was a different time and the child had not been taught not to talk to strangers. Smiling, she got up and went to Darci, who put the Touch of God on the child's chest, over her heart.

"You're beautiful," the child said.

"Thank you. Do you feel anything?"

"Yes. It feels very nice. You're the prettiest lady I've ever seen, but your clothes are funny."

"Very funny," Darci agreed, concentrating on the ball. It wasn't easy keeping her balance, and in the end she had to leave only her left foot on the other side of the circle. After several minutes the ball grew cool and stopped vibrating in her hand, so she knew that the hole in the child's heart had been healed.

Darci started to leave, but she stopped

and smiled at the child. "When you grow up, you're going to look just like me, and you're going to marry a man named Adam who loves you very much. You'll have three adorable children and a very happy life. But, Diana?"

"Yes?"

"Make sure he stays out of the tunnels."

"What tunnels?"

"You'll find them someday. All in all, it might be best if he stays away from Fontinbloom Nokes. Can you remember that name?"

"I think so," she said. "Will I see you again?"

"I don't think so, but, yes, maybe someday I'll meet you in Camwell when I'm there with Jack. If I do, I want you to remember that two people *need* to die."

The child stepped back from Darci, clutching her doll tightly to her chest. "Die?"

"Yes," Darci said, smiling, "but it's all right. Remember all that I've told you. Can you do that?"

"Yes," the child said. "I will remember this always."

"Good, now I must go. Have a happy life, Diana." With that, Darci stepped back through the circle and into the room.

For a while she leaned against the paneling and willed her heart to calm down. Had she done the right thing?

The enormity of what she'd just done frightened her. She had just changed history! But then, as Jack pointed out, maybe she'd changed history for the better.

Turning, she started back to the circle, but on impulse she looked at the folder of papers. It was back now, so that meant that Tom had lived to put Simone's papers in the box. Holding her breath, Darci opened the folder, flipped through the photo-copies, read one, then closed it, smiling.

"Yes!" she said as she danced around the room. Simone had enclosed a birth announcement for the third child of Adam and Diana Drayton. There was nothing about Adam having died in the tunnels.

Suddenly, she wanted to talk to Jack. She started to go into the bedroom to call him, but she had no idea where he'd been taken. Turning back, she went to the circle. "Show me where Jack is now," she said. Instantly, she saw a bed in a pretty room that could be identified as a hospital room only because of the machines in the corner.

Jack was lying on the bed, one arm behind his head, and staring up at the ceiling. Darci stepped halfway through the circle.

"Holy —" Jack began when he saw her — or saw half of her. She was standing beside his bed, but her left arm and leg weren't there. "You did it without me, didn't you?"

"Please don't be angry. I promise I'll share everything with you when you get out of here."

"If I ever leave, that is. Where's the rest of you?"

"In the room in your father's bedroom."

"And to think that not long ago I didn't believe in such things as you."

"Things?" she asked, her voice rising.

"Don't try that on me. You know what I mean."

"I want to know what you mean by saying that you might never leave here. I'll go back and get the Touch of God."

"No!" he said before she could disappear, then he lowered his voice. "You know how you said that you felt that I *needed* to come here?"

"Yes."

"You were right. I met Lavender."

"You what?"

"She's my father's private physician. My old man has great taste, doesn't he?"

"That's wonderful," Darci said. "Truly wonderful."

He was still looking at her half-in, half-out stance. "What happens if you leave that . . . that whatever-it-is . . . fully?"

"I don't know. I'm afraid that it'll close up and I'll not be able to get back."

"Try it here. If it disappears, you'll be in this century and all that will happen is that you'll have to hear me tell you in detail about how wonderful Lavey is, although her name here is Lillian."

"Pretty awful punishment," Darci said seriously.

Jack made a lightning fast movement, grabbed her arm, and pulled her out of the circle.

"What have you done?" Darci stared in horror as the circle disappeared. "Now I'll have to find a car and drive all the way back to your father's house. I'll — Someone's coming."

"Think they'll be able to see you?" Jack asked.

In the next minute, the door opened and in walked Dr. Shepard. Darci, standing to the side of the door, knew right away that the woman was Lavender. Same spirit; same aura. She'd changed a bit over the hundred-plus years since her Victorian life, but basically she was the same.

"Feeling better?" the doctor asked Jack.

"Not much," he answered, lying back on the bed as though in great agony.

"Sorry to hear that." She marked something on his chart, then walked behind him to fluff his pillows. When she saw Darci, she jumped. "How did you get in here? There's a guard outside. I'll have his hide for this, and Mr. Hallbrooke will fire him."

"No," Jack said, putting his hand on her arm. Darci saw the sparks in the touch from across the room. "It's all right. Please don't tell my father. Darci's so small that she slipped past the man when he blinked."

Darci concentrated and tried to make the woman believe him. She wanted to so it was easy to persuade her. She wanted to do whatever Jack wanted, Darci thought. But right now, Darci wanted to see if she could get back to the circle. She had other things she wanted to do in history. Concentrating, she sent the thought to the doctor that she had to leave the room immediately. Abruptly, the doctor left.

"Why'd you do that?" Jack asked. "I wanted her to get to know you."

"The real me or the made-up me?"

"I want her to hear every detail of a lie that you and I make up." He was grinning. "It's her, isn't it?"

"Oh yes, and she's as mad about you now as she was then. Jack?"

"Yeah?"

"What do you remember about Adam Drayton?"

"He was a great guy, with a pretty little wife who looks a lot like you. Don't *you* remember them?"

"Yes, I do, but I was wondering if you did. How did he die?"

"I have no idea. Simone sent us the clipping about their third child, but nothing else about the man. What are you up to? You aren't going to change them, are you? I remember that you liked Drayton a bit too much."

"Maybe I did," Darci said, looking at the wall where she'd come in. She saw no sign of the circle that had brought her there. "Open!" she said, never expecting to see anything, but the circle opened immediately.

"Think I could go with you?" Jack asked, his eyes longing for adventure.

Darci could tell that he wasn't nearly as ill as he was pretending to be. "I don't know. Come here," she commanded the circle and it moved closer to them. "Truly wonderful, isn't it?"

"I haven't decided yet. If I can use it, I'll

love it, if not, I'm going to give you a lecture on how dangerous that thing could be."

Darci laughed. "Try it and see what happens."

Looking as though he was about to stick his hand into a fire, Jack reached out toward the circle. When his hand disappeared, he drew back quickly.

"Exactly what I did," she said. "Now try your face."

"Why not? Now that I know Dad can buy me a new one, I feel safe." Jack put his face through the circle for a second, then drew back. "How do I see things? All I see now is the hidden room."

"Tell it what you want to see."

"Lavender," he said quickly. "Show me Lavender on the day we met." He put his face through, then withdrew it. "Nothing. You try it."

Darci asked to see Lavender on the day she met Jack and when she looked, that's what she saw. "Looks like it's only me who has the power and the control," Darci said cheerfully.

"That's not fair. I've been in on this from the beginning. I've — Where are you going?"

"Back. I have a date with a witch." In the

next moment she was gone and Jack lay back against the bed, thinking about what he'd just seen and heard, and wondering why she'd asked him about Adam and Diana Drayton.

For a moment he felt bereft because he knew that the closeness that had been between him and Darci was gone. He knew that he was now going to become like Lincoln Aimes, a man she said she "adored," but didn't seem to have a lot of contact with.

As Jack lay there and thought, he knew that his life had been changed by Darci. He knew that he'd never be able to return to his undercover work. Too many people had seen him with this face and knew that he was Hallbrooke's son.

But deeper than that, Jack knew that he didn't want to return to what he'd once done. Now he wanted to . . . He knew that he wanted to marry Lavender and have a bunch of kids, but what else did he want to do? Work with Darci, he thought. Maybe with her talents and his father's money, they could do something together in the future.

Smiling, he closed his eyes, and after a while he went to sleep.

Upstairs, in a room sectioned off from

the attic, the security man pulled the CD from the machine and hurried down the stairs to where Mr. Hallbrooke had set up an office.

"Yes?" Mr. Hallbrooke asked.

"Sir, I think you should see this."

"What is it?"

"It's the video from the surveillance camera in your son's room. There's something odd on it."

"Such as?"

"A young woman came to see him, but she didn't use the door. She came out of the air, and for a while only half of her was in the room."

"I think you're wrong," Mr. Hallbrooke said, taking the CD from the man. "You saw nothing, did you?"

"No sir, not a thing."

"Good," Mr. Hallbrooke said, dismissing the man.

He put the CD into a machine and settled back to watch.

Chapter Twenty-one

The first thing Darci did when she got back was to remove the jewel from the base. Within seconds it cooled off, and the big circle closed. For what she planned to try next she wanted all her strength, and for her mind to be at its peak.

Once she'd disabled everything, she left the room, closing the door securely, and went to the kitchen to find something to eat. An hour later, she climbed into Mr. Hallbrooke's bed. She set the alarm for ten minutes to midnight, then went to sleep instantly.

Hours later, she awoke a few minutes before the alarm went off, and began to prepare herself for what she was going to try to do.

She was going to try to use the past to save her husband. If she couldn't get him out of wherever he was now, then she was going to do what she could to prevent his being in such a place.

But how did she do that without taking herself out of Adam's life was her dilemma.

By the time she'd showered and dressed and was ready to go back into the hidden room, she'd decided that she'd do whatever it took to save the man she loved.

She carried a chair into the room, put the jewel back into the base, and commanded the circle to open.

"What if Adam were not kidnapped?" she asked first.

When she first saw her husband, alive and well, her heart seemed to leap into her throat. But then she relaxed and smiled. Part of her had feared that all she'd been through since she'd seen him would have dulled her feelings for him. After all, she'd spent time with an actor who was considered one of the most beautiful people on earth, and then there was Jack. She'd watched in two centuries how women's eyes followed him. His charisma had caused a woman to kill for him, then attach her spirit to his for over a hundred years.

But when she saw Adam again, it was as though they'd never been apart. He couldn't see her, but she could see and feel him. He wore that same look that said he was responsible for all the world's problems — and that was the look that made her sit up straighter. If he wasn't kidnapped as a child, then shouldn't the adult Adam be happier?

She investigated further, going back years. She had to look away when she saw that Adam's parents had been taken by the witch, because who she'd really wanted was Boadicea.

No, Darci thought, she couldn't just stop Adam's kidnapping. She had to go farther back.

The mirror, Darci thought. It had all started with finding the Mirror of Nostradamus. The witch's sister had found the mirror in a shop in Paris and the witch had killed her to get it.

What if Darci kept the sister from finding the mirror? Smiling, she asked to see that. But when she saw a world destroyed in a nuclear war, she decided not to go that route. "What in the world happened?" she whispered. "Who found the mirror and what was done with it?"

The circle started to show her, but she waved her hand. She didn't have the time or the stomach to watch that.

No, the sister *had* to find the mirror. "What if the witch didn't take it from her?"

Darci asked and was shown that the sister, with good intentions, began to predict people's futures. But she was a kind and generous person who wanted to share with others, so she told people about the mirror. Within weeks, evil people had taken over and had formed a cult meant to dupe people out of their money.

"No," Darci said. She felt bad about it, but the sister had to die.

Frustrated, Darci leaned back in her chair. It couldn't be that the best way would be for the witch to kidnap Adam and Bo, could it? "No! Of course not!"

"Back," Darci said. "I want to go back. I want to see the history of the mirror." What she was shown wasn't good, and she wasn't surprised to see that the mirror had grown fed up with being used for nothing but money. "Where is a mountain of gold?" it was asked. "Where are the riches?" "When will it be safe to rob that house?"

It was also shocking to see how the mirror had tricked people. It never lied, not directly, anyway, but it told what it wanted to. Bo had said that long ago. She knew the mirror well and had had to learn how to ask the right questions.

"So why was it in that antiques shop?"

she wondered. "Who did the mirror want to find it?"

The circle cleared, then Darci saw herself holding the mirror.

She waved her hand. No, she thought. It was too much. She had enough power now and could do more than she'd ever wanted to. If she could get her husband back, all she wanted to do was . . .

She didn't finish her thought because she knew that she was lying if she said that all she wanted to do was live with him and their family. She knew that in the years since Adam had been taken from her, she'd changed drastically. A few days with no power had been enough to make her appreciate what she'd been given.

Darci looked back at the circle and told it to show her the witch after she took the mirror. She'd killed her sister and had to run away to hide. For years she was content. Like all the others, she'd used the mirror to make money.

"Odd that the mirror allowed her to do that," Darci said aloud. But then came the day when the witch gave herself to a young man under a flowering pear tree, and with the loss of her virginity, she was no longer able to read the mirror.

The loss of her only "friend" in her life,

the mirror, had nearly driven the woman insane. After that . . . Darci didn't want to look at what had happened after that, as the woman tried to find someone who could read the mirror.

"So that's how the mirror tricked her," Darci said. The mirror hadn't shown her that if she went to bed with a young man she'd never be able to see the future again. "Mean little thing!" Darci said.

"What would happen if she saw in the mirror that to lose her virginity meant she'd lose her ability to see the future?"

The circle showed an old, rich, miserable woman.

"Miserable because she never had a man?" Darci asked. "I don't think so! She just needs something to do besides make money." What if . . . ? Darci thought, then asked some more questions, watched, asked more, then watched more. Yes, she thought, it might work.

For three hours, Darci worked. She asked questions and moved things around until she figured out a way to keep the woman from making herself into a witch.

The problem was, how would all this affect Adam Montgomery?

Darci took a break, then trembling in fear of what she would see, she asked what would happen if she did change the witch. Where would Adam and his family be?

When the circle began to change, Darci put her hands over her face, afraid to see what was going to come up. She'd met Adam through the witch and what had been done to his family. To take away the witch meant taking away Darci.

Slowly, she raised her head and looked. She saw that Adam was a professor at a big university — and he was married. Darci watched as a young woman came up to him, kissed his cheek, and asked what he wanted for dinner that night. She was from his own class, someone like him.

Darci had to swallow hard. Their children, Adam's and hers, didn't exist, would never exist in exactly the same form. And her father would never meet Adam's sister, much less marry her and have a child.

"And what about me?" Darci whispered. What would happen to her if she didn't meet Adam and marry him?

The circle changed and she saw herself married to Putnam, the rich boy from her hometown who'd begged her to marry him. He'd said he'd pay off all the debts of the townspeople if she'd marry him. Without Adam to save her, she married Putnam.

"And my daughter and niece?" she asked. She saw that both spirits would be put into the bodies of children born to her and Putnam. The girls would have different bodies and . . . and less power, she saw. It seemed that an ancestor in the Montgomery family had had Second Sight and that gene had united with the genes in Darci's father's family to form two extraordinary children.

For a moment Darci put her hands over her face and her eyes filled with hot tears. Adam was happy, she thought, and wasn't that what she'd always wanted for him? He was married to a tall, skinny, blueblood of a woman who probably rode horses all day long. "Someone like him," she whispered. "Not a freak like me."

And the children wouldn't be such oddities as they are now, she thought, and this would be good. As for her father, if Darci changed history, he'd never know what he'd missed. It would be like Jack not remembering that he'd never met Diana Drayton.

She took a breath and looked back at the circle. Adam was at home now, staring out the window at his wife, with her blonde hair floating about her shoulders as she tossed a stick to a dog. "No time travel,"

Darci said. "No witches. No FBI showing up at two in the morning saying that a child had been kidnapped and asking, 'Can Darci help?' No raising anyone from the dead. Just normal."

Darci decided to carry out her plan for the witch, and she'd leave Adam to this new future. She'd let him be happy. She'd let him have the wonderful life that he deserved.

As for her, she could divorce Putnam. She could pop back in time and tell herself — or write herself a note, maybe — and . . .

She looked back at Adam as he stood by the window. She'd seen him look exactly like that a thousand times, and she'd used her mind to calm him down, to make him at peace with himself. But what did he have to be sad about now? she thought. He had everything, so why was he looking as he had when he'd been carrying around the burden of a destroyed family?

"Show me what's inside his head," she said softly. "Show me what's really, really inside him."

For a moment Darci became dizzy, and in the next moment, she could hear the thoughts of Adam Montgomery.

He was looking at his beautiful wife, but

he felt only fondness for her. What's wrong with me, he asked himself. I have it all. I have everything. But why do I want more?

Darci saw him turn away from the window. What do I want, he asked himself.

He ran his hand over his face and she saw him give a little smile. I want what so many of my ancestors seemed to have. I want a love that overpowers me, engulfs me.

"Enough," Darci said softly, and the circle closed. She got up, poured herself some juice, and thought about what she'd just heard. This Adam hadn't been kidnapped, yet he was still an outsider, still different from the other people in his family.

"And so am I," Darci said. "I'm about as different as you can get."

She sat back down on the chair, stared at the droplet that was the circle, and said, "What would happen if I were to go back in time to before Adam was married? What if I went to his university? Would he notice me?"

The circle opened, but all she saw was the glassy, wavering surface. There were no images. She stood up and put her face into the circle, but still there was nothing to see.

She collapsed back against the chair and knew without a doubt that this emptiness was yet another test of her. She wasn't going to be told whether or not she could make Adam love her again. When they'd met they'd been put together in extraordinary circumstances and had been forced to work together. At first there had been no physical attraction from him to her, and he'd even laughed at Darci's passes at him.

"I don't know if I can do it," she said. "How can I compete with all those long-legged girls who grew up in country clubs? Adam and his family are . . ." She couldn't finish as she put her face into her hands.

It was while she was trying to decide if she could bear to see Adam and be rejected that she thought, I can try. I can just, plain old-fashioned *try*. If I lose, then . . .

After she'd made her decision, she desperately wanted to see her daughter and niece. Using the circle, she went to them, and saw that they weren't in the least surprised to see her stepping out of a horizontal pool next to their swing set. Darci romped and played with them for an hour, then knew she needed to go. She needed to do what could be done to bring Adam back to all of them.

As she prepared to leave, she couldn't keep from crying and hugging and kissing them, all the while thinking that she might never see them again. If she didn't connect with Adam, neither of them would be born.

At last, she got back into the circle and returned to the hidden room. Using every bit of concentration she could muster, she put aside her personal fears and began her task.

First, the witch. She needed to change that woman's life.

The plan that had taken Darci so long to come up with was actually very simple. All she did was make the witch ask questions that the mirror had kept her from asking.

First, she made the witch ask the right question so that she saw that if she slept with a man, she would lose her ability to foresee the future.

The second question had taken more work. Darci had had to ask to see what it was that the woman really wanted in life. Darci would have guessed that she wanted power, but, no, the woman had wanted to be respected. She'd thought that money would get her respect, then that evil power would make her respected, but both had failed.

Darci made the woman ask the mirror what would happen if she used the mirror for something besides making money. It took Darci a while to get the witch to ask the right questions, but she'd been able to use her True Persuasion to put the thoughts into the woman's head.

In the end, what the woman did was write books about what she saw. Unlike her stepsister, she had no desire to share anything about the source of her knowledge, so she kept the mirror a secret all her life. She told people that she'd been born with paranormal ability, and as a result, she became a renown psychic. Presidents and kings called her in secret and asked for her predictions.

The witch became a celebrity, and her elevated status kept her happy. She especially loved to play up her virginity, and she was credited with cutting down teen promiscuity by twenty-five percent.

However, without gaining any evil power, she was not able to unnaturally prolong her life. She was to die when Darci was only six years old.

What happened to the mirror after the woman's death was ugly. It fell into the hands of three of the woman's caretakers and they used it for evil.

Darci made the woman ask the mirror about her own death so that she saw when it was going to happen and what would become of the mirror. It would be found out that she'd killed her stepsister to get the mirror, and that would be all that people remembered of her. Her hard-won respectability would be gone. Darci showed the woman where to hide the mirror two days before her death. She also told the woman to take a supply of Jerusalem salt and some dried raspberries with her, and showed her what was to be done with them.

Smiling, Darci leaned back in her chair. She felt she'd accomplished a lot in a short time. It had taken hours to make sure that the woman's not becoming a witch wouldn't hurt the world. She had murdered a lot of people. It was horrible to think of, but would any of those murdered people live to be worse than the witch? "Show me all," she'd commanded, then felt sick at the sheer number of faces that flashed by her. She looked at auras, watching for irregularities and muddy colors. She was happy to see that several of the people contributed significantly, whereas the others just lived ordinary lives.

Her next task was to return to her hometown of Putnam, Kentucky. This was hard for Darci and at first all she wanted to do was pop back to the old stone building where she'd had the witch hide the mirror and the little man in his cage. But Darci knew she was being cowardly. Instead, she made herself go back to her own room in the run-down house where she'd lived with her mother — or, more rightly, lived by herself since her mother had rarely been there.

Closing her eyes, Darci stepped halfway into the circle, then visualized where she wanted to go, and took a step forward. When she opened her eyes, she was in her bedroom in Putnam, and, immediately, sensations overwhelmed her.

The room itself was ugly, with peeling wallpaper and a bed frame and mattress that someone had thrown out. She and her mother had lived on what her mother could make in one cheap job after another. Almost always, her mother had quit because the boss expected everything from her. Sex had never been enough. Men had wanted to possess Jerlene Monroe — and they still did, which was the secret of her current success in the movies.

Sitting down on the bed, Darci could see so much more than she had before. Her own daughter had extraordinary powers, but Darci understood them. How must it have been for a woman to give birth to a child who talked to rocks? Who could do things with her mind?

As Darci sat there, looking around the cheap, awful room, she saw many things about herself, about her mother, and about the town.

Getting up, she opened her closet and saw the ghastly, hand-me-down clothes there. Now, looking back, Darci realized that it had never occurred to her to use her True Persuasion to gain money and worldly goods. She'd always been so ashamed of what she could do that she'd done nothing for herself. And she'd naively thought that no one around her knew what she could do.

As Darci touched the cheap, worn clothes, she felt sorry for that child who was half-starved and left on her own so much.

For a moment she was nearly overcome with self-pity, but then she straightened and smiled. She had changed. She was no longer afraid of her power — no, her Power. She had seen how she could help people, even to helping the world, and from now on instead of spending her time wishing she were "normal," she was going

449

to thank God for choosing her, for whatever reason He had, every hour of every day.

She closed the closet door, looked around the room one last time, then left it. She walked through the small house, not looking at anything. She was done with looking back, done with regretting and wishing that this had been that way, and that that way. From now on, she was going to look ahead — unless history needed a bit of tweaking, that is, she thought, smiling.

Darci was brought up short when she saw her mother sitting at the kitchen table, polishing her perfect nails. This had not been part of her plan! As it often did, her mother's beauty startled her. But now, having seen that gorgeous face on the big screen, it was even more startling.

"Where are you going?" Jerlene asked, her tone cold.

When she was a child, her mother's constant coldness had terrified her. For all that Darci had abilities, she'd never been able to see that her mother loved her very much.

"I'm going . . ." Darci began, then stopped, realizing that, out of necessity, when she'd been a child she'd never told her mother anything but lies. What could she have said, that she was going out to visit her friends who had died long ago?

Suddenly, Darci remembered how her mother had saved her life, and the resentment she'd felt all her life toward her mother left her. "Mom," she said softly, "I know that you and I haven't always been the best of friends, but I also know that when the chips are down you'd risk your life for me."

Jerlene, who usually refused to move her face for fear of causing wrinkles, looked up at her daughter in astonishment, then her face began to crumple. Tears formed in her eyes. "I didn't know you knew that."

"I found it out," Darci said as she kissed her mother's cheek. "Don't worry, Mom, everything will be all right."

Smiling, Darci walked out the back door of her mother's house and up the hill. For behind the house was an old stone building, built by pioneers and now falling apart. Darci had spent a lot of her childhood in that roofless shelter. She'd talked to the ghosts and listened to them and sometimes found things for them. They'd helped her survive her childhood.

When she reached the building, the ghosts came out to greet her, even the grumpy old man who'd fallen down the well and had never forgiven his wife for being happy that he'd died. They knew that she'd been gone for years and they wanted to hear all that she'd seen and done.

Darci shot them images of her life while they excitedly told her about the old, sick woman who'd come there and hidden two things.

"Yes, I know," Darci said as she went to the corner and pulled the rotting bucket out of the mud. It hadn't been moved in many years. Under it, safe, was the mirror, beautifully packaged in silk and waterproof plastic. Darci could feel the tears of the old woman. The mirror had been the only real friend she'd ever had in her life.

Beside the mirror was a little homemade cage with a rock inside it. There were still a few pieces of Jerusalum salt left and one dried raspberry. The little man had eaten only one of each a year so they'd lasted for the years it took Darci to grow up. The cage was made of cardboard and string and should have rotted, but it was intact, clean and new.

"Are you going to wake up now?" she asked, holding the cage aloft.

The rock didn't move or change form,

but Darci heard him in her mind. "Depends on what's going on."

"I have a circle that I can see history in and change it."

He sent her images of the iron egg with a question.

"Forgot to look inside," she said, then felt him go back to sleep.

"My sternest critic," she muttered, then, holding the cage and the mirror, she commanded the circle to appear. Seconds later she was inside the hidden room and she placed her treasures on the long shelf.

She took the iron egg from the base and looked at it, but she could see no way to open it. It took several minutes of twisting and tugging before she finally thought of blowing on it. Her breath made the two halves part. Inside was a necklace, small and plain, except for the three blue stones on it. When she held it up to the light, the stones seemed to give off a radiance of their own. Not from this planet, she thought, then started to put the necklace on. "Not yet," she whispered. Adam was next, but first she had to go to a hairdresser and to the mall. She had some shopping to do.

Chapter Twenty-two

Darci was standing in the doorway of Adam Montgomery's secretary's office, and she was having to work hard to keep from running away. After she'd had her hair cut and had bought a St. John suit, she'd lain awake most of the night planning what she'd do to make Adam fall in love with her again. She'd had her hair cut and highlighted just the way he liked it. And she told herself that she was going to use her True Persuasion as little as possible — if at all. If she got him through trickery, it wouldn't last. As a child, she'd learned that when she tried to make people fall in love with each other, it couldn't be done.

The university where Adam taught was a prestigious Ivy League school. In other words, full of Yankee snobs who'd never said a kind word to anyone in their lives.

His secretary, who looked like she'd grown up in Greenwich, Connecticut and been educated at Miss Porter's school, was looking Darci up and down in a way that would have once made Darci cringe.

But now, Darci looked the young woman in the eyes and said, "I'd like to speak to Dr. Montgomery, please."

"He's not here. Come back some other time," the woman said, looking back down at her work.

The headache I could give you! Darci thought, but instead she smiled. She stared at the top of the woman's head and concentrated. So much for not using her powers.

The secretary looked up and said that Dr. Montgomery would be away all afternoon. "I have no idea where he is."

A tough case, Darci thought, still smiling. She stared deep into the woman's eyes until she said, "Hiking. Whitnell Woods."

"Thank you," Darci said politely, then started to leave, but she stopped and looked back. "How are Dr. Montgomery's parents?"

"Fine. They were here last week."

"And his sister?"

For the first time, the young woman smiled. "Beautiful, as always."

"What was her name again?" Darci asked.

"Elizabeth Montgomery."

"Yes, of course. She . . . ?"

The woman pointed to a large poster pinned to the wall behind her. It said *Elizabeth Montgomery in Concert.*

"She plays the piano," Darci said in wonder, staring at the poster. Bo was truly beautiful, with clear eyes. There was no horror in them. "Is she married?"

"No, but she's engaged."

Staring at the poster, Darci smiled. Adam's sister had been named Boadicea for a great queen in one life, and in another life she'd also been named for a great queen.

"You wouldn't have tickets to the concert, would you?" Darci asked, concentrating on the woman.

"Why, yes, I do. They were to be given to the head of the department, but I'm sure he won't mind missing the performance." She reached into a desk drawer and, smiling, handed Darci two concert tickets.

Darci took a pen and paper off the woman's desk and wrote a note.

Dear Mr. Raeburne,

I'm a great admirer of your work. Would you please come backstage after the concert and meet me? Perhaps we could have dinner together.

Elizabeth Montgomery

When Darci finished, the woman was holding out an envelope to her. Darci put the tickets and note inside, then addressed the envelope to her father. "Would you please mail this for me?"

"I'd be happy to," the woman said, still smiling.

As Darci walked away, she thought, I bet her face hurts tomorrow.

Darci cleared the wooded area of all hikers except for the one who she could feel was now walking toward her. She'd chosen a beautiful spot just off the trail by a little stream, and spread a cloth on the ground. She'd changed out of her pretty suit into a shirt and khaki pants, with a little straw hat with a ribbon on the back of it. Adam had always liked her in hats. She'd purchased many of the foods he liked, and had even gone to a wine store and bought something that was supposed to be excellent.

While Darci had sworn she wouldn't use her powers on Adam, she thought it was perfectly fair to use what she knew about him.

In the minutes before he arrived, Darci closed her eyes and felt him. She could feel his presence, feel his aura even through the trees. Would he recognize her? Would something inside of him know that he'd never met her, but that he was madly in love with her?

By the time he came through the clearing, Darci's heart was racing. When she saw him, it was all she could do not to run to him and throw herself on him. He was even more beautiful in person than she remembered. She'd found out that he'd spent a lot of his life traveling, bumming around the world working on steamers and anywhere he could get a job. He hadn't used his family's money to travel from one mansion to one yacht to one exclusive hotel after another. Instead, he'd paid his own way and worked with the crews of ships. Darci liked that about him. She'd always wondered if he'd been so independent because of what had been done to him and his family or if it was natural to him. She was glad to know that all the things she liked about him were his own.

"Beautiful day," he said as he passed her on the trail.

"Yes, isn't it?" Darci said, her heart pounding. She wanted to jump on him and yell. Where had he gone that day he'd disappeared? What had happened to him?

Neither the mirror nor the circle would tell her that.

After his polite greeting, Adam kept walking down the trail.

Now what do I do? Darci asked herself. It was one thing to be altruistic and noble and think that she'd let the man she loved marry someone else, but it was another thing to actually *do* it.

She sat still on the cloth, her mind in turmoil. She tried to think of what to do, but she couldn't seem to think clearly. The man she'd vowed to love *forever* had just walked past her. He'd not recognized her or even been interested in her as a woman.

"Excuse me."

She looked up to see Adam Montgomery standing over her. "Do I know you? Are you one of my students?"

"I'm much too old to be a student," Darci said demurely, knowing she had always looked young for her age.

Adam looked at the stream, then back at her. "I guess you're meeting someone."

You! Darci wanted to shout, but she just smiled. "No one. It's just me and too much food."

Adam looked back at the water, seeming to be at a loss for words.

But Darci knew him. He'd always been

awkward when it came to romance. After they were engaged that had changed, but before then . . .

"What about you? Are you hungry?" she asked. "Or do you have an appointment you have to go to?"

He looked down at her, seeming to be considering something very important. "Actually I did, but I think I'm going to skip it." He looked into her eyes. "I don't want you to think I'm being forward, but I feel as though I could stay here forever."

"Yes," Darci said. "Forever."

Epilogue

Devlin looked at Darci's time traveling with disgust. "Will she be popping into all her old lives now? I rather like the time when earth had pirates."

"Don't you listen? She had no other lives," Henry said.

"Had no other lives?" Devlin asked. "But of course she did. All these earth people had other lives. Even I had a time when I was in a body. Not like theirs, too few arms for my taste, but I did have a few lives." He turned himself into one of his old bodies.

"She had no other human lives," Henry said pointedly.

"But only . . ." All four of Devlin's eyes widened.

"Only what?" Henry asked impatiently.

"Only angels have no past lives, and that woman can't be an angel. She's much too human. She has many human faults."

Henry sighed. "Don't we all."

As Devlin looked at Henry, the outline of his body began to grow dimmer.

"Don't fade on me now," Henry said. "It's not a matter of what she is, but *who* she is. I thought you would have guessed that by now."

"*Who* she is?" Devlin asked meekly.

"My goodness, but I don't have time to educate you. We have a great deal of work to do."

Devlin brightened as he turned into one of his beloved pirates. "What are we going to do to her next? She knows nothing of worlds other than her own, so maybe we should send her to another planet. Or she could explore this time-travel thing more fully. Next time you could send her back in time with her power. She could —"

"Don't waste my time," Henry snapped. "We're going to do nothing to her. She's now learned that she has a purpose in life, so we must begin to show her what that purpose is."

"And what is that?" Devlin asked, studying his fingernails. He was now wearing a tuxedo and looking very bored. "To open a detection agency with her little friends?"

"No, Darci is to prepare the earth for the Second Coming."

At that Devlin was so shocked that he reverted to his true form: a wizened little man with three white hairs growing out of his shiny scalp. In the next second he disappeared in a puff of gray-green smoke.

Smiling, Henry said, "Coward," then turned back to the fog where he could see Darci. He was pleased with her, very pleased indeed.

About the Author

Jude Deveraux is the author of thirty-two *New York Times* bestsellers, including *Holly*, *Wild Orchids*, *Forever and Always*, *Forever . . . *, *The Mulberry Tree*, *The Summerhouse*, *Temptation*, and *A Knight in Shining Armor*. She lives in North Carolina with her son, Sam.